WE'LL NEVER TELL

WE'LL NEVER TELL

WENDY HEARD

Christy Ottaviano Books

LITTLE, BROWN AND COMPANY

New York   Boston

Cover art copyright © 2023 by Bex Glendining. Cover design by Tracy Shaw.
Cover copyright © 2023 by Hachette Book Group, Inc.
Interior design by Torborg Davern.

Christy Ottaviano Books
Hachette Book Group
1290 Avenue of the Americas, New York, NY 10104
Visit us at LBYR.com

First Edition: May 2023

Christy Ottaviano Books is an imprint of Little, Brown and Company. The Christy Ottaviano Books name and logo are trademarks of Hachette Book Group, Inc.

The publisher is not responsible for websites (or their content) that are not owned by the publisher.

Little, Brown and Company books may be purchased in bulk for business, educational, or promotional use. For information, please contact your local bookseller or the Hachette Book Group Special Markets Department at special.markets@hbgusa.com.

Library of Congress Cataloging-in-Publication Data
Names: Heard, Wendy, author.
Title: We'll never tell / Wendy Heard.
Other titles: We will never tell
Description: First edition. | New York : Little, Brown and Company, 2023. |
Audience: Ages 14 to 18. | Summary: While investigating an infamous
Hollywood murder mystery for their final YouTube episode, four teenagers
visit the scene of the crime, but one does not come out alive, leaving the others to
solve crimes old and new—or die trying.
Identifiers: LCCN 2022030605 | ISBN 9780316482332 (hardcover) |
ISBN 9780316482653 (ebook)
Subjects: CYAC: YouTube (Electronic resource)—Fiction. | Murder—Fiction. |
Mystery and detective stories. | LCGFT: Detective and mystery fiction. | Novels.
Classification: LCC PZ7.1.H4314 We 2023 | DDC [Fic]—dc23
LC record available at https://lccn.loc.gov/2022030605

ISBNs: 978-0-316-48233-2 (hardcover), 978-0-316-48265-3 (ebook)

Printed in the United States of America

LSC-C

Printing 1, 2023

For my mother and daughter.
Our story is my favorite.

WE'LL NEVER TELL

THE HOLLYWOOD REVIEW

SILVER SCREEN TRAGEDY AT SILVER LAKE

Saturday, April 15, 1972

Two shocking deaths in the night have shaken Hollywood. At seven o'clock this morning, the household staff of Mr. and Mrs. Andrew Valentini discovered their master and mistress, Hollywood's leading man and lady, dead in the living room of their palatial mansion in the Silver Lake hills.

"It was a grisly scene," say neighbors who managed a glimpse: twenty-three-year-old Rosalinda Valentini, the cinema darling known for her roles in *On the Water* and *He Loves Me Not*, prostrate on the plush living room carpet in a pool of blood, while studio mogul Andrew lay crumpled near the window in a similarly terrifying state.

Neighbors heard no disturbances, which is unsurprising given the locale. Estates are large and wooded, and the hills provide residents a measure of privacy to protect them from prying eyes... or perhaps they invite evil in.

Is the culprit an obsessed fan? A jilted lover? Tonight, the world will grieve a star-studded couple while the Los Angeles Police Department begins their investigation into who may have had a motive to cut down this dynamic duo in their prime. We'll be covering the story as it unfolds.

ONE

Tuesday, April 4

"CASEY, LOOK," ZOE SAYS, CLUTCHING MY HAND. It's lunchtime, and we're out in front of Hollywood High in the blazing April sunshine, waiting for her mom to drop off Starbucks.

"What?" I ask, confused. "Is your mom here?"

She points at two people sitting on the steps, riveted by something on an iPhone. "They're watching one of our videos."

"No way." What are the odds?

"*Look,*" she insists, pulling me toward them so we can peek over their shoulders. On the screen, glowing eyes blink twice and vanish into pitch blackness. The camera moves closer, searching for the eyes again. The creature is revealed: a monkey, high in the branches of a tree. A zoo enclosure.

A smooth narrator voice says, "These are capuchins. They're from Brazil, and they're endangered." The camera pans across the exhibit, and more monkeys appear, curled up on branches, clearly having been awakened from a sound sleep.

"Aww, look at the baby monkeys," coos the girl holding the phone.

I meet Zoe's eyes. Hers are full of contained glee, and I'm sure mine look the same. It's the first time we've seen people watching our videos in public.

The couple switches to a different clip, the one at an abandoned, burned-down clothing factory in Downtown LA. That was a cool episode; we'd found all the old sewing machines, some of them untouched by fire, collecting dust.

"What's the name of this channel?" the guy asks.

"*We'll Never Tell,*" his girlfriend replies. "I can't believe they don't get caught."

"I bet it's not that hard to sneak into these places. Come on. The zoo? Some old factory?"

"I'm sure there's security," the girl argues. "If it were easy, there wouldn't be a whole channel about it. Besides, that's not the point. You and I aren't going to go break into the zoo in the middle of the night. So they show you. It's about satisfying people's curiosity. Seeing something off-limits. You know?"

I meet Zoe's eyes. She's wearing hot-pink eyeliner, and when she purses her lips and gives me a mischievous smile, her hazel eyes glow like a cat's.

A horn honks twice. It's Zoe's mom, at the curb in her white Expedition, and we hurry down the steps to meet her. The passenger's side window opens smoothly, and Zoe reaches in for the drinks. I accept the one offered to me and call, "Thank you, Maria!"

She blows me a kiss, as always looking too beautiful and petite to be driving this behemoth. She was a pageant contestant back in the Philippines, even competing in Miss Universe, until she met Zoe's dad. "Love you guys," Maria calls in her always-cheerful singsong voice. "Have a good day! Be safe at work, Casey!"

I smile and wave as she pulls away. "Your mom is seriously the best," I tell Zoe.

"I know." She flicks her eyes left and right. "Have you seen Liam?"

The guy she likes. "No," I reply, sipping my caramel macchiato. "Want me to go find him and tell him you want to have his babies?"

"I'll kill you in your sleep."

I grin at her for a minute, feeling a sudden rush of nostalgia for her many crushes over the years and all the times I've tormented her about them. Two more months and we'll be done with high school. Another two months after that, she'll be gone, off to MIT, as far geographically as a person can be while still in the continental US.

"What?" she asks, noticing my expression. "Tell me."

I feel suddenly stiff and awkward. "Just thinking about how you're going to freeze to death in Massachusetts. Do you even own a single coat?"

Her eyes go wide. "That's a great point, actually. Major

5

fashion opportunities await in the coat department. It's completely unexplored."

I bite my tongue. That isn't what I mean.

She wraps an arm around my neck, and we wander along the sidewalk, killing time until the bell rings. "You excited about the murder house?" she asks.

I brighten, thinking about our next—and last—episode. "I am."

"A million subscribers. Did you ever imagine we'd get here?"

I make a face. "No." She knows how I feel about internet fame. Some of our douchiest classmates will talk your face off about their follower counts.

She laughs. "Whatever. We're legends. People will be watching our channel for years to come."

"We can never tell anyone," I remind her.

She rolls her eyes. "Please. I don't want to lose my spot at MIT because I'm out here doing time. Orange is *not* the new black."

I try to imagine what the other programming students at MIT are going to be like. I wish I could see their faces when they meet her. She's the most vibrant person I know, from her halo of curly, blue-streaked hair to her bright outfits and the eyeshadow that changes daily.

"Casey, Zoe!" We turn toward school. It's Jacob and Eddie, trotting down the steps. From far away it's not always easy to tell them apart; both are medium height, slim, with dark hair. As they get closer, their differences are more visible: Jacob is fair-skinned, with shaggy, messy brown hair, freckles, and sharp, pretty features, while Eddie has a tan from hours of playing basketball, shiny black hair cut short, strong, straight brows, and a square jaw. Eddie is hanging back behind Jacob, scowling like they've just finished arguing.

Zoe greets them cheerfully. "Hey, losers."

Jacob grabs the Starbucks cup from my hand and takes a long sip. "Rude," I say.

Making unwavering eye contact, he licks the lid daintily with the tip of his tongue. He's such a brat.

His eyes wander down to my clothes. "I'm liking this look," he tells me, stepping back. "What is this, a vintage bowling shirt?"

I point to the name patch on the left breast pocket. "Look, I'm Marjie." We share a love of thrifting and have delved into some truly esoteric parts of town looking for deals. In Hollywood and the surrounding areas, thrift stores are as expensive as regular ones, which completely defeats the purpose.

I notice a yellow paper folded in Eddie's hand. "Is that a tardy slip?" I gasp, stealing it. Sure enough, it says *Eddie Yu, 8:55 a.m.*

He shoots Jacob a glare. "Not my fault."

"Ho-ly crap," Zoe whispers dramatically. "Mark this freaking day. Eddie was late for something."

Jacob shakes his head, lips pressed together. "Ix-nay, ladies." Eddie clearly doesn't think this is funny.

Zoe shoots Jacob a wink and changes the subject.

"We just saw people playing one of our videos. We were standing out here waiting for my mom, and the couple next to us was totally watching that one we did at the zoo."

Eddie's scowl has relaxed. "Did you stay cool, or did you give us away?"

Zoe makes a pouty face. "After three years of total secrecy, why does everyone still think I have a big mouth?"

All three of us chorus, "Because you do."

With her non-Starbucks hand, she starts slapping at us in turn, hitting our arms. There's a minute where we engage in a four-way play fight, and then Jacob calls a truce so he can finish my coffee in peace.

I take a moment to look at them, really look. Eddie and Jacob, friends since elementary school, have such different personalities, it's sometimes hard to believe they're as close as they are. Zoe and me, same thing—no one would match us up on the street, but here we are, best friends since freshman year. We're definitely not popular, but I like to think we're a unique little band of misfits: Zoe is a programmer by day, lock picker by night, brilliant and stylish; Eddie is the strong silent type, like someone out of a Calvin Klein ad; Jacob is a hundred percent punk rock, teleported straight from early eighties New York; and I'm...I don't know. A brunette with bangs and glasses whose entire wardrobe is secondhand. "If your eccentric grandma were young and cute," Jacob had said in the group chat once, which...thanks?

"This last episode needs to be perfect," I tell them.

Jacob lifts his stolen drink in a toast. "All good things must come to an end. *We'll Never Tell*, you've had a sweet ride. Time to go out with a bang."

Zoe and I make little hooting noises, but Eddie furrows his brow and doesn't respond. Zoe looks at me quizzically, noticing it, too. Eddie is always quieter than Jacob, whose energy is so unpredictable, he'll give you whiplash. But Eddie's quiet is usually calm, not gloomy like this. Can he really be this out of sorts just because Jacob made him late for school?

Jacob forges ahead. "You guys want to have a planning session tomorrow? If we're doing the murder house this weekend, we need to be tighter than ever." He grins, his excitement palpable. I think he's happy we took his suggestion for our last episode. I had wanted to do a different location—the oil rigs in San Pedro, which are terrifying at night—but I'd been unanimously overruled when Jacob had suggested the Valentini murder mansion.

We all agree to meet at Zoe's. The bell rings, and the guys hurry back toward school. As they walk away, Zoe asks, "Are they in a fight?"

"I don't know," I reply, analyzing the back of Eddie's stiff shoulders. "Something's definitely off, though."

✧

The evening bus hosts the usual assortment of people: normies getting off work, homeless folks sleeping, an older woman with a dog in a stroller, and of course the guy selling incense, who you absolutely do not make eye contact with under any circumstances. I have a personal hygiene policy of never sitting down, and I keep my balance with practiced ease, tucked into the little vestibule by the door. I'm tired, having gone straight from school to work at Sunset FroYo, and I reek of sour, melted frozen yogurt from cleaning the machines.

I get off at LaBrea and Franklin, turn right, and trudge uphill; we live near Runyon Canyon, at the base of the Hollywood

Hills. Our street is lined with large apartment buildings and is always congested—cars circling endlessly, searching for parking spots they'll never find.

Our building is one of the older, less-nice ones on this street, but I don't mind. One thing I've learned the hard way—you have to appreciate what you've got because things can always get worse, and rent control is as good as it gets. I let myself in the front gate and hurry through the courtyard to our unit on the ground floor. I find Grandma stretching on the carpet in front of the TV. She looks up when I enter. "Hi, baby." Her smile is weary, all her makeup worn off. She's pretty, with warm brown eyes and short blond-brown hair. She always seems younger than my friends' grandparents.

I love the way she smells coming home from the flower shop, like roses and Oasis—the spongy, wet material inside vases—along with a cool refrigerator scent. I have so many memories of helping her on holidays, sticking flowers into Oasis and learning to tie ribbons into fancy bows.

"Hi, Grandma. Tired?" I drop my backpack on the floor by the small dining table and kick my shoes off.

"I'm fine." She's lying. Her job has been wearing her down since she turned sixty, but she has no other skills; she's been doing floral design for forty years.

I wash my hands in the kitchen sink and sit next to her on the carpet. It's not a big place; the little galley kitchen, dining nook, and living area are all one space, and half the living room is partitioned off with Ikea room dividers to serve as my bedroom.

She wraps an arm around my shoulders and squeezes me

affectionately, then examines me, straightening my bangs and smoothing my ponytail. "How was work? School? Friends?"

"All fine. A chill day."

"You need dinner?" she asks. "I made some chicken soup. A big pot for the week. Oh, and I brought some chocolates home from work."

I groan at the idea of more sugar. "I had way too much froyo."

She twists her mouth into a playful grimace and hands me the remote. "Okay, then, I'm heading to bed. When you're old, eight thirty is the new midnight."

"You're up at three to go to the flower market every day," I point out, turning the TV off. "I've got homework anyway."

She pushes up to a standing position. "I recorded *Jeopardy!* for you. It's the college edition. The kid who won was *so* smart."

I can't help but smile. "You know I can just stream it."

"It's more fun to watch on the big TV!"

"Thanks, Grandma." She's right; it is more fun to rewatch it together. Only a few people know about my secret dream of being on *Jeopardy!*

She kisses me good night and heads for the bathroom. I can tell that her back hurts from the arch of her spine. Somehow, after high school, I need to figure out how to contribute more to the bills while going to community college. She can't keep working this much forever.

I heave myself up from the floor, grab my backpack, and push the divider aside to enter my room. It's just large enough for a twin bed, dresser, and bookshelf, but the way we divided the space means I get both windows. Because I don't want to get murdered, I never sleep with them open, but I do like to air out my room before bed. I crack the windows now, letting in the cool night air and the smell of fresh weed; someone must be smoking right outside.

My homework's done, but I still have research to do for Saturday. I pull up my Drive folders of notes and feel a twinge of sadness, scanning through the file names. Each episode we've done has its own folder. Our last three years lined up like this makes it all so final. I hover over the folder for the first urban exploration we ever did, titled "CityWalk." It wasn't even a real break-in; CityWalk is easy to get into. But we got great footage from inside the neon-lit outdoor mall, and it went viral.

Then there was the gated-off, burned-down fire station in North Hollywood, which got a similar number of views, and the next thing we knew, we were doing one every month or two, thinking bigger and more dangerous with each installment. We've broken or snuck into twenty-eight different off-limits places around Los Angeles, giving people behind-the-scenes access to the city in a way I like to think hasn't been done before, not like this. And now it's over. Almost.

I switch to an incognito window and log into my secret Notion account. It's unbelievably organized, dozens of tiles in a perfect grid. Each is titled with the name of a woman. "Lacey Hannity," "Kaisha Jennings," and "Melissa Ramirez" are on top, the last few I worked on. Each tile, when clicked, opens up a board dedicated to that woman, a victim of a murder. I've collected links and information on each case.

I despise true crime junkies. I'm not satisfying some sick need to obsess over murderers, and I hate the idea of rubbernecking other women's deaths. It's just that maybe, someday, I'll run across a case that reminds me of my mom. Maybe I'll stumble across her killer. Maybe then we'll finally have some answers.

My eyes lift of their own volition and land on the photo of my mom and me, hung on the wall facing my bed. We're smiling; I'm three years old and she's twenty-five. She has long brown hair and a wide, pretty smile. We were at Griffith Park for a picnic, and the background is emerald green. My soft little arms are wrapped around her neck and we're cheek-to-cheek, grinning at the camera. I didn't have glasses yet; my vision started deteriorating when I was nine, one year after she died. I always wonder if the two events were related, like when you hear about someone's hair turning gray after a war.

I hung this photo above my dresser so she'd always be watching me while I sleep. It's stupid, I know. But I used to have nightmares of her dead, all bloody and torn like I imagine she ended up. The picture anchors me to her whole self, a reminder that she wouldn't want me reducing her memory to what she was at the end.

That's the thing with being the victim of a crime. It collapses an entire life down to its violent conclusion. It's perverse and wrong that victims are remembered for a crime committed by someone else—in my mom's case, a complete stranger.

The murder house has a different story, though. The woman there, Rosalinda Valentini, was killed by her husband. Like my mom, she was found dead in a pool of her own blood. But Rosalinda was a celebrity—a beautiful blond actress—so her death and life will be memorialized for ages, while my mom's will only be remembered by my grandma and me.

And whoever killed her.

TWO

Wednesday, April 5

EDDIE DRIVES, JACOB BROODING IN THE FRONT seat, flicking the flame on his lighter off and on, while I sit in the back, nervously observing the tension between them. Of the four of us, Zoe is the only one who lives in a house instead of an apartment, and she has a pool, so her house is often our de facto hangout spot, with Eddie playing chauffeur.

This will be our last production cycle. It's become such a fundamental part of my life. My role in the group is researcher and voice-over script writer, and I pour hours and hours into learning everything about a place and translating that into an interesting narrative for Jacob to read in his smooth baritone after he edits the footage in Avid. What am I going to do with all this excess mental energy once I'm no longer nurturing something secret, something that's just ours?

What am I going to do without Zoe?

Eddie looks at me in the rearview mirror. "You good, Casey?" He always senses when something's simmering beneath the surface.

I force a smile. "Of course."

He returns his eyes to the road. "You finalize your plans yet? Still thinking about LA City College?"

"Yep. Gonna live at home, help Grandma pay the bills. Can't rack up a bunch of debt."

They glance at each other. It's Jacob who says, "You know, it's okay if you need to, like, do your own thing."

Eddie nods. "You have good grades; you're super smart. It seems like a waste to go to community college."

The words sting. I'm tired of people saying stuff like this to me. I just sat through an after-class lecture from my AP Econ teacher, who wants me to study library science at one of the UCs because of my "head for research." But I can't abandon my grandma. I'm all she has. When you've been through what we've been through, the rules are different.

I redirect, tapping Jacob on the shoulder. "How 'bout you? You pick a college yet? I know you've been debating."

He looks back at me. "Yeah, actually. I decided I'm going to skip college and try to get a PA job, work my way up."

I consider that. It's not a huge shock. He ditches school more than anyone else I know, and he relies on Course Hero,

Wikipedia, and the three of us, his loving enablers, for the work he does turn in. That said, this no-college plan is going to be a tough sell to his dad.

Jacob continues, "Let's be honest. I have ADHD. I hate school. I want to *do* things." He talks with his spidery, expressive hands, animating his words with a sort of desperation.

In a sharp tone, Eddie says, "A lot of people have ADHD and still go to college." It occurs to me that this reveal isn't news to Eddie.

Philosophically, I say, "To be fair, we're lucky he's had the YouTube channel to get him through high school. Imagine the trouble he'd have gotten in without it. Sixteen-hour PA shifts might be just what he needs."

"I knew the ladies would have my back," Jacob says merrily.

"You're not helping," Eddie snaps over his shoulder, which is so out of character that I shut up instantaneously.

Jacob returns his attention to the window, grumbling something unintelligible under his breath.

"Sorry," Eddie says after a minute of silence, glancing back at me. "I didn't mean to be so..."

"Dickish?" Jacob supplies, and the three of us laugh, the tension diffused but still hovering in the air.

Eddie turns onto Zoe's street, which climbs and weaves into the hills. He makes a right into her driveway, and then we're in the paved area in front of her house. I get out and turn to look at the view, the flat basin of LA with its grid pattern of streets, and Downtown like stalagmites clustered to the east, brown-gray smog hovering around the buildings like a fogbank. Zoe's house isn't quite high enough in the hills to see the ocean, but it's there, the city's western barrier, cold and bright.

Zoe's mom answers the door, stunning as always in designer exercise clothes. "Come on in, she's in her room," she says, beckoning us into the marble foyer. "I can make some snacks. Are you hungry?"

"Yes," the guys chorus.

"When are they not?" I wonder aloud.

Her eyes twinkle. "Go on in. I'll bring you food."

We leave our shoes on the rack, then head through the living room, past the picture windows and fancy white couches I refuse to sit my clumsy ass on. The hall is full of photographs of Zoe's dad with various rappers, singers, and musicians, framed alongside album covers, plaques, and pictures of him and artists receiving awards. He's a music producer and executive, having moved to LA from Atlanta in the nineties when the West Coast rap scene was blowing up. Every once in a while, a music buff will ask Zoe, "Wait, is your dad *Terrence Wilkins*?" He's great, though, totally warm and normal, so it's easy to forget when you're hanging out with their family that they're going to be in Malibu at some celebrity's dog's birthday party the day after. (No, but really, that's exactly what they did last Sunday. I helped Zoe pick a present.)

Zoe is sprawled out on her bed with her pink Beats on, watching something on her phone. When we enter, she throws off the headphones and grins. "You're here!" She squeezes me first in one of her attack hugs, then gets on her tiptoes to embrace Eddie and Jacob as one. Her mom enters with a platter of mangoes and sandwiches and a warning not to eat on the bed. We sit on the floor around the platter and happily slurp down the fruit.

"I'm excited about Saturday," Zoe says, wiping her mouth with a napkin. "It's going to be epic. Go big or go home, right?"

"Hell yes," Jacob says.

"Your mom is seriously the best," I declare, biting into a jelly-on-Hawaiian-sweetbread sandwich.

"I know," Zoe replies, patting my knee. I realize I said the same thing yesterday when Maria brought us Starbucks and feel pathetic, the sad orphan with a mom complex.

Eddie burps loudly, which challenges Jacob to belch even louder, which Zoe takes as an affront and one-ups them with a huge burp of her own.

"Okay, okay," I say, fanning away the smell. "Can we please start talking logistics? We have three days to get everything figured out."

"I think we're in good shape," Zoe says, grabbing her laptop and moving to her desk.

"Ready for Silver Lake," Jacob says, a sly smile crossing his pretty face.

I can't resist dropping some trivia. "Did you know that in 1967, one of the nation's first gay rights protests happened in Silver Lake after a police raid on a nightclub on New Year's Eve?"

Jacob's eyebrows lift. "Sick."

Sitting on the bed beside Jacob, Eddie reaches for his Mac-Book Pro. "I just need to open up my files. . . ." Jacob leans in to look over his shoulder, and Eddie pulls away just a bit. I pretend not to notice this flash of tension between them.

"Let's go chronologically," I suggest. "Eddie, I'm going to walk us through our route, and you can call out exactly what shots you want us to get." I pull up images of the house's interior I've been collecting from articles.

Eddie nods, referencing his own notes. "Okay, so we're entering through the back kitchen door."

Zoe chimes in. "That's our friendliest entry point. I'll have disabled the alarm system, so it's just the deadbolt and the door-knob. I'll pick the locks, of course. Easy peasy."

I pull up a photo of the kitchen. In the picture, which was taken for an architectural magazine, it's painted bright yellow with floral curtains on the windows. I turn my laptop so they can see it. "So now we're in the kitchen. Eddie—any ideas for that room?"

He studies my screen, rubbing his chin. "I'm interested in finding a way to show their before and after narrative. They were a perfect couple—a beautiful movie star and doting wife to a hot shot studio executive. She would make him breakfast, send him off to work, never realizing what was about to happen. That kind of thing."

"You're not in film school yet," Jacob mutters.

"What's that supposed to mean?" Eddie claps back.

"You're not, like, some professional director, so you can stop acting—"

Zoe holds a hand up. "No bickering, boys. Casey's going to kill you."

She's right. I may kill them. I ask, "So then what? We leave the kitchen, we're in the hallway that leads either up the stairs or to the living room where the crime happened. And it's a big house; there's a dining room, maid's quarters..." I flip to another photo, which features the living room and gives a peek of the hallway behind. "Should we try to find everyday items that haven't been disturbed? I'm picturing canned goods in the kitchen cabinets, toiletries in the bathrooms, clothes in the closet, that sort of thing."

"Totally," Eddie says.

Jacob chimes in. "But please try to keep the lighting consistent. It's hard when one of you is using a flashlight and one is using your phone, then the third one is using the light on the camera, and I have to edit all of that together."

"We should all make sure to use the lights on the cameras," Zoe suggests.

I realize this warning is for my benefit because last time I forgot and used my phone. "Sorry," I mumble. "I won't forget this time."

"Cool," Eddie replies, typing something into his notes. He's the reason we have access to studio-quality cameras; he borrows (steals) old ones from his dad's collection of gear. You'd think Zoe could just buy us what we need, but her parents are careful not to spoil her and they give her a normal-sized allowance. If they ever found out about *We'll Never Tell*, it's entirely possible she'd spend the rest of her life padlocked in her bedroom.

Zoe looks up from her laptop, eyes dreamy. "The Silver Lake Murder House. We've come a long way from fake-breaking into CityWalk."

"This is our Everest," Eddie agrees.

I don't say anything. I'm glad they're happy about this, but I'm...not.

Jacob says, "We're going out with a bang."

Zoe takes his hand. "I can't believe I'm moving to the East Coast."

"After college, I bet you move to New York," I say. "You have very main-character, lead-singer energy."

"I know, right?" She fans herself dramatically. "Remember that one time at karaoke? I'm surprised Jacob and I didn't land a record deal."

We bust up remembering the night spent at a restaurant in nearby Thai Town, where we'd discovered they had a karaoke *and* lights machine. Jacob and Zoe had entertained Eddie and me for hours, with Jacob's finale rendition of "Midnight Radio" from *Hedwig and the Angry Inch* bringing the house down.

"Can I just say something?" I ask, heart pounding as I try to find a way to put feelings into words. "You guys have been, like...the best..." I trail off, embarrassed.

"Aw, Casey's trying to be emotional and can't." Zoe cracks up.

I groan. "Never mind, I hate you."

Jacob mimes being a robot. "I am Casey. Machine learning human emotions. Is this love?"

I pull a pillow off the bed and hurl it at him, dislodging my glasses. Jacob cowers, protecting his laptop with his body, and Eddie says, "Whoa, watch the hair," which makes Zoe laugh harder.

She grabs a fork off the tray and brandishes it, pretending to stab Eddie. "You're Rosalinda," she says in a mock-scary voice. "And I'm her evil husband, Andrew. You're dead!"

He falls backward on the bed. "But, darling, I thought we were so in love."

Jacob says, "Can you believe it, though? Killed by her husband? Damn."

Zoe quips, "Statistically, women are far more likely to be murdered by an intimate partner than by anyone else."

I'm frozen, halfway through cleaning my glasses, feeling like I've turned to stone. There's nothing good for me to say right now. How can they make jokes about a woman getting stabbed right in front of me?

"Hey," Eddie says, nudging Zoe. He glances at me, and the three of them stop, clearly sharing this realization all at once.

"Sorry, Case," Zoe murmurs, putting a hand on my arm. A horrible part of me hates her for her perfect life; her gorgeous house; her cool, nice, and very much alive parents.

I jerk away, not wanting to be touched. "I'm fine. Let's just move on." I shove my glasses back onto my face. An awkward silence hangs between us. I take a deep, shuddery breath. I hadn't realized it, but I'm kind of hurt and angry that they pressured me into agreeing to this as a last episode. Well...did they pressure me? Or were they just so excited that I couldn't see a way to speak up?

None of them seem to have even considered how I'm supposed to feel at the scene of a crime that's so similar to the way my mom died. They've been caught up in the novelty of breaking into such a famous location and the romance of the murder itself: a crime of passion, of jealousy, of possession.

But in reality, there's no romance in a crime of passion. There's just the ending of a life, small and quiet, and the broken people who get left behind.

THE HOLLYWOOD REVIEW

WHAT HAPPENED TO THE VALENTINIS—
AN ANSWER AT LAST?

FRIDAY, APRIL 28, 1972

After two weeks of Hollywood's elite grieving the late Valentinis, the Los Angeles Police Department has answered the world's most pressing question: Who killed Andrew and Rosalinda? The answer is even more shocking than we expected: It was Andrew himself.

The LAPD confirmed Rosalinda's cause of death was a series of stab wounds, and her husband died from a gunshot wound to the head. All injuries seem to have been inflicted by none other than Andrew Valentini. "The investigation is ongoing, and we're exploring other avenues of inquiry," stated Chief Mason

at 9:00 a.m. in a press conference at the Central Police Station downtown. "But we believe a domestic crime is the most likely scenario."

Those close to the couple recall that Andrew was no angel. "He could be jealous," Anita Allan (*The Way Forward*, *The Lost Summer*) told us. A confidential source confirmed Mr. Valentini's jealous nature, going so far as to say he was "obsessed" with his wife, keeping close track of her whereabouts. In light of today's revelations, there is no denying Mr. Valentini had a dark side.

Speculations abound as to the cause of Andrew's rancor toward his starlet wife. A separate confidential source said, "She could be flighty. You never knew what she was up to. He had his work cut out for him, keeping tabs on her." Another close friend shared doubts about Rosalinda's faithfulness. Eyes are turning toward her on-screen lover, Mr. Ken Keaton, whose chemistry with Rosalinda tantalized crowds in the recent release *Love in the Islands.* The famous beach scene between the two had tabloids raging; now, friends of the late couple can't help but wonder...could there be some truth to the rumors?

The shock rippling through Hollywood this morning is palpable. A neighbor said, "The Valentini house always stood at the top of the hill as a shining beacon of Hollywood success. Now its darkness looms over all of us." Beautiful Rosalinda, only twenty-three, with her long blond hair and shining blue eyes, will forever be remembered as a treasure taken too soon.

Memorial services will be private.

THREE

Saturday, April 8

IN THE BLINK OF AN EYE, IT'S SATURDAY NIGHT, and we're piled into Eddie's car. He drives us through the Silver Lake hills, and I'm quietly staring out the windshield, reminiscing about all the other times he's driven us around the city in the middle of the night, all the adventures we've had.

The memories come with a side of guilt. If my grandma knew the places I've been, she'd have a heart attack. After losing my mom, you'd think I'd be extra careful with my personal safety, and usually I am. I've never fully understood why I do this. It's almost a need. It feels like freedom.

These hills are pitch-black in a way my neighborhood never is. This is an interesting part of Los Angeles, with hidden pathways and staircases leading to secret sidewalks; I'm riding shotgun, helping

Eddie navigate through the darkness. Zoe and Jacob are in the back, looking out the windows like I am, and I wonder if they're finally feeling some of the sadness that's been haunting me for weeks.

"What's this music?" I ask, frowning at the instrument panel.

Eddie turns it up. "'Everybody Plays the Fool.' A popular song from 1972. I made us a playlist for tonight."

"My dad has this album," Zoe says. "It's got that parents-getting-romantic vibe."

"Gross," I tell her. "Turn left here at the stop sign," I instruct Eddie. "Then the street will dead-end, and we'll park on the cul-de-sac."

Eddie pulls onto the side of the road, flips off the headlights, and opens his driver's door. "Let's do it."

We start our usual routine: slipping on latex gloves so we don't leave fingerprints, pulling hair into a bun (Zoe), double-knotting laces that always come untied (me). Jacob opens the trunk and starts handing out our clunky movie cameras. They're twenty years old, which is the only reason their absence from Eddie's father's storage space goes unnoticed. At this point, I assume he doesn't even remember they exist. Zoe passes out the four burner phones from a gallon Ziploc, and we each pocket one. We obviously don't want to have our phones traceable while committing crimes, but we like to have a four-way call open during our explorations so we can keep track of each other. "You charged them?" Eddie checks, and Zoe nods.

Eddie locks his car, and I lead the way along the quiet side-walk lined with overgrown bushes. It takes us to a narrow flight of concrete steps where the air smells like blooming roses and it's so dark I could almost imagine we're not in Los Angeles at all. The stairs let us out onto the landing of another sidewalk, this one a tiny, two-foot-wide walkway between houses. We creep single file along the path. It's silent but for the crunching of leaves under our sneakers, and we're struggling to hold the cameras against our bodies so they don't bump into the fences on either side.

I slow down, searching, and then I find what I'd expected from my recon: the beginning of a high concrete wall that continues along the footpath as far as the eye can see. "This is the rear of the property, right?" Zoe says, unzipping her backpack.

"Yep," I confirm.

She pulls out her laptop and squats down, fingers flying across the keys. The screen lights up her face, and Eddie says, "That would be a great shot if we could use it."

My stomach is full of jitters. Anticipation? Excitement? Fear? Images creep in—Rosalinda Valentini, surprised, turning to face her attacker, her husband, Andrew, and then the sharp punch of a knife through breastbone. I wonder if it made a sound, like a crunch, or if—*Stop*, I command myself. Forcefully, I shove these thoughts aside.

Zoe finishes deactivating the alarm, and at last we're climbing the fence with the help of our favorite rope ladder. Eddie goes over first, then Zoe, then Jacob, and I go last, crouching on the top of the wall to pull the ladder up and toss it down to Jacob on the other side.

I jump and land on the soft earth. We're at the far end of the expansive property behind the pitch-black swimming pool, a gaping hole gouged in the land. The bushes and hedges are overgrown, the grass mostly dead. Ahead, the house looms. It's tall and stark white, a sharp-cornered, Spanish-style collection of angles and tiles. Against the pallid stucco, the vines marbling its walls make it look like some haunted creature being dragged down into the earth, screaming out of hollow window mouths.

When I was researching the Valentinis, I listened to a true crime podcast that unpacked the original crime. The host lives in LA, and when she described the house she said, "I'm not one for vibes and auras—that's the opposite of evidence—but this house has seriously dark energy."

Staring up at our quarry, I feel a chill forming in my lower abdomen. Suddenly, I don't want to go inside. What if there's something lurking in there, waiting.... What if something dark and residual, from the violence that took place within these walls, can stick to us—follow us home—

Jacob snaps me out of it. "Cover up," he reminds me. They all have their ski masks on already.

"Sorry. It's creepy, right?" I whisper, pulling my own over my hair and settling the eyeholes in place over my glasses. We always wear black ski masks to avoid accidentally showing up in each other's shots. We learned this trick the hard way after having to toss tons of footage.

"Totally creepy," Zoe murmurs.

We slip earbuds in under the masks, and Zoe starts a four-way call. "You guys hear me?" she checks.

"We hear you," Eddie says.

"I hear you," Jacob echoes.

"Same." My stomach is in knots.

This is it. We're going in.

FOUR

Saturday, April 8

WE CROSS THE UNKEMPT BACKYARD AND PASS the swimming pool. I can't help being drawn to the edge; it's been emptied, but a black pond has formed at the bottom. Through the woolly ski mask, I get whiffs of brackish water, algae, and a piercing sewer smell.

"Gross," Eddie murmurs. He's beside me with his camera, shining the light down into the scum. Talking on camera's not a problem; we always replace the audio with voice-over narration and music.

"Hurry up," Zoe hisses at us. She's already at the back door with her lock picking tools, two different picks in hand as she manipulates the deadbolt. Jacob is filming the process; people love to see how we manage to break in so quickly without getting caught. There's no "we," really. It's all Zoe.

"Textbook," she whispers, and the door swings open, screeching loudly on its hinges.

The kitchen is quiet and dark, and it smells musty, like no fresh air has entered for half a century, which I guess it hasn't. We tiptoe single file, already filming as Zoe pulls the door shut behind us, sealing in a hollow silence. Eddie and Jacob wander around, their cameras' narrow beams of light illuminating the counters.

It's a large, linoleum-floored room with a retro vibe. I mean, duh; it's been time-capsuled since 1972. On the Formica table by the window, a dusty vase holds the blackened remnants of dead flowers. I lift my camera, settle it on my shoulder, and get comfortable looking through the shutter. I flick the light on and press record. Zoe's doing the same thing. We've agreed that she and I will take the upstairs while Eddie and Jacob explore the ground floor.

"Ready?" I ask her.

"Sure. Hey, look at this." She's squatting to record something. I bend down and focus in on what she's found: a book of matches from a place called The Red Room.

I poke at them, carving a streak in the dust. "Are these from 1972? They look newer."

"We're not the first people to break in here," she replies, which is a fair point.

We leave the guys in the kitchen, opening cabinets and

whispering excitedly over ancient canned green beans, and the two of us head for the staircase, which is out in the hallway. "Hang on, I need to see something," I tell Zoe, surprising myself. I didn't plan this. I turn down the echoing, massive hallway with squeaking wood floors and yellowing walls, cracks like dry creek beds veining the drywall. I find myself in the arched entrance to a grand, cavernous living room. One side of the room is dominated by a beautiful, Spanish-tiled fireplace that stretches up to the twenty-foot ceiling. The sofas are low to the ground, square and modern in their lines. On the grand piano, which looks pale because of the layer of dust on it, sits a generic teddy bear, totally out of context, propped up by a pile of antique books. Its bright black eyes glint eerily in the light from our cameras. It's medium-sized, with arms that stick straight out like it wants a hug.

"They didn't have a kid," I say to Zoe, who's right at my shoulder. "Why is this here?"

"Maybe someone left it when they broke in. You know how people do those altars to victims of car accidents? They always leave stuffed animals."

In my earbuds, Eddie says, "You found a stuffed animal?"

"Yeah, on the piano," I reply.

"There's one in here, too. A bear. Sitting on the top of the fridge."

I exchange a look with Zoe. "That's..."

"Creepy," she supplies.

Jacob says, "Get a good shot of the bear, and make sure you can see exactly where it is. I want to edit them in next to each other, and it's only going to work if you can really see they're in different rooms."

"I'm on it," Zoe says, approaching the toy and focusing her camera.

And then my eyes land on what I came in here to see, on the carpet that was once plush and soft but is now crusty with grime: a dark, horrible splotch in the middle of the room. Another black stain marks the floor by the picture windows, which are covered with dirty damask curtains. I feel drawn to them, like they're magnetized.

"That was Rosalinda," I tell Zoe, pointing at the stain closest to the piano. Squatting down, I see not just the shape where the blood had pooled but streaks and spatter stains where the blood must have splashed during the stabbing.

"Dang," she breathes. "This is spooky as hell."

I can't take my eyes off the dried blood, and I feel one hand drawn unwillingly forward, reaching out a gloved finger to touch it.

Stay away. Run.

I stumble to my feet, panic seizing me. I clutch my camera, which swings heavily, trying to knock me off balance, trying to force me down to the carpet, back to the bloodstains. "I've got to get out of here," I tell Zoe. I pull her arm, hurrying us out of the room, glancing back like the blood will follow me somehow.

Good thing you didn't touch it. The words shiver through me, superstitious and enigmatic. I push Zoe ahead of me to the stairs, and we dash up.

"Everything good?" Eddie asks. The voice in my ear shocks me, and I jump a little.

"All good," Zoe says. "We found the bloodstains, but we'll let you record the footage down there. Going upstairs now."

The grimy wooden stairs groan under our feet, but otherwise, the darkness is stuffy, stale, and dead silent. I let Zoe get artsy shots of the little plumes of dust our feet dislodge on the staircase, and once we're up on the landing, I assess the floor plan, which consists of a main hallway with rooms leading off it. An alcove looks down on the living room, framing a settee placed just so, its burgundy velvet ashy with dust.

Zoe points left. "I'll take those rooms, you take the other side?"

I nod. My heart is pounding so hard and fast, I don't trust myself to speak. In my ear, Jacob says, "Do you guys dare me to eat one of these Wheat Thins?"

"No," chorus the rest of us.

"Seriously, don't—" Eddie says, and then the line goes dead.

Zoe pulls her burner phone out of her back pocket. "He must have hung up on us." She presses the button, restarts the call, and I pick it up, but Jacob and Eddie let it ring out.

"Should we go check on them?" I ask.

She tries again, but it rings six times without a reply. "We probably have bad service up here. It's fine. I'll call again in a few minutes."

I agree, and we part ways to film. I start with a powder room where decorative soaps have fossilized into rocks. The toilet is empty and smells bad; clearly the water was turned off long ago.

I find an office with a *Mad Men* aesthetic, and I poke around in the desk drawers filled with clipped ads for hair spray—the blond model has epic, feathered bangs—and catalogs filled with women in bright, bell-bottom pantsuits, which I riffle through on camera.

Something creaks in the hallway. I jump, electrified with fear. Silence settles on me like a weighted blanket, and I realize I'm not breathing. I force in a chestful of air, which makes my head feel dizzy.

Nothing is there. I'm alone. "Get a grip," I whisper to myself.

We've been in so many abandoned places. This is not my first rodeo. That burned-out clothing factory downtown had been vast, empty, with the hungry feeling that ghosts were waiting in every pool of darkness. Why is *this* house putting me so on edge?

I know the answer as soon as my brain poses the question: because at every other site, the four of us were never disconnected. Somehow this house has managed to lure me into complete isolation.

Just get this over with. I turn to the bookshelves, pulling out a few volumes and flipping through them, not recognizing any of the titles: *The French Lieutenant's Woman* by John Fowles; *The Crystal Cave* by Mary Stewart. I'm tempted to steal one, but it seems wrong. I've read about cultures where they burn all the dead's porous belongings: paper goods, clothes, blankets—anything a spirit might be able to embed itself in.

Something occurs to me: The police investigated this murder for years. They must have searched the house a thousand times. Why is it so neat in here? I examine the desk. It's dusty, but not fifty-year-old dust. This makes me uneasy, though I know the house has an owner. Our research says it was passed to a relative of Andrew's when he died, and it's since changed hands between family members. Maybe they have a cleaning service come in every so often. They probably check for vermin, make sure no one's squatting in here. There's a functioning alarm system, after all. But why haven't they just sold it or torn it down yet? None of the crime podcasters seem to know.

I leave the office and discover a guest room with a floral bedspread and a rose-colored armchair by the window looking out at the backyard, as though this was someone's favorite spot. I approach the chair, next to which sits a small side table, and wonder if this could have been somewhere Rosalinda liked to hang out. It must have a nice view in daylight. I picture her reading here, and I wonder if she kept stationery nearby for writing letters.

I adjust my camera on my shoulder and examine the side table. At first glance, it doesn't seem to have any storage, but when I grip the underside and pull, a drawer slides out. Sure enough, there are all kinds of things in here: pens, vintage stamps, cards. I pull the paper goods out and notice that some of these are letters addressed to Rosalinda. How did nobody get to them before now?

On second thought, it's plausible enough: This is clearly a guest room, and the little table is hidden unless you're on the other side of the armchair. For anyone breaking in to steal Rosalinda's personal belongings or valuables, this corner doesn't exactly scream "jackpot." I bring one of the letters into the light cast by my camera. In loopy cursive, I read *Dear Rosie, It's been too long.*

A thunk from downstairs—something heavy, like a piece of furniture falling over. I freeze, letter in hand, and hold my breath. Silence.

I set the letter down, get my phone out of my back pocket, and call the group. Zoe alone picks up. "What was that?" she asks.

"No idea. Where are the guys?"

"I assume downstairs. They're not answering."

"Let's go check on them," I say, uneasy.

The same nervousness I feel is echoed back to me in her voice. "Good call. Meet me at the staircase."

I hem and haw for a moment, and then I quickly go through the papers and cards and extract the stack of letters. They're too precious to leave behind. If Rosalinda were my mom, I'd want someone to get these to me. I decide I'm going to find her descendants and mail them the letters anonymously.

I stuff the letters into the pocket of my hoodie and hurry back to the landing, where Zoe is waiting at the top of the staircase. "You should see the dresses in the master bedroom closet," she says. "I can't believe they haven't been stolen. I'm talking yellow satin, seventies pink chiffon. Incredible."

"Right? I found—"

The alarm goes off.

It hits us like a tsunami, the air suddenly pierced with ear-splitting sirens. We shriek in surprise, and Zoe cries in protest, "I disarmed it!"

"That's a little beside the point. Let's get out of here!"

We tuck our cameras under our arms and run down the stairs, through the hall, into the kitchen, and out into the backyard. The guys aren't out here. It's marginally quieter, but the wailing of the alarm is echoing through the hills. In a neighborhood like this, the cops will be here any minute.

"Where are they?" I cry. "They should have beaten us out here."

She turns in a circle, looking for them. "They must still be inside. What the hell?"

"I don't know!" I rush across the patio, returning to the house.

Inside, the volume of the alarm is unbearable. I search the kitchen—no one—and the pantry. I notice an open side door potentially leading to the garage, and another leading to a bathroom and a study I hadn't realized were there. The noise is piercing my temples, slicing into my forehead.

Zoe appears behind me, shouting to be heard. "Find them?"

"No!"

She turns, panicked, and I follow her through the kitchen into the living room. She stops short, and I bump into her back.

Jacob is on the ground. His body is stretched across the carpet in the middle of the room between the two antique bloodstains. Eddie is kneeling beside him, hands pressed to Jacob's chest. Jacob's face is calm, serene, eyes closed. A dark stain spreads on the pale carpet beneath him, growing as I watch.

Zoe breaks free from the frozen horror first. She sprints the last few yards to Jacob, tosses her camera onto the carpet and kneels beside him, hands flying to his neck, searching for a pulse. She presses here, there, apparently finds nothing, then grabs his wrist. She leans down and listens at his mouth for breath sounds. I'm shocked she can think or act or hear at all above the alarm; it's vibrating in my bones. Eddie is sobbing, doubled over now, and I catch an expression on his averted face that I've seen before, on my grandma.

Jacob is dead.

FIVE

Saturday, April 8

I CAN'T BE HERE, WITH JACOB BLEEDING OUT on the carpet. It's too much. Images of my mom's death flood my pounding skull, horrible scenes I've pictured a million times, my imagination filling in all kinds of grisly details. The blood, flowing out of Jacob—this is what she looked like. This is how the life left her body.

Zoe yells, "We have to get out of here!" Eddie and I don't reply, don't react. We can't tear our eyes off Jacob's face. He looks peaceful, lips parted slightly, fair skin glowing in the half-light. She grabs Eddie by the arm, drags him to his feet. "You guys! You aren't thinking straight! Someone else is in this house. We're in danger, we need to go!"

Eddie finally speaks, and I have to read his lips to catch the words. "I'm not leaving."

"Shut up," Zoe commands. "Take Jacob's camera and let's go. Now." She keeps glancing around at the darkness, paranoid—obviously afraid someone is going to pop out and attack us, too.

I point at Jacob. "He doesn't have his camera."

Eddie and Zoe whip their heads down to Jacob, and then we exchange a three-way, petrified stare.

Zoe says, "Either someone is still in this house, or someone *was* in this house. No matter what, the cops are about to respond to this alarm, and we are going down not only for this but for all the stuff on our YouTube channel. Our lives will be over."

"Jacob is dead," Eddie roars, so suddenly furious I almost cower in terror. "What is wrong with you?"

"Zoe's right," I tell him, barely able to see through my tears.

"Let's go," she insists, pushing us. "Come on. Go!"

I grab my camera, and Zoe picks up both hers and Eddie's, shoving his into his arms. I take Eddie's hand and drag him with me. We run through the kitchen, out the back door, and into the yard, where the alarm echoes outward. As we sprint to the back fence, cameras bruising our legs as they bump against us, I imagine someone springing out of the darkness and thrusting a knife into my back.

Zoe has the rope ladder in position and is climbing it. Tears pouring down his cheeks, Eddie follows her, knocking his camera carelessly against the wall, and then I'm climbing with the urgency of someone about to be knifed in the back. When I jump down, I stumble to my knees, sending my camera toppling to the asphalt. Zoe helps me up, hands me my camera, grabs the rope ladder, and then we're running down the narrow, dark walking path. Branches whip against my cheeks, and the pulsating of the security system fades in the background, now replaced by the wail of police sirens. We tumble down narrow concrete stairs, along another path, and I'm convinced we're lost until Zoe leads us onto the street where we'd parked.

Now a complete zombie, Eddie walks right past his own car. Zoe grabs the back of his shirt, goes through his pockets, and finds the car key. "Get him in," she tells me, but I'm useless, too, my hands so numb, I'm not even sure if I still have my camera. I do, though; I'm clutching it so tight, my knuckles and fingers are dead white.

Zoe unlocks the car, shoving Eddie into the back seat. As she takes my camera and throws it in behind him, she says, "Casey: I need you to pull it together." I try to shake some sense into myself as I get in the passenger's seat.

She adjusts the mirrors and starts the car. I'm trembling from head to toe. This can't be real. We were only in the house for what...fifteen minutes? Maybe twenty? I can almost imagine it didn't happen. Fifteen minutes isn't long enough for death.

Then again, my mom was gone in five. Stabbed on the way to her car at the end of her bartending shift. A customer had come along five minutes later, and she was already gone.

Eddie's face is buried in his knees. His voice comes out muffled as he says, "Who would do this? Why?" Zoe's expression is grim. She turns right at a stop sign and speeds up, the road a little wider now. We're almost out of the hills, heading in the opposite direction from the sirens.

"I just don't understand how we got here," I hear myself say.

Zoe drives in silence. We're fleeing the scene of a crime; what we just did could implicate us in Jacob's murder. By running away, we've incriminated ourselves.

"Turn off this freaking song," Eddie moans from the back seat. I don't know what he's talking about, and then I realize— loud, happy music is blaring out of the speakers. It's Paul Simon's "Me and Julio Down by the Schoolyard." Lips pressed into a grim line, Zoe turns the volume off.

Eddie's staring, blank, at his hands. He peels off the gloves, leaving only his bare skin, sticky and shining with blood. Zoe turns left onto Glendale Boulevard and floors it, speeding east, putting as much distance as she can between us and Silver Lake.

"Get out my laptop," she tells me. "I want to listen to the police scanner."

I robotically start digging through her things, and Eddie begins crying again, his sobs quiet. It's his first encounter with death, I think. Oddly enough, it's the first time I've seen it up close, too. It was anticlimactic. Jacob was just quiet, as though he were asleep.

I don't think it was like that for my mom. I've always imagined her face frozen into a scream. In my darkest moments, I think she must have gone into the cremator like that, face fixed in an eternal expression of terror. At least Jacob will look peaceful in his coffin.

I know these thoughts are no good. There's a reason I never say what I'm thinking.

SIX

Saturday, March 25 (Two Weeks Ago)

JACOB

I WAS IN THE LIVING ROOM, FACING OFF WITH my dad, when I heard Eddie let himself in the front door. "Anybody home?" he called. He was wearing his favorite jeans and fitted black T-shirt, backpack slung over his shoulder.

My dad narrowed his eyes at me. "You want to tell him, or should I?"

Eddie halted, alarmed, when he saw us. We were both obviously fuming, my dad's tattooed arms folded across the chest of his white cook's uniform.

"It doesn't matter," I said. "Go ahead. I've got nothing to hide. I'm not doing anything wrong."

Eddie cleared his throat. "Sorry, I didn't mean to interrupt. I can go."

My dad ran his hands through his graying hair, which he wears in an undercut. "Eddie, see if you can talk some sense into this kid."

"About what?"

"Did you know he pulled his applications to the Cal States?"

Eddie turned to me, face full of concern. "Why did you do that?"

His expression pissed me off. "I'm going to be a PA and work my way up. I don't want to waste four years of tuition on something that's not even going to help me get a job." What I didn't say is that my grades probably only qualified me for community college anyway. "Besides, you're one to talk," I told my dad. "You didn't go to college. You came out here to be a musician. At least I have career goals that will pay my bills."

"Yeah, *look at me*." He laughed bitterly. "I'm a line cook, Jake. If I'd gone to culinary school, I could be a chef, I could work in fine dining or open my own restaurant—"

"You can do that now," I argued. "Literally no one is stopping you."

He put a hand to his forehead. "Why don't you talk to Mike? See what he says." Eddie's dad. A successful director. "I bet he says you need a college degree. I love you, kid. I just want you to have more than I did."

USC-bound Eddie did not need to be here for this. I gave my dad a glare that was probably unfair and said, "Sorry you raised such a loser."

"Jake, stop," my dad ordered, his voice doing the authoritative thing that always made me want to throw something at a wall. I spun, heading for my room before I started destroying things. I knew Eddie would follow.

And he did. He was right on my heels, probably waiting for us to be alone so he could lecture me about not being organized and getting my life together, like he did effortlessly. In my room, I commanded, "Close the door." He did, opening his mouth to say something but I cut him off. "Just shut up. Please." I crossed the messy floor, fumbling for my phone on the nightstand clutter, and hit play on Spotify. From the Bluetooth speaker by my bed, the Misfits blared, intrusive and aggressive and exactly what I wanted.

"You don't have to be a dick," Eddie said, calm as always. "Just tell me what's going on. Are you afraid of getting rejected by colleges? Is that why you pulled your applications?"

"I already told you why I did it. There's no other secret reason. Jesus." I raked my hands through my hair and we met each other's eyes. After ten years, we didn't always need to argue out loud. Sometimes we could do it telepathically. In that moment, I was as jealous and irritated by Eddie as I was pissed off at my dad.

I stepped closer to him. He tracked me with narrowed eyes.

"I'm never going to be perfect like you," I said between my teeth.

"That's bullshit and you know it." His tone was infuriatingly calm. I wanted a reaction, to know he cared enough to shout.

I put a hand on the wall by his head, leaned in, and kissed him. He sucked air in through his nose. Pulling back a little, I looked him in the eyes. We were silent for a few seconds, and then he tangled a hand in my hair. "I missed you today," he murmured, kissing me again. His lips were rough, searching. He pulled back a few inches. "Maybe we shouldn't right now. Your dad—"

I dismissed this. "He's rage-cooking. Can't you hear him?" I pressed him back into the wall and kissed him again. I unbuckled his belt and pulled it off in a swift motion, and now I had his full attention and that reaction I needed so badly. He locked the door and shoved me backward, down onto my bed, and I felt the first true smile of the day spread across my face. He stripped his shirt off, lifted mine over my head, and we were skin on skin, everything blurring into a haze of sensation.

Afterward, in bed in our boxers, arms wrapped around each other, Eddie whispered, "Why didn't you tell me?"

I sighed. His cheek was on my chest, and his head moved gently with my breath. He waited me out, patient to a fault. "College makes sense for you, but it doesn't for me. I don't want to be a screenwriter or some fancy director. I want to *work*. I want to be out in the world. I don't want to spend four years in a holding tank."

Eddie propped himself on an elbow and ran a hand through my hair, his dark eyes melting me, so close and intimate. "I didn't ask why you don't want to go to college. I know that; I know you. I want to understand why you didn't tell me."

"You're better than me," I murmured. "In every possible way. Why would I keep reminding you?"

He frowned.

"I'm afraid to lose you," I blurted out, which was...maybe more than I should have said. We didn't talk about what it meant, being together like this. We hadn't talked about it when we first kissed, drunk one Saturday night last year, and we hadn't talked about it when we first slept together, or when we did it again, or when we started snuggling under the covers after every hookup.

Eddie rubbed a thumb across my cheek. "You figured I'd stop talking to you if you didn't go to college? It's stupid to think you'd lose me over that."

"Do I even have you to lose?" I replied, and I couldn't believe I'd said it.

He lifted his eyebrows. "I mean..."

With my usual recklessness, I said, "Because I love you."

Silence. I could feel his shock.

I gestured wildly at the door, at the world beyond. "I don't need anyone else to know about us, but I need..." Who was I kidding? I needed everything.

"Jacob," Eddie said, voice low and serious. "We can't."

"I'm not saying we have, like, a coming out party. I mean, I—"

He pulled away, the softness between us hardening into cement. His back to me, he said, "I can't."

Just like that, he sucked all the air from my lungs and the blood from my veins. I felt weightless, like I was floating on a cloud made from his words: *I can't*. I turned away from him, drew a pillow toward me and pressed my face into it. Everything in my bloodless, airless body hurt. That was it, then. He was saying no.

In a cruel, swift confirmation, Eddie got up, put his clothes on, and left.

SEVEN

Saturday, April 8

WE'RE SILENT AS ZOE DRIVES THROUGH ECHO
Park into the bright lights and tent cities of Downtown LA. This
isn't the way home, but Eddie and I don't question it. I'm not
exactly ready to see my grandma right now.

Wait, no. I'm supposed to be spending the night at Zoe's.
We're "at a show." I can't go home yet anyway. "This is so bad," I
murmur, not intending to say it aloud. I'm stick-straight, sitting
with my knees clenched together, hands pressed between my
legs. Every muscle in my body is tensed to keep from shivering.

Eddie suddenly leans forward between the front seats. "Hey.
Do you think this could be a joke? You know Jacob likes pranks."

Zoe and I exchange an anxious look. We're at a stoplight

in the financial district, brightly lit but populated only by the homeless people who own downtown at this time of night.

"Eddie, I don't think so." I turn to put a hand on his shoulder. His face shines with desperate hope, something even worse than his grief.

Zoe takes a right and finds a tucked-away street with almost no lights and a row of tents whose occupants have gone to sleep for the night. She pulls over and puts the car in park. Killing the headlights, she says, "There's an easy way to find out." She takes the laptop from me, and I only notice she still has her gloves on when she starts typing, her secure personal hotspot thankfully going strong. Behind us, Eddie leans back, curling up against the window.

Noise blares from the laptop speakers, and my nerves are so raw I jump. She ignores this, adjusting the volume. Static white noise fills the car.

"I need two units to 1269 Glendale Boulevard for a possible 647," says a female dispatcher.

"Working on it," says a male voice. "What's the status of the 459 in Silver Lake?"

"Units just arrived."

A different voice says, "On scene. 459 confirmed, back door wide open. We're going in."

"Roger that," dispatch replies.

I tell Zoe and Eddie, "459 is the code for breaking and entering."

Eddie has leaned toward the speakers and is gripping the shoulders of our seats. The voice comes back on the scanner, sharper now. "10-52, we need an ambulance. We have a possible 187, teenage kid bleeding out. Repeat, 10-52, immediately, to 29 Lakeview Terrace." The house alarm echoes behind him, frenzied and shrill on the airwaves.

I put my hand on Eddie's. He rests his forehead on my hand, and I feel hot tears make tracks down my cheeks. Zoe is a statue, staring lifelessly out the window. The scanner hisses. "Ambulance en route to 29 Lakeview."

Another voice asks, "Do we need more units to Silver Lake?"

The now-familiar deep voice answers, "No, we've got this. We're sealing the perimeter. No suspects in custody; we're searching the house."

"Creepy old place."

"That it is. Stand by." A pause, during which a different voice says, "Units arrived at Glendale Boulevard. Drunk and disorderly confirmed; we're handling it."

A panicked tone cuts in from the cop at the murder house. "What's the status of the 10-52? This kid is alive!" Eddie shoots upright.

The dispatcher replies, "Two minutes out."

"We're in the living room. Tell them to come straight in through the front door. Officers are waiting."

"Roger."

Zoe, Eddie, and I all talk at once. "Alive?" Zoe exclaims.

"I thought you checked," Eddie chokes out simultaneously.

"I'm not a doctor!" she wails.

"He's alive? And we left him there to die?" My voice is the quietest of the three.

The scanner crackles, and we all suck our words back into our chests. "Ambulance arrived at 29 Lakeview. Kid is hanging on, just barely. He's definitely one of the intruders. Looks like one turned against the other. We've got a 664 here. Multiple stab wounds to the chest."

"Is the scene clear?" the dispatcher asks.

"Almost. Doing one last sweep of the house. Detectives on the way?"

"Confirmed."

"What's a 664?" Eddie asks me.

"Attempted murder," I reply.

The rest of the chatter on the scanner is about a different scene, a drunk guy in Echo Park, and then a liquor store robbery, and then they don't come back to Jacob at all.

Zoe closes the laptop, and we look at each other in silence. "What a mess," she says.

Eddie's face is stricken. "He was alive, and we left him."

"I know," I reply, just as horrified.

"I don't think he'll ever forgive me." This comes out as a whisper, like he hadn't meant for anyone to hear.

Zoe makes a frustrated noise. "Try to pause your feelings for five seconds. Think rationally. We are completely and totally screwed." Despite her pretend control, she's clearly losing it, cheeks flushed, eyes hot, lips pale. "They're calling in detectives. That house is now a crime scene—*again*. They're going to do forensics, CSI, come *on*." She flails a hand in a frantic gesture. "What do you think all that investigating will turn up?"

I reply sharply. "Hopefully, the person who tried to kill Jacob."

She almost yells at me, "Don't you think they'll be able to tell we were all there? Who knows what evidence we left behind? It won't take a genius to piece together who was with him. And I hacked into the alarm company's site. What if they get smart enough to trace that back to me? Then what? Eddie and Jacob are eighteen, and Casey, you and I are almost there. We're looking at felony charges, even before they start pinning Jacob's attack on us!"

I grab her hands in mine. "Stop. You're panicking." Her chest is heaving. Eddie is stricken, mute. I say, "They might not be able to tell as much as you think. I can say from personal experience, everything you've seen on TV procedurals is fiction. You're forgetting there was a fifth person in there tonight. Someone stabbed Jacob, Zoe. We need to come clean to the cops so we aren't muddying their investigation with any evidence we left. They need to know the full story so they can look for that fifth person."

"No." Eddie is the one who says it. He clears his throat and wipes his face with both hands. "We're not talking to the cops." I make shocked eye contact with him, and he shakes his head. "No. We are never telling them about *We'll Never Tell*. That was our deal. And we can't say we were at the murder house tonight without risking them figuring out that we're behind the channel."

"We have to," I protest. "We can tell them we're just stupid

53

teenagers breaking in on a dare, and then Jacob got stabbed. They might not even charge us with the breaking and entering."

"They won't look any further than us once they know we were there!" Zoe cries. "You really think they'll believe that a random fifth person just swooped in and stabbed Jacob? The only evidence of a fifth person is that Jacob's camera is missing, but we can't reveal that without telling them about our channel."

I try to argue, try to come up with a solid rebuttal, but I can't. My stomach twinges with fear. It's starting to sink in: We could be blamed for what was done to Jacob. That's a real possibility. Eddie leans back against the seat and pinches the bridge of his nose. I look out the window at the tent city. Zoe rubs her mouth, as though she might wipe off tonight like old lipstick.

I'm the one who breaks the silence. "So we do nothing? Seriously?"

"That's what Jacob would tell us to do," Eddie says. "We'll meet him at the hospital and explain everything so he knows what's up."

"What should we tell our parents about tonight?" Zoe asks, more to herself than to us. "Casey and I are supposed to be at that show...Eddie and Jacob..." She swivels to face him. "Where did you guys say you were going?"

"We didn't. My parents are out of town, so Jake just told his dad he was coming to my house to sleep over."

When Zoe thinks hard, her hazel eyes flit back and forth like she's reading. They do this now, and I get the impression that she's not really processing Eddie, though her face is turned toward him.

"What are you thinking?" I prompt. Outside, a man has emerged from one of the tents and is pacing around in front of it, hands fisted in his armpits against the light chill in the night air.

Zoe turns her eyes on me, and they're steady now. "Eddie's building is pretty high-security. They have cameras in the lobby, a buzzer."

"So?"

"So let's say we got ourselves on camera going into Eddie's building and I altered the time stamp on the footage. That's a solid alibi that would show we weren't with Jacob."

Eddie sits forward, elbows on knees, like he's worried about being overheard. "Or the cops will be able to tell you tried to mess with it, and we'll look ten times guiltier."

"Yeah," I agree. "That seems way worse than just going to your house."

She holds a hand up. "You guys. I've been breaking into security systems for three years. Ye of little faith."

This feels like we're digging ourselves a deeper hole. I double down. "I really think we should ditch the cameras, delete everything off our computers, and just tell the cops that we broke into the murder house with Jacob out of curiosity, just you know, teenagers being teenagers. They won't question it. People have broken in there before. We'll tell them exactly what happened, minus the fact that we were filming it. We'll say we got scared, that there was someone else in the house, and we'll—"

Eddie and Zoe are both already interrupting me with "No way, Case," and "Have you lost your mind? Do you want to go to jail for attempted murder?"

"Wait. Wait!" I wave my hands around to shush them. "You're forgetting something crucial. There was no murder weapon. Jacob was stabbed, but there was no knife in him. They won't have our prints on anything; we were all wearing gloves. Whoever did this took their knife away with them. So it couldn't have been us."

Eddie looks down at his hands, which he must have wiped on his pants, because the blood that had covered them is almost gone.

Zoe says, "Casey, that's not entirely correct." She nods to Eddie. "He pulled the knife out of Jacob. He threw it aside."

"What?" I gape at Eddie.

"He had a knife in his chest, Casey. Of course I pulled it out!" His voice cracks, and he sounds like he's about to cry.

I take a deep breath. He clearly feels horrible. I don't want to make it worse. I say, "No matter what, your prints won't be on it."

Zoe says, "No way in hell am I telling the cops we were there. Jacob would never ask that of us."

"He wouldn't," Eddie agrees. "If it happened to me, I'd tell you guys to get out and pretend you were home all night." I consider that: If this had happened to me, what would I want?

I'd want the person who stabbed me to get caught. And they aren't going to get caught if the police don't have the complete and accurate story to work from. So yeah, I'd expect my friends to tell the cops the truth and face the consequences. But I can't make that choice for Jacob. This is a democracy, I guess.

All my Notion pages flash across my imagination, the names

of women, the black-and-white photos of their smiling faces pulled from yearbooks and driver's licenses. "You guys don't know what it's like," I say in a low, dark voice I've never heard come out of me before. "You think it's more important to stay out of trouble than find the person who did this. But you don't know how bad it is, the not knowing. The world moving on while whoever did this is just—out there."

Zoe puts a hand on my shoulder. Her face is full of compassion. "I know how you feel about justice. We won't mess that up for Jacob."

I meet her eyes, then Eddie's, both shining in the streetlights. "What if we do? Can you live with that?"

They look at each other, then turn back to me. Eddie is the one to answer. "If Jacob says he wants us to come clean, we will. I promise." Zoe nods her agreement.

Jacob's the victim. He should have the final word. "Okay," I concede. "That seems fair."

"Okay," Zoe replies. "So let's go to Eddie's. We'll be there all night. I'll doctor the footage."

I say, "We should get rid of all our *We'll Never Tell* stuff in the next day or so. Just to be safe."

Zoe responds, "I can wipe our computers, take all the software off. I'll need to get into Jacob's room, though. Eddie, do you have any ideas for that?"

He waves it off. "I have his laptop at my place."

Zoe breathes out a huge sigh of relief. "God, that's lucky. How long have you had it?"

"Just a few days." He doesn't look at her when he says this. I wonder if he feels guilty for some reason...if there's more to the story than he's telling us.

I say, "One last time, I just want to make sure you realize—if the police find out we were there, and we didn't tell them right away, this looks a hundred times worse. Especially if we're doctoring security camera footage to fake an alibi. There's no coming back from that."

They nod in unison. "We know," Eddie replies. I'm struck with the feeling that there's more at play here than I understand. It's the first time I've felt like my friends are strangers.

"Let's go," Zoe says, starting the engine.

EIGHT

Sunday, April 9

THE RIDE BACK TO HOLLYWOOD IS QUIET. EDDIE and Zoe switch seats so he can drive now that he's calmer. She and I keep our eyes out the windows, watching Koreatown and then East Hollywood move past in a series of barred windows, gated, closed restaurants, and rows of tents and shopping carts. We stop at a dumpster near one of these encampments to dispose of our ski masks. We tuck the cameras into Eddie's trunk and hide them under his pile of forgotten sweatshirts and papers from school.

Eddie lives in a four-story building off Hollywood and Vine. His parents rent three parking spaces in their underground garage, and he pulls the Honda Civic into his designated spot.

"Will anyone think it's weird that we're in all black on the security camera footage?" I ask as he closes the driver's door. "I mean, considering it matches Jacob's outfit?"

Eddie wordlessly grabs a white sweatshirt out of his trunk. Zoe rearranges the papers on top of the cameras, and we head across the parking garage toward the door.

I'm part of this now, contributing ideas. I have zero deniability.

Eddie unlocks the door with his building key, letting us into a hall that leads to the two elevators. Zoe presses the call button. She smiles brightly and says, "Casey, that's hilarious. Where did you even hear that?"

She gives me a meaningful look, and I realize she's attempting to seem lighthearted for the sake of the camera, which I'm trying desperately to ignore even though I see it positioned above the elevators, a dark glass sphere affixed to the ceiling.

I do my best to play along. "Some girl at school. You know Candace?"

"Oh yeah." We do know Candace; she's in my English class. I recall my last conversation with her. "She said she was going to get a VW Bug, one of the vintage ones, but her mom said no way, those are death traps."

Eddie pipes up. "They are death traps. That's legit."

Zoe says, "You have no sense of adventure."

The elevator dings and the doors slide open. Eddie leads the way and presses the button for the third floor. As the elevator rises, I try to remember if there is a camera inside here as well. I sneak peeks up at the ceiling.

"There's no camera," Zoe says. "I've checked before."

I nod, looking down at the toes of my Converse. A horrible

thought—what if we have Jacob's blood on our shoes? What if we're tracking it in? It occurs to me suddenly that we need to make sure there's no forensic evidence from the house on our clothes. We should really dump everything we're wearing.

The door slides gracefully open, and the clean, white hallway stretches to the left and right. Eddie's place is three doors down from the elevator, with a palm tree–printed doormat. Inside the unlit apartment, he tosses his keys on the kitchen counter, kicks off his Nikes, and heads straight for the fridge. "You guys want something to drink?"

We chorus an affirmative, and he grabs a few cans of Passion-fruit La Croix and hands them over.

"I'm worried about there being blood on here," I say, checking the soles of my Converse as Zoe and I untie our shoes. They check, too. Nothing. I'm slightly reassured.

Zoe plops her backpack on the counter and unzips it. "Your phone, Casey." She hands it to me.

"I don't think we should all power our phones on at the same time," I say.

"Agreed," Zoe replies. "Eddie, why don't you turn yours on now. If they're going to call one of us with news about Jacob, it's going to be you." He takes his phone out of his pocket and presses the power button. The Apple logo appears, and then the Home Screen. His wallpaper is a photo he took in Malibu. The time surprises me—two a.m. It's later than I'd thought.

"Who should power up next?" I ask her. "My grandma will be getting up to go to the flower market in an hour, but she'll assume we're sleeping."

"I'll go next," she suggests. "In an hour or so."

We take turns washing our hands, and then we retreat to Eddie's room, where we flop down in various places: Eddie on the bed, Zoe at his desk, attention focused on her laptop, and me on the beanbag chair that's usually Jacob's spot. Eddie's room is neat as always (unless you look in the closet or drawers), but something feels different. I let my eyes run over the walls and notice a *Star Wars Episode VI* poster, formerly affixed to the wall with putty, is now at a haphazard angle, like it fell and was put back in a hurry. I get up and start to fix it.

"Wait," Eddie protests, but it's too late. I've seen the hole in the drywall behind the poster.

"What's this?" I ask. It's a few inches in diameter, just below eye level for me, which would be shoulder level for him. "Did you punch the wall?"

He takes the poster from me and replaces it, straighter this time. He insists, "It's nothing. It's been there for a long time. I did it when I was thirteen."

I frown at his back. He's obsessively leveling the poster now, and once he's done, he returns to the bed, slumping into place. Zoe isn't listening to any of this; she's in the zone. I swallow down more questions. That hole has definitely not been here for five years.

"We should get rid of all our clothes and shoes from tonight," I say after a minute. "There has to be trace evidence from the house on them."

"Fine by me," Eddie replies, head cradled in his hands.

I muse aloud, "We should scatter them in different dumpsters. And then make sure we have similar clothes in our closets. Like, if the cops see us on the footage wearing black Converse but we don't own any black Converse, that will raise suspicion. But we can't be seen buying black Converse...." I turn the problem over and over in my mind.

"I have like ten pairs of Nikes," Eddie says. "The ones from tonight are black, but I have navy-blue ones that probably look identical from far away."

Zoe says, "I wore the same shoes you did today, Case."

"We'll have to get replacements."

"I'm sure we can. Converse are everywhere. We can pick some up at a little shop that doesn't have cameras or something." I nod. She's right. And the rest of our clothes are not distinctive. It's going to be fine.

Without my phone to distract me, I have nothing to do but stare at the stuff in Eddie's room. He's got his eyes closed now, but I can't imagine he'll be falling asleep anytime soon.

On top of his dresser is a neat row of picture frames, lined up in order from largest to smallest. I notice a few of them are empty; the rest are of his family. I linger on a photo of his parents and him, posed in front of the famous *Friends* fountain on the Warner Bros. lot. They must have been at a party; his mom is wearing a black mini dress and heels, her blond hair curled, her smile white and glamorous. His father is an older, more broad-shouldered version of his son, with a strong jaw and thick, dark hair that falls just so onto his forehead. Posed between them, Eddie has his mom's wide smile, but his is careful, guarded. I notice his hands are stuffed into his pockets, his forearm muscles tight like he's making them into fists out of sight.

"Ah!" Zoe says, startling me. "There they are. Oh my god,

this is going to be easy." She types, pauses, types, pauses. "I wish people knew how simple it is to get into security systems. Take them off the network." She's said this approximately one thousand times in the past few years.

Eddie's phone buzzes. He sits straight up, eyes wide. "It's JJ." Jacob's dad.

Zoe turns in her chair and looks at him with owl eyes.

"Well, answer it," I prompt.

He slides the button and puts the phone to his ear. "Hello?" A pause. "No. I wasn't asleep. I'm sitting here in my room with Zoe and Casey. What's going on?"

Zoe and I exchange an anxious glance. So far, so good.

"Wait, what?" Eddie asks. "What happened? Where was he?" His voice has the right note of panic and confusion, a very realistic portrayal of shock. "Okay. Yeah, of course. Where do we go? Is it okay if I bring the girls?" Another pause. "Yeah. Of course. Bye." He hangs up and sets the phone on the bed. "He's hanging on, but he's critical. He's in surgery now." He puts both hands to his face, and his shoulders fold forward.

Critical. That's not a good sign.

Zoe looks stricken. I'm sure I do, too. "Did JJ ask you to go to the hospital?" I ask Eddie.

He nods into his hands. "If I want. He said I don't have to, but he knew I'd want to—" His voice breaks. I think what he's saying is, in case Jacob doesn't make it, Eddie would want to be there, would want to say goodbye.

I turn to Eddie and put a hand on his shoulder. "We're here with you every step of the way, okay?" Zoe gets up, and we sit on either side of him for a hug, a weird ball of arms and elbows that I hope he finds comforting.

I feel his shoulders shake with small, contained sobs. I smooth my hand across his forehead, something my grandma does to me when I'm sad. His face still buried in his hands, he murmurs, "I've been so mean to him lately."

"Stop that," Zoe commands. "Jacob knows you love him."

I say, "Come on. You can tell him whatever you have to say when he wakes up. You can bring him ice cream in the hospital. Sound good? And he can live happily ever after, borrowing your favorite shirts."

He drops his hands from his face and smiles weakly. It's a truth universally acknowledged that Eddie has the best clothes and Jacob is always stealing them.

"We should hurry," I say. "We need to change our clothes in case the police are at the hospital. We can swing by your house, Zoe. Eddie, you should change now. Something close to what you're wearing that will look the same on camera." Eddie gets up and rummages through his dresser, then shrugs out of his shirt and jeans and replaces them with similar items. From the kitchen, I get a plastic grocery bag and collect his discarded outfit.

We get our stuff and lock the apartment behind us. In the elevator, we exchange a worried glance. I feel like I've aged a thousand years tonight. The Casey who left my apartment was excited, a little sad, proud of our channel's success. She was a kid with no idea what lay ahead.

The elevator doors slide open. "Here goes nothing," Eddie whispers.

NINE

Tuesday, March 28

JACOB

THE ELEVATOR DOORS SLID OPEN. BEFORE I could exit onto Eddie's floor, he stepped into the elevator. He'd been waiting right outside.

"What are you doing?" I asked, confused.

"What are *you* doing?" The doors slid shut behind him, and the elevator hovered on the third floor, waiting for instructions.

"I wanted to talk to you. Can we go into your room?"

He hit the button for the lobby, and the elevator sank downward. "No. My parents are home."

In the brushed-steel doors, my reflection looked back at me, bewildered. "Eddie, I've been inside your house a million times."

"It's different now." He crossed his arms, which made his pecs bulge a little under his shirt. I refused to be distracted.

"It's not different," I protested. "What the hell are you talking about? We've had sex in your room like a hundred times."

He glanced around. "Shhhhhh."

"Are you kidding me right now?"

The doors slid open, revealing the lobby. "Come on. We can talk over there." Eddie indicated the seating area with two white leather couches and glass-and-mirror end tables. Reluctantly, I followed him out and sat beside him on the couch farthest from the mailboxes. He turned to face me, a knee up on the cushions.

I reached for his hand and he allowed it, but he didn't meet me halfway. "Eddie, what is going on with you?" I scooted closer. "This is stupid. We're...us. Why are you acting like you don't even know me?"

He looked down at our hands. Mine had writing on them; I was always drawing on myself in class. My nails were bitten, my hands pale and spidery. His were clean, the skin smooth and moisturized, the nails neatly filed. I loved his hands. I loved everything about him.

He flipped his hand palm-up and gripped mine. He brought our joined hands to his cheek and rested them there, just for a moment, before he released me. His eyes flicked up to the security camera by the mailboxes, then back to me. "Sometimes, I wish we'd never crossed that line. Things would be so much less confusing."

I shook my head, mute. I'd never once wished for that.

He said, "You know we can't be together. We can't be a couple. We've talked about this."

"*You've* talked," I retorted. "I don't mind telling my dad. He won't care. You really think your parents will be mean about it? They have gay friends. They're not homophobic."

He took a deep breath, closed his eyes, then reopened them and met mine. His voice was deep, even, and steady. "It's not about that. You know how hard I've worked to get into USC. You know how hard my dad's worked. My mom. It hasn't been easy. And here I am..." He shook his head. "This isn't the same stuff you're dealing with. I'm not saying your situation is easy. It's just different."

Eddie's family had money. They had status. His parents were both successful in the industry. My dad was a line cook and my mom had a drug addiction. For all I knew, she could be dead. I kept all that in and just said, "What does any of that have to do with us?"

"I can't get distracted. I have plans."

I bristled. "So I'm a distraction?"

"Yes. You are."

"Wow." I sat back. "Have you considered that I might be able to support you, that we could go through this next phase together? Or am I just some gay temptress who's going to keep you from, what, marrying the perfect actress you meet on set?"

"Maybe," he snapped. His eyes traveled up to the camera again, and I nearly screamed.

"You're so full of shit, Eddie." I hoped the acid on my tongue would burn him. "You say you need to focus on school and your future, but I see you worrying people will see us." I tried to be gentler. "You're scared of coming out. I get it. I'm here for you."

"It's not about that, it's about *you*. Look at you, Jacob." The way the words slipped out of him, unguarded and cruel, stopped me in my tracks.

I looked down at myself. Ripped jeans, tattered Clash T-shirt, dirty sneakers, hands covered in writing, uneven hair flopping over one eye. I knew what he meant. I didn't belong beside him.

"You're a mess," he finished quietly, like he was hammering the last nail into a coffin. I felt myself crumble forward, my head falling into his lap, dignity lost.

"Please, no," I said into the leg of his jeans. "Please don't mean that." He allowed it for a few moments, a gentle hand on the back of my head.

He scooted aside, helped me rest my forehead on the arm of the couch, and got up. Without a word, he walked away, leaving me alone in the sterile lobby.

You're a mess, he'd said. Well, he wasn't wrong.

TEN

Sunday, April 9

THE EMERGENCY ROOM WAITING AREA IS CROWDED when we enter through the sliding glass doors, Eddie in front, Zoe and I on either side a pace behind. Once we'd parked, he'd gone into overdrive, legs flashing as he rushed through the parking structure.

He stops in the crowded, antiseptic-scented room, looking around in obvious confusion.

"I'll find out where Jacob is," Zoe says, patting his arm. She works her way around the line and flags down a harried nurse. "We're here to visit our friend who was brought in a few hours ago."

"Ask at the desk," the lady snaps, and Zoe gets in line, disgruntled. She's not used to waiting for things.

"I'll text JJ," Eddie mutters, getting out his phone. His thumbs flash across the screen, and a minute later he says, "Jake's still in surgery. We should meet him in the waiting area of the ICU."

Zoe gets directions, and we follow her out of the ER into a series of hallways to an elevator, up to the fourth floor, and through another maze of corridors. I don't know how she never gets lost. There's really nothing her brain can't blueprint.

We find Jacob's dad standing by a window, looking out. It's almost five o'clock, and the sky over Hollywood is moving through shades of charcoal. He spots us right away and gives us a pained smile. "Hey, kiddos."

A pair of uniformed cops is standing sentry by the double doors that must lead into the patient rooms. When we arrive, they glance at each other, and one of them messes with the walkie-talkie on her shoulder, speaking into it. Zoe squeezes my hand, a secret little anxious gesture. I squeeze hers back. The cops are a confirmation of the obvious: A crime has been committed, and the police will be investigating. This is real. This is happening.

"How's he doing? Do you know when he'll be out of surgery?" Zoe asks JJ, and I think I'm the only one who would recognize the note of guilt in her voice, the little twang that always tells me when she's hiding something.

"No. They said it could be up to eight hours. Maybe longer." He collapses into a chair and steeples his hands, elbows on knees. I notice he's in plaid pajama pants, flip-flops, an ancient Guns N' Roses T-shirt, and a leather jacket. He must have been yanked out of bed; his tangled hair hangs down over his face, shielding one of his bloodshot blue eyes from view. He's covered in tattoos, and I've always particularly admired the red roses on his hands, but I've never really looked at him before. He's just a dad, an older person in the background, but right now, he's a hundred percent human and real, and I could sink into the floor with shame for the pain we've caused him.

This YouTube channel is turning into a curse. I was always worried we'd get charged with a misdemeanor for breaking and entering, but it never occurred to me that one of us could get seriously hurt. If JJ knew why Jacob was really in the hospital, he'd never forgive us.

There it is—the true guilt, not the little taste of remorse I get for staying out late or breaking into places, but the crushing, bone-deep shame. I've been living beside it for so long, watching it slowly eat away at my grandma, that I almost forgot what it feels like when it's fresh, before it's fermented into a tumor you get used to housing inside your body.

A suited man and woman approach us. From the badges attached to their belts, I assume they're detectives. He's in his fifties, a Black man with gray hair, and she's a thirtysomething Latina woman with a low ponytail. They both look extremely serious.

"Sir?" the woman asks JJ. "Can we speak with you?"

"Of course. These are Jacob's friends. Detective Martinez and Detective Adams, this is Eddie Yu, Casey Costello, and Zoe Wilkins." Clearly, JJ's already been talking to them for a while; he seems comfortable in their rapport.

Zoe asks, "So what happened?" She looks back and forth between JJ and the detectives.

The two officers sit facing us across a coffee table full of old magazines. The man—Detective Adams—says, "Are you three familiar with the Silver Lake Murder House? Have you heard of it?"

We glance at each other, not sure how to respond. I answer first. "I am. It's where Rosalinda Valentini was killed."

Zoe interjects, "We call her Human Google. Ask her anything. You should see her play *Jeopardy!*" I elbow her, willing her to shut up.

Detective Martinez smiles at me. "That's probably helped you out in school. You must have good grades."

"Yeah, I guess so." I look down at my feet. I'm wearing a pair of Zoe's black Vans. They're a size too small and are pinching my toes.

Eddie says, "Is that the house that's abandoned or something?"

I tell him, "Yeah, they never cleaned it up after the murder. A lot of the tourist buses stop there."

He frowns. "But what does that have to do with Jacob?"

Detective Adams says, "It looks like Jacob was there tonight, and he wasn't alone."

JJ is listening closely, but it's clear none of this is news to him.

"Who was he with?" Zoe asks.

"We don't know. We're working the scene now. Did he say anything to any of you about going there?"

We shake our heads in unison. I look at Eddie. "Do you know what he was doing tonight?"

We rehearsed this approximately thirty times in the car. On

cue, Eddie replies, "No. I asked him in school yesterday—or Friday, I guess it's technically Sunday now. He just said he was busy."

Detective Adams says, "Were there any other kids who might've known about his plans? Anyone else we can ask?"

After a moment of consideration, I say, "I mean, he has other friends at school. We could give you a list of people to call." We spend a few minutes giving the detectives the names of all of Jacob's school friends, who of course will know nothing.

"What about girlfriends?" Detective Martinez asks. "Is he seeing anybody?"

JJ clears his throat. "He's not interested in girlfriends. But no, he's not seeing anybody that I know of."

Adams redirects his attention to us. "Is he seeing anyone?"

"He's not," Zoe answers. "For sure. We'd know."

A nurse hurries out, calling, "Sir? I have an update about your son."

JJ stands, face dead white behind his beard. She approaches and acknowledges him with a nod, then directs her words to the detectives. "He's still in surgery, but I wanted to give you an update. They were able to repair the damage to the lung and myocardial wall. They're still working, but that was the most difficult part of the operation, and the fact that they were able to successfully get through it—that's very good news. You can breathe a little bit. He's lost a lot of blood, and we're not sure how long his brain was without oxygen, so we certainly aren't out of the woods. They'll know more when surgery's over. Okay?"

JJ collapses into his chair. He hides his face behind his hands, and I realize he's crying. Detective Martinez fetches some tissues from the nurses, and Adams gestures that we should move to the side of the room with him and give JJ some space.

He drops his voice and faces us, eyes moving from one of us to the other. "I want to tell you three something," he says. "I've worked with teenagers before. I know y'all aren't going to give me the truth on the first try. Is there anything else you care to share out of earshot of Jacob's dad? Any romantic partners, any enemies at school, any family members he has issues with? Anything at all?"

We shake our heads. Eddie says, "There's no one else; it's just him and his dad. His mom's MIA. They don't know where she is, but I get the impression that JJ thinks she's dead. JJ is adopted, and he's not close with his family. He came out here to be a musician back in the nineties, and they kind of lost touch. I get the feeling they're pretty conservative."

Zoe adds, "And in school, everyone likes Jacob. He's funny, he's lovable. He's the best. No one would do this."

It's so well-put, and I feel Eddie start to fall apart, hearing what could be the beginning of Jacob's eulogy. He turns, has nowhere to hide, and I pull his head down so he can bury his face in my shoulder. "They're best friends," I mouth to Adams.

His eyes are sympathetic but calculating. I get the horrible feeling that he misses nothing.

This is the beginning. Like I told Zoe and Eddie, we've set something in motion by lying, and now the train is leaving the station. We'll see where it goes.

ELEVEN

Sunday, April 9

AT THE DOOR TO MY APARTMENT, I PAUSE WITH A hand on the knob and take a deep breath. The courtyard smells like bacon and weed, and the common area is rustling with the sounds of people waking up: babies crying, music playing, the woman upstairs rudely FaceTiming for work on the walkway in front of her apartment. "I work with international clients," she'll tell you indignantly if you call her out for doing this at six in the morning on a Saturday.

I fix my bangs, straighten my glasses, and open the door. It's quiet and bright, the room dividers having been slid halfway open to let in the morning light. Grandma is on her yoga mat in front of the TV, obviously at the end of her workout. I'm always amazed she can grab the soles of her feet with her whole hands. I did *not* inherit the flexibility gene; I can barely touch my toes.

She smiles up at me in her happy-morning way. "You're home early. Did Zoe's parents kick you out? Do they have to go to another dog party in Malibu?"

I set my overnight bag down on the dining table. "Something happened. I've actually been up all night."

That gets her attention. She grabs the remote and turns off the TV. "What's up?"

I sit cross-legged on the other end of her mat facing her. "Don't freak out, okay? It's been a hard night, and I just...I need you to be calm."

She's stick-straight, face stricken. "What happened?"

I gather my courage. "Jacob got attacked last night. I was just at the hospital with Zoe and Eddie. And his dad."

"What?" The word comes out a decibel higher than human hearing, such a panicked screech I wince and almost clap my hands over my ears.

"Grandma. Keep it together, please."

"How did this happen? Who attacked him?"

"We don't know." I'm completely exhausted, and the idea of running through the story again is too much to bear. "I was with Zoe and Eddie. We got a call late, like around one or two. Jacob had been out in some abandoned house. He got attacked by someone, they don't know who. He was badly injured. He just got out of surgery, and now he's in the ICU."

"The ICU? What kind of injury?" Her voice is setting me off balance, making my blood pressure rise. I can't do my normal thing right now where I calm her down and keep her anxiety at bay.

"He got…" I can't say *stabbed*. I can't use that word with her. "Hurt with a knife," I finish uselessly.

"Stabbed?" Her face is gray with horror.

I get up and go to the kitchen for some water. I fill a glass up from the sink and take a deep drink. I didn't realize how dehydrated I was.

She's right behind me. "Oh my god. Casey. Who did this to him?"

I already told her this. "They don't know. The police are looking into it."

"Who found him?"

I take a deep breath and set my glass down. The edges of my vision are dark. I don't think I can stay calm for both of us, but I reach down into my reserves. "I don't know, Grandma. I'm sorry."

"But why would someone do this? Who could have—"

"I don't know!" I scream the words so loud she takes a step back. We stare at each other for a moment. I clap a hand to my mouth, face going hot, humiliated to have erupted. I'm the one who keeps my emotions under control. She's the one who falls apart.

She reaches for me. "Hey, it's okay, honey." Her voice is soft now, soothing. Her hands land on my shoulders and squeeze. "It's fine. I'm so sorry. You must be so upset."

"I'm fine." I try to back away, but she draws me into a hug.

"It's okay to not be okay, sweetie." She rubs my back, and

pressure is building in my chest. *Now* she can be calm? Once I've given her something I didn't want to give—a peek into my private emotional world—now she can be the steady, reasonable adult I've needed her to be all along?

Something sudden, fierce, and violent spikes up inside me, and I squirm out from her grip. "I'm fine. I just want to be left alone." My jaw is clenched so hard, it hurts. Her face softens, and she looks at me with what feels like pity. I wait for that look to incite another wave of rage, but the moment has passed, and my limbs are getting heavy, the adrenaline trickling away, leaving me hollow and tired.

"I'm going to lie down," I say.

I grab my backpack and step over her yoga mat to get to the room dividers. I slide one aside, slip behind it, and close it. The windows have a view of the sky above the apartment building next door. It's a bright, clear blue, a beautiful day brewing. I expect tears to well up again, but they don't. I'm dried up. Over the last decade, the walls of this apartment have witnessed so many scenes like the one in the kitchen. How many tears can one place contain?

I plug in my phone, make sure the ringer is on in case anyone needs to reach me, kick off my shoes, and set my glasses on the nightstand. I hide under the covers, only my eyes peeking out. The photo of my mother is watching me, her wide, carefree smile lying to me, telling me everything is going to be all right.

I reach under the mattress and pull out a notebook. It dates back to when I was ten, in fifth grade. I'd realized suddenly, horribly, that I was starting to forget her. It had only been a year and a half, and some memories were already growing foggy. So I'd started writing down everything I could remember. Sometimes what I write now is just memories of remembering, but that doesn't matter. I flip to the beginning.

Mom loved baking muffins. I don't know why she liked them so much, but she made all different kinds. Here are the muffins I remember her making: lemon blueberry, cinnamon sugar, apple cinnamon, plain blueberry, vanilla, chocolate, raspberry, and I think she also made one with maple syrup. They were good, but never as sugary as the muffins from the store. Sometimes I'm worried that I hurt her feelings by not liking her muffins enough.

That one stings. I flip to a page toward the middle.

We went to this one motel in Carpinteria three times, always on spring break. I was five, six, and seven. She said she wanted this to be our spot forever, even if we got rich someday. We ate pancakes at McDonald's and went to the beach a lot. The beach was crowded, and sometimes it was annoying. She really loved the water, and we skipped stones together. Once we found a sand crab. We drove up to Santa Barbara and went to the mission. I loved the church. It was Catholic. I never went in a Catholic church before, and I liked the stained-glass windows.

Another one I'd written not too long ago:

I remember she was soft. When she hugged you, you felt like you'd been hugged all the way. She wasn't skinny, not at all. When I was little, I remember thinking I was so lucky because my mom gave better hugs than anyone else. I felt sorry for other kids whose moms didn't look like they gave such good hugs.

I shut the notebook. My eyes burn, dry and hot.

Jacob, you have to pull through. You can't leave your dad like this. You can't leave me like this. I can't handle another one. What a selfish thought. But then, that's how pain works: When you're in enough of it, there's no thinking of anything or anybody else.

THE HOLLYWOOD REVIEW

THE WONDERS OF THE VALENTINIS

Months into the Valentini investigation and the Los Angeles Police Department has made no further announcements, nor do they seem to show any progress. When questioned, representatives say they cannot comment on active investigations, but this humble rag must wonder: What's left to investigate? Was Andrew Valentini not identified as the culprit back in April? The Valentini family has quietly filed a civil suit against the LAPD. At the head of the lawsuit is Andrew's younger brother, Rudolph Valentini, resident of New York City and rumored man-about-town.

Swooping into the fray is medium-to-the-stars Adrian Wonders. The charismatic and eccentric Mr. Wonders has grown quite famous over the last two decades for serving as a channel to departed loved ones and providing peace to those left behind. Most recently, Mr. Wonders performed a televised séance on board the *Queen Mary*, where he was at last able to ascertain the identity of famous child spirit Jackie, whose alleged drowning has been a point of contention since the ship's permanent residence in Long Beach in 1967. After an emotional séance attended by as-yet-unnamed Hollywood elite, Jackie revealed herself to be the child of a war bride who jumped overboard in 1945 during a voyage to the United States from Europe. Jackie (whose real name Wonders claims to be Sadie) leaped to her death into the Atlantic after her mother fell or jumped into the sea.

Wonders gave an interview to the *Star* last week, stating, "There's more going on in the Valentini house than a simple murder-suicide. Andrew and Rosalinda are still in there, and they're trying to communicate. They're holding on to that house; they don't want anything moved an inch until this crime is solved. We need to get in there and hear what they have to say."

The LAPD has not responded to a request for permission to hold a séance in the house, but Wonders is undeterred. "If Andrew and Rosalinda want this to happen, it will happen. Believe you me."

TWELVE

Monday, April 10

I'M BACK INSIDE THE VALENTINI HOUSE. IT'S dark; I can see nothing except the glow of candles, and I'm being summoned. Someone is calling me to the living room, a wordless, magnetic cry, and I'm running up the stairs, away from the call. I should scream for help. I try, but my throat closes, and I realize I can just as easily be killed on the stairs as on the living room carpet.

I open my eyes, fear whooshing around inside me. I'm on my side in bed, facing the windows. I forgot to close the blinds, and Hollywood is sparkly and restless out there in the distinct muted way that means it's late at night. No traffic, no horns, just an echoing rush of cars on Hollywood Boulevard and fog creeping around the edges, rolling down off the hills behind us.

I blink at the view for a while, disoriented, memories jumbling together and reorganizing themselves. How long was I asleep?

I fumble through the sheets until I find my phone. There are a bunch of Signal notifications, and I open it up to find our group chat cluttered with messages between Eddie and Zoe. We have it set up anonymously, and Eddie's screen name is Blondie, a throwback to his bleached blond days last year. Zoe is FancyLike, the name Jacob gave her when he stole her phone and changed it. Mine is Frankenmouse, because, as Jacob says, I am "a sarcastic little goth mouse."

BLONDIE:
His dad called me. Says he's in a room now but can't have visitors at least till tomorrow.

FANCYLIKE:
Is he still unconscious from the anesthesia?

BLONDIE:
Yeah.

FANCYLIKE:
We need to talk to him as soon as he wakes up.

BLONDIE:
I know.

FANCYLIKE:
We can take turns waiting with him. Do shifts or whatever.

BLONDIE:
I really can't go back there right now.

I'm surprised he left at all. Maybe JJ asked him to go home, wanting some privacy. Or maybe Eddie's parents insisted.

FANCYLIKE:
Get some sleep.

BLONDIE:
Yeah right.

I check the time. It's one in the morning. I must have fallen asleep around noon. I'm wide awake, no chance of sleeping now, and my stomach is growling aggressively. I get up and tiptoe into the living room, which is dark and silent. I sneak into the bathroom to pee, then to the kitchen, where I grab a banana and a slice of Grandma's homemade bread. Back on my bed, I eat without interest, watching Hollywood, picturing what's going on out there right now. The tourists have gone home. It's too early in the season for the Hollywood Bowl, and anyway, it would be over by now. The clubs and bars are still open, and I'm sure if I cracked the window, I'd hear sirens and the occasional screech of tires as someone peels out in a fancy car. Crimes are happening in darkened corners—assaults, rapes, burglaries. I sigh, the banana suddenly slimy and disgusting. I set it aside.

I think back to the events at the Valentini house. It all happened so fast. That's something I've always wondered about with eyewitnesses: When a crime happens, you aren't expecting it.

Your brain is jarred, shocked. No wonder witness statements are so contradictory and unreliable. With my mom's case, every single person from the bar she was working in had a different account of her movements that night.

I get my laptop, painfully aware that anything I do could become evidence. The seven-year-old MacBook was a hand-me-down from one of my grandma's friends, and it still works great as long as you leave it plugged in. I pull up Chrome and think about what would be reasonable from the police's perspective for someone in my situation to search.

Silver Lake Murder House, I start with. It loads up a million hits about the house, none of them particularly promising. I click through a few articles anyway, reading about the original murder. "Rosalinda Valentini, formerly Rosalinda West, a movie star in the late sixties and early seventies, was stabbed to death by her husband, studio mogul Andrew Valentini, in 1972." I knew that. I scroll through photos of her, never having studied her closely. She was blond, with stick-straight, waist-length hair. Her skin was lightly tanned, exuding health and vigor. She was very thin, with a tiny waist and small breasts. I find photos of her and Andrew, a tall, handsome man with dark hair that fell around his temples and a crooked, wolfish smile. I'm sure this photo was intentionally selected for this article because it makes him look predatory, but still, it gives me goose bumps the way he loops his arm around her waist, possessive and arrogant and at least ten years older than her.

I'm reading another take on the crime, an article from the eighties with a bent toward satanists' involvement, wondering why

I'm even looking at these, when I realize what's nagging at me. The alarm.

Why had it gone off? What had we done to trip it? I remember Zoe panicking, insisting this shouldn't have happened, that she'd disarmed it. I've never seen her make a mistake with an alarm, not once. Zoe misses nothing, forgets nothing. So… what the hell?

I type into Google, *Who owns the Valentini house in Silver Lake?*

I have to try the search a bunch of different ways. Eventually, I get to a true crime article with an accompanying podcast episode that says the house is owned by the Valentini family; it was inherited after the murder and is still in their possession today. I google *Andrew Valentini family* and several variations, all of which produce nothing definitive. I'll have to dig deeper on this.

I grab a different journal from my underwear drawer—the one I use for random research projects and trivia factoids—and flip to a blank page. My last entry was a bunch of numbers, a budget for saving up to visit Zoe at MIT. I start listing some things to look into.

Valentini family—who owns the house?

Alarm company—who could have access? Did Zoe make a mistake? If so, how?

Then I realize: If the cops get a search warrant, they could access this journal. I tear the pages out and crumple them. I feel like a rat trapped inside a sinking ship.

I can't help but remember that Eddie was downstairs with

Jacob when the stabbing happened. I know this line of reasoning is ridiculous—what we actually need to do is search for clues in our footage from that night. I get my phone and check the time. Almost two. I text Zoe.

You awake?

She answers back right away. **Yeah. Slept all day so now I'm wired.**

Same.

Want me to come pick you up?

My grandma won't expect me to go to school, and she'll be glad I'm at Zoe's instead of home alone while she's at work. **Yeah, come get me. I'll wait outside.**

Before I leave, I pen a note to my grandma and leave it on the kitchen counter by her car keys.

Going to spend the day with Zoe at her house. I'm sorry I snapped. I didn't mean it.

I hesitate, pen hovering over the scrap of paper. My throat aches, so many unsaid words backed up into the limited space behind my tonsils, years of painful truths and fears left unspoken.

I love you, I scribble at last—because that's all that really matters, isn't it?

THIRTEEN

Monday, April 10

I'M SHIVERING IN THE COOL NIGHT AIR WHEN
Zoe pulls up in her mom's Expedition. Double-parked, she gestures for me to hurry in. I open the door and climb into the
lemon-scented leather interior. Like Maria, Zoe looks much too
small to pilot such a beast, but she does it with ease. "I'm glad
you're up because I have a lot of thoughts" is the first thing she
says as I buckle my seat belt.

Immediately refreshed by her presence, I nod my agreement.
"I did some research."

"Good!" She slaps the steering wheel. "You want coffee?"

"Yeah, but I don't think there are any twenty-four-hour Starbucks around here. You'll have to settle for 7-Eleven."

She makes a show of grimacing. "Desperate times call for desperate measures. We can also get snacks."

I don't reply. I don't have money for snacks. I can do a couple of bucks for a coffee, but that's it. My froyo paycheck isn't play money; my grandma needs it to pay the bills.

"I was thinking about the alarm," I say as she pulls off the side street and onto LaBrea, heading south.

"What about it?"

"Well, it's weird that it went off. Right? You've never had that happen before."

"Never. It makes no sense. It couldn't have re-armed itself—even if there were some kind of glitch that allowed the system to automate something like that—because we left the back door partway open."

"We did?"

She nods. "I'm ninety percent sure."

"So if it wasn't automated..."

"Someone triggered it manually."

I stare at her profile, briefly highlighted pink by a neon sign. "But how?"

"Well, I didn't get a good look at the panel. I didn't interact with it at all, remember? Sometimes there's a panic button, which someone could have pressed. I'm going to see if I can find any images of that panel in photos of the interior of the house."

"There could be images on our footage," I point out.

"I know." Of course she's already thought of this.

"That reminds me. Have you heard from Eddie since you guys chatted on Signal?"

"No."

While she drives, I text him. **You awake? Zoe and I have insomnia. Let me know if you want anything from 7-11.**

He doesn't answer. "I guess he's sleeping," I say.

In the bright convenience store that smells like coffee and nachos, I can almost forget about Jacob, about the horrible images of blood on a plush carpet. I get plain drip with hazelnut creamer, which always makes cheap coffee feel like a latte, and Zoe pumps a combination of things from the slightly-more-expensive machine. From the food racks, she picks three packages of mini chocolate doughnuts and a box of strawberry Pop-Tarts. "You want something?" she asks me.

"I'm good. I ate at home." It's my alibi whenever people want to eat in restaurants.

She narrows her eyes at me, then grabs a fourth package of doughnuts. "Liar."

I flush. "No, honestly."

"Shut up." She says it kindly, though, and nudges me with her elbow as we get in line. "You know it's on me."

"You don't have to," I protest.

"I know I don't. And if I ever can't, I won't. But it's just a few bucks, and I love you." Her smile is so warm, I want to hug her.

"Thanks," I say awkwardly, with no idea how to put all my feelings into words.

The guy ahead of us, a twentysomething in skintight leather pants who has clearly been hitting something much stronger than coffee, takes his cigarettes and leaves, and the clerk turns to us. Zoe deposits her stuff on the counter and says, "Her coffee, too." She pays for everything, and we carry our loot to the doors. She hands a package of doughnuts to each of two homeless guys out front, and we get in the car, shivering audibly. It has to be in the fifties, freezing. I realize she'd noticed the guys on our way into the store and bought two extra packages of doughnuts with them in mind.

I'm used to Zoe quietly looking out for people. It's the way her mom raised her. "If you have something good, share it," I've heard Maria say a thousand times. Zoe's older brother, who's a sophomore at UC Berkeley, is the same way. I remember being in ninth grade when he was a junior, and Zoe and I were eating in the cafeteria when he passed by and casually dropped two bags of Sour Patch Kids onto our table. Zoe knowingly smiled up at him, but I was confused. "Why?" I asked.

He showed me a third bag. "I was getting some for myself." That's just their way.

"Eddie hasn't texted me back," I tell Zoe as she drives, checking my phone again.

"I'm worried about him."

"Me too. If you were in the hospital—" I stop myself, horrified to have said it aloud.

"I know." She leans over to pat my knee, and I feel warmed up from the inside.

We're quiet the rest of the way to her house, watching late-night Los Angeles fly by. It's such a documented city, but there are so many little things they leave out. For example, all the roadside vendors selling flowers and fruit, and the entrepreneurial families starting tiny little food businesses outside the Hollywood Bowl. Movies don't show the mobile barbecues with lines of people waiting for fresh carne asada or the millions of food trucks selling everything from sushi burritos to Korean barbecue. Los Angeles is all about layers, and middle-of-the-night Hollywood is one from the deep interior, all the for-show stripped away, displaying only what's at its core, what's usually hidden under all the tourism and partying and beauty and wealth. In the middle of the night, everyone is gone except the residents of tent cities, the people whose habits keep them up all night, the sex workers searching for stragglers from the bars, and the cops like vultures circling for carrion.

In the quiet that weaves through the foggy, tree-scented hills, we sneak into Zoe's house, careful not to wake her parents, and tiptoe barefoot to her room. She closes her door and we relax into our usual positions: Zoe on the bed, me on the rug, leaning against the wall with throw pillows for support. We enjoy our little feast while Zoe opens her laptop.

She says, "I'm re-checking the security system at the murder house. I want to make sure I didn't miss anything."

"I'm sure you didn't." I take a large bite out of a doughnut. "Hey, we've got to figure out what to do with the footage."

She glances up at me. "You want to say that again in English?"

I laugh, mouth full, and spew doughnut crumbs onto my knees. She laughs, too, and then we make eye contact and stop, guilty. How can we be laughing right now?

I swallow. "We should watch the footage from last night,

and then find a way to hide those tapes." The cameras we stole/borrowed from Eddie's dad are old, and they use these digital cassettes that get exported into the computer. So they're digital, but they still have tapes.

She says, "I think we're fine if Eddie holds on to the cameras. He's a film student, or he will be in the fall."

I nod. "As long as they aren't all together in one place, which implies they're being used at the same time."

"One in his room, one in his dad's office, one in his car."

"That should be okay. But we need to think about a spot to hide the tapes. Not in any of our houses. We really shouldn't throw the footage away. We could get charged with a felony if they figure out we were with Jacob that night and destroyed evidence."

Zoe muses aloud. "Could we, like, bury them in my yard?"

"Hmmmm. A little too close. But the burying thing isn't a bad idea." I consider. "We could put them in a Ziploc like the one we use for the burner phones.... What about somewhere in Griffith Park? We could go on a hike. That wouldn't be suspicious. People hike."

She smirks, going back to her laptop. "People. Not us. But fine. Griffith Park it is."

My phone buzzes in my back pocket, and I lift off the ground to pull it out. "It's Eddie," I tell her, answering the call on speaker. "Hey, it's Casey and Zoe."

"Hey." His voice sounds hollow. "I'm back at the hospital."

"How's Jacob?" Zoe asks, setting her laptop aside and scooting closer.

"Not so good." His voice cracks. He clears his throat. "He's in a coma."

"A coma?" we echo in unison. Our eyes meet. "What does that mean?" I ask.

"They don't know. They said there's nothing to do but wait."

"Eddie," Zoe says, voice full of sympathy. "Are you okay? How's his dad?"

"Not great." He laughs, a sad, teary sound. "Anyway, I don't really feel like talking. I'm going to go home. I haven't slept yet. I think Jacob's dad wants to sit with him alone, you know."

Zoe says, "Do you want us to come get you? Casey can drive your car home if you're really out of it."

"I'm fine. I'll talk to you later."

"Call us tomorrow," I say, but he'd already hung up.

We stare at each other, breathless. Zoe grabs her laptop and starts typing.

"Looking up prognosis of coma after trauma." She scans and clicks, scans and clicks. "Seems like every case is different."

I don't know what to say, how to feel. When Jacob survived surgery, I'd assumed he was on the road to recovery. I should know better. Nothing is ever quite as it seems.

FOURTEEN

Tuesday, April 11

"GOD, THIS FEELS WEIRD," ZOE MUTTERS TUESDAY morning as we walk up the front steps into school. She's right; it's bizarre to have to be here right now. I didn't sleep well last night, and I can see Zoe didn't, either. Her eye makeup is minimal, hair pulled loosely into a puffy, blue-streaked bun. I dealt with the sleep deprivation differently, putting on too much eyeliner, not that anyone will notice behind the glasses. On a good day, I'm ten percent eyeliner and ninety percent hair anyway.

"Let's wait for Eddie. We have a little time," I suggest.

"Sure." We step to the side of the entrance, out of the flow of foot traffic, and lean against the railing, looking out at the street. Hollywood High is on a busy corner right in the middle of this disaster of a neighborhood. Congestion today is as bad as usual, cars inching painfully through the intersection.

The first bell rings. "I'll call him," I offer, pulling my phone out of my back pocket. It goes straight to voice mail.

"He's probably inside already," Zoe says. "Come on, we can't put it off any longer."

We head in and are immediately confronted by Emerald Cain and her two main followers, Katie and Maya. This is the first time they've ever turned their heads in our direction.

"Hey, I heard about Jacob," Emerald says in a sweet tone I've never experienced in person. She's on a Disney Channel show, but you'd assume she'd won an Oscar from the size of her ego. "God, it's so awful. I can't believe it. Is he going to die?"

Anger rises in my chest like heartburn. It's a familiar feeling. "Wow, you must be really good friends with Jacob. You guys talk a lot? Hang out all the time?" Sarcasm drips from my words, and Emerald's pretty face sets into angry lines.

Zoe puts a hand on my arm. "Come on, Case. Let's not be late."

Emerald says to her friends, "I guess this is what I deserve for showing some actual concern."

"You're *such* a saint," I reply, imitating her annoying vocal fry.

"Okay, moving on," Zoe says. She pulls me away from them, down the hall. "You can't pop off every time someone asks about Jacob, or you're going to be setting the school on fire by lunch. If Emerald knows, everyone knows."

Turns out, she's right. Every class throughout the day is full of sympathetic smiles and curious stares. Teachers stop me and ask how he is. Random people ask me if it's true he's dead, or that he got mugged, or maybe he got shot by the cops while he was committing a crime. Part of me wants to tell each person their story is right, absolutely, and let the rumors compete against one another, gladiator-style.

Instead I fold inward and keep quiet, gathering my hair into a bun, tearing it down, then pulling it into a ponytail, and then pulling the rubber band out and flinging it across the hall in frustration. I text Eddie between classes to see if there's news. No answer.

Zoe and I eat lunch in her car, neither of us very hungry, dawdling over granola bars and yogurt. "Still nothing from Eddie," I tell her. "You?"

She shakes her head. "Nope."

I sigh. Out in the parking lot, kids are coming and going, living their normal lives.

"There's a new girl in my English class, from Costa Rica," Zoe says absently. "Imagine moving to another country in the middle of your senior year."

I perk up a bit. "Did you know that Costa Rica has no military? Since 1948."

"I did know that one, actually." She pokes my arm.

I narrow my eyes. "Did you know that twenty-five percent of their land is reserved for nature conservation?"

She pokes me harder. "Maybe I knew that."

I poke her back. "You did not! Did you know they play the national anthem every morning at seven a.m. on the radio? Did you know they have more than nine hundred species of birds and five active volcanos?"

"I give up, oh my god," she groans, and I cackle with satisfaction.

It hits me—we shouldn't be joking while Jacob's in the hospital. I settle back into my seat, chagrined. She does the same, eyes drifting out the windshield.

"After school, I'm going to try to find out more about the house," I say.

"On your own computer?"

"No, at the library."

"Good."

"Hey, why'd your mom let you drive the Expedition again?"

"She feels sorry for me."

"Aw."

We sit in silence. I guess it's going to be like this now. We can't talk about normal things without feeling guilty, but we also can't talk about Jacob all the time, not when there's no news and we're just waiting to hear if he wakes up.

Zoe folds the wrapper of her granola bar. "I'm done doctoring the security camera footage. Oh, and I wiped all the YouTube stuff off Jacob's laptop. And I got rid of the burner phones."

"I deleted my research folders from Drive."

"And I'm assuming Eddie cleaned up his own tech. Case, I'm seriously worried about him."

"Same."

We lapse back into silence. Zoe breaks it eventually. "We

should really get rid of the tapes from that night. We've already waited too long."

I nod. My phone jangles an alarm; it's time to go back inside. I silence it, and we robotically gather our things. I assume my expression matches Zoe's grim face. It's like we're in a bubble, waiting for it to be popped.

I picture Jacob, more full of life and personality than anyone I know, silent in a hospital bed. *No.* I can't deal with that right now. I shove the image aside.

✧

I turn my phone off before fifth period—goodbye, GPS—and when school is finally over, I catch the bus to the Echo Park Public Library, a branch that's nowhere near any of my usual haunts. Inside, the library carries a faint smell of urine and sweat. It dates back to 1925, a fact I inexplicably remember. I scan the ceilings—no security cameras—and relax a notch. I'm wearing latex gloves, a black surgical mask, and a baseball cap, hoping the look is both anonymous and unmemorable.

I take a seat at the most tucked-away computer available. I follow the instructions on screen and proceed as a guest even though I have a library card. I start by looking for articles addressing the ownership of the house and what happened to it after both residents died. My findings are convoluted. It seems that, in 1974, the police still hadn't closed the case, which feels unusual given their very public certainty that it was an open-and-shut murder-suicide.

I find a long article titled "What Happened After: The Murder of Rosalinda Valentini." It describes the next few years as "bedlam," reporting that the LAPD fumbled the case and maybe even destroyed evidence. (I half-smile wryly. *Not* the LAPD!) In 1974, people were certain the FBI was now involved, but that was disproved when the LAPD started re-interviewing people in 1975 under the leadership of a new chief of police, Bartholomew Rogers.

A few lines toward the end catch my attention: The Valentini family was hung up in court trying to sort out the property ownership. Andrew's will had been written before his marriage and gave everything to his now-deceased mother. Rosalinda didn't have a living will herself, and no one on her side of the family came forward to stake a claim; apparently her father was out of the picture, her mother was dead, and she was an only child. Andrew had a brother, Rudolph, who was bickering with the rest of the Valentini family about who would inherit everything. Some felt it should be his uncle, and apparently there was a stepfather in the mix as well.

It makes me frown. Why couldn't they all just split the assets? I'm sure Andrew Valentini was loaded, and Rosalinda was a movie star who must've had her own money. Wasn't there enough to go around? I fiddle with the search terms again, looking for mentions of the outcome of their court case. Since it was here in Los Angeles, it should be pretty easy, and I'm sure it made the papers....

There it is. Andrew's brother, Rudolph Valentini, won the case in 1978, inheriting the house and estate. I have to google—what does it mean when someone inherits "the estate"? Ah, I see: He got the house *and* all the money.

I look up Rudolph Valentini and find an obituary dated 1979. He'd died one year after winning his court case. In the photo he looks like a tool, chin lifted arrogantly, smile wide and self-satisfied. Another round of googling, and I discover Michael "Baby" Valentini, Rudolph's son. The number one search result is from the eighties—an article titled "Baby Valentini—Prepared to Handle Massive Estate?" featuring the photo of a twenty-something white guy partying on a yacht.

"Douche," I mutter, looking at his white shorts, Hawaiian shirt, messy hair, and wide, inebriated smile. I click around some more, wondering why he hasn't had someone deal with the house in the last, what, forty years? It seems ridiculous.

The next thing I find is a 1984 obituary: "Baby Valentini dead in tragic boating accident. He's survived by his widow, Jenny Valentini, and son, Trevor." A gossip rag article from the same year surfaces titled "Valentini Estate Cursed! Tragic Legacy Takes Another Life."

"Jeez," I mutter, scribbling all this in a notebook I plan to dispose of once I commit this information to memory. I don't believe in curses, but it really seems like every time someone inherits this house and the money that goes with it, they end up dead.

I follow the trail of articles, my back stiffening. After Michael died in '84, the estate went into trust for his son, Trevor, and was managed by his widow, Jenny. She remarried some guy named Robert and had more kids. Trevor grew up to be kind of a washout like his dad and was big into the nineties surf/skate scene in Venice. The next thing I read about him is a few lines in the *Times* in *2009.*

Trevor Valentini dead at 40. Police suspect a drug overdose. The owner of the infamous Silver Lake Murder House and the inheritor of the Valentini estate, Trevor leaves behind long-term girlfriend Cammy (Camila) Klein and two daughters, Dallas (age 4) and Morrison (age 2) Valentini-Klein. Services will be private.

The trail stops there. I've already switched computers twice to extend this little research project into two hours, and I have a few burning questions—namely, where are Dallas and Morrison? Dallas would be my age, and Morrison would be two years younger. Could they be here in LA? "Dallas Valentini" and "Morrison Valentini" turn up zero search results.

In a flash of genius, it occurs to me that property records are public. I just need to figure out which government agency to hit up for the records of ownership. It takes more googling, but the answer is simple. They'll dig up the records for a small fee. I need Zoe's advice before I do this. I'm sure the cops would think it was weird if they saw that transaction on my bank statement. Maybe she can hack in and get the records for me.

Before I pack up, something occurs to me. I type "Dallas Klein" into the search engine, curious if the daughters opted to use their mom's last name. Results populate, and I'm electrified with excitement. She's a senior in a performing arts magnet on the west side; she does theater, and her name and photo are on a bunch of online programs. She's a thin, dark-haired girl with piercing, ice-blue eyes and a fierce expression in every picture. Her sister, Morrison, goes to a different school and does Academic Decathlon. I find very little on their mom except a blurb on a head shop with her picture and a bio—she's the owner. She's a white lady with blond hair and a tired, stoned smile.

I check the wall clock. It's six. I need to get back on the bus; when I'm not working, Grandma likes me to be home for dinner. I pack up my bag, thinking about Dallas, Morrison, and their mom. They might be able to shed some light on why the alarm went off that night.

The air outside is soft and cool, redolent with the urban stench of exhaust, weed, and urine. I turn my tired steps toward the bus stop, and suddenly the weight of this city with its sordid history and glimmering limousines and hordes of invisible, trampled people feels heavier than I can possibly bear.

THE HOLLYWOOD REVIEW

SÉANCE AT THE VALENTINI MANSION

MONDAY, JUNE 12, 1972

Tongues across town are wagging: Adrian Wonders, Hollywood's most eccentric medium at-large, hosted a star-studded séance at the Valentini mansion on Friday, June 9. Attendees included Academy Award winners Joan Waters and Anthony Madsen; producer Craig Brighton; the Radley brothers; rock band Angel Cake; and any number of hangers-on and starlets. A crowd of hundreds, along with the press, witnessed Mr. Wonders organizing a large circle of participants on the front lawn around the fountain, which now sits silent. The *Hollywood Review* was in attendance, of course.

Mr. Wonders asked the press and onlookers to hang back and provide some space for the séance. Night was falling, and candles were spread out evenly upon the lip of the fountain. Police lurked at the back of the crowd, including the two detectives heading up the investigation into the Valentini deaths, Detectives Guzman and Schmidt. Many wondered at their presence; if the LAPD's intention was to protect the house from intruders, surely detectives were not required. Could there be some internal speculation about an external culprit? Could the authorities secretly hope the real attacker might surface at just such a soiree?

Once all attendees had spent a few lingering moments in quiet contemplation, Mr. Wonders began his ritual for summoning spirits. Dressed in layers of silk robes, black mustache neatly combed, hair slicked back to his collar, he presented as the quintessential spirit guide, solemn yet full of repressed energy.

After half an hour of murmuring and swaying, he declared that he had made contact. "I have them! They're here!" Many in the crowd cried out in excitement. "They haven't left," he declared, eyes closed. "The trauma of their deaths created a bond with the house that can't be broken. They're trapped."

His eyes snapped open, moving from face to face. Each famous visage glowed in the candlelight, hands clasped in a perfect ring around the lifeless fountain. To the group, he said, "This was no murder-suicide. They suffered a horrible betrayal. God, poor Rosie. Poor Andy." Tears ran down Mr. Wonders's cheeks. He seemed to be struggling to speak. "I'm sorry. They're showing me what happened. They've been trying so hard to break through." He shook his head, as though denying something painful being whispered in his ear. "They're showing me the murder over and over, but they aren't..."

"Who killed them?" The blunt question came from Craig Littleton, executive producer at Sunset Studios and best friend to the late Andrew Valentini. "Spit it out, man. If you know something, say it."

Mr. Wonders said, "Spirits aren't linear or literal.

They're caught in a hurricane of emotion. They're stuck in a moment. In this case, the moment of death, the shock of betrayal. That's the word I keep getting. Betrayal. Betrayal." Cheeks wet, he shook his head. "Honey, please. I see you, I hear you. I know it's hard. Can you try to see who's doing this to you?"

Moments passed during which nary a breath was drawn.

"Please," he repeated. "Who's in the house with you? Who's there?"

A rush of wind swept through the night, and every candle was extinguished. A chorus of alarm rose from the crowd, gasps and cries of fear. Mr. Wonders let out a delicate sigh and opened his eyes. The lighting was now provided by the moon alone, soft and white.

"They can't see it," he said. "They're stuck. They're reliving that one moment over and over and over—" Mr. Wonders's voice cut off, and he turned to face the detectives, who looked on without expression. "You have to figure out who did this to them. They're trapped."

FIFTEEN

Wednesday, April 12

AS PLANNED, ZOE AND I MEET AFTER SCHOOL in the student parking lot, which is complete and total chaos today. A rock band is inexplicably playing on the corner of Highland and Sunset, having set their rig up in front of the Chick-fil-A, causing a massive traffic jam. It's clearly a publicity stunt; someone is filming it, and the lead singer keeps running into the street to serenade cars. Groups of students have gathered to heckle them, half of them taking selfies and videos.

"Phones off," I call to Zoe over the din.

"You don't have to tell me." She shows me her black screen. We cast one last glance at the band. A pair of guys from our school has now joined them and is doing a choreographed Tik-Tok dance with the guitar player.

"I can't tell if I'm going to miss this when I'm gone or never look back," Zoe says.

We climb into her mom's Expedition. "You really have the car all week?" I ask.

She buckles up and starts the engine. "Yeah. I think they're going to buy me my own ride soon. I heard my parents talking. They say I'll want it when I'm in college."

"And do you?"

"Not really, actually." She tosses me a half-smile. She never even wanted to learn how to drive, but her parents insisted. I, on the other hand, would kill for a car, anything to get me off the bus. "Hey, what's up with Ho-Yo?" she asks, her little nickname for Sunset FroYo. "Aren't you supposed to work today?"

I wince. "I asked for the day off, and my boss was pissed. I didn't come in on Sunday, and he was cool about that, but now he's, like, very done being patient."

She gives me a sympathetic look before turning her attention to backing out of the parking space. "Well, if you want, I could handle this on my own. You can still go in."

"No, I wanted to see the footage before we, you know. Bury it."

"Oh." She's clearly surprised. "I didn't realize. I thought we were going straight to Griffith Park. I already watched it."

"You did? Did you see anything? I was especially hoping there'd be something on Eddie's camera."

"Nothing. Just the kitchen, the stuff in the cabinets, the hallway. You know, all the stuff they were talking about. And then Jacob leaves the room, and Eddie stays in the kitchen until the alarm goes off. After that, the camera is just hanging by his side, with the lens pointed at the floor."

I'm disappointed. "What about the alarm panel?"

"I did see that. There's no panic button. So, yeah. I have no answers about how the alarm got tripped." She merges into traffic and focuses on getting into the left lane. "Okay, so we'll start at the abandoned zoo and go from there?"

"Yeah, there are a bunch of trails, but this one in particular takes you through the woods. And there are these old concrete ruins we can use as landmarks."

"You're the boss."

"What are we going to do about Eddie?" I ask. "He can't miss school forever."

"I don't know. He's not answering me, either."

We fall silent, anxious with no solutions.

"Maybe we should go to the hospital later," she ventures.

"Do you think? If Jacob's in seriously bad shape, JJ might just want family."

"I know." She bites her lip.

It's a twenty-minute drive north along picturesque lanes that weave through Griffith Park, overlooked by the hills and clustered with trees and greenery—an oasis inside city limits.

"Turn left here," I tell her, having memorized the directions since we can't use Google Maps. It's hard to believe people ever lived without GPS, just winging it all the time. It must have been way easier to commit crimes and way harder to be a detective.

We park next to the Crystal Springs playground, which offers us lots of options if we're ever asked where we went from here. We can say we walked along the base of the hills on the jogging path, or we can say we took any number of other trails.

We both wore clothes today that work for hiking, which for me means jeans and a T-shirt, but for Zoe means black leggings and a black crop top. Shouldering my backpack, I tell her, "You look like a sexy cat burglar."

She kisses the air at me. "Taking that as a compliment."

She's also wearing hot-pink lipstick. "We might be underestimating how suspiciously out of character this little adventure looks," I observe, slamming the door. "Maybe they'll arrest us the second they hear you went into nature." She fluffs her hair and sashays to the tailgate in an exaggerated way that makes me giggle.

Beneath it, I feel a twinge of resentment. Sometimes she makes everything such a production, even when it's completely unnecessary, engineering situations so she's always on center stage. What does that make me? Set dressing? It's an unfair thought, and I'm ashamed every time it pops up. Zoe doesn't mean anything by being constantly fabulous, larger than life, and good at everything.

Extroverts just have such an advantage, and...I guess I'm jealous. I'm jealous that she can sing karaoke uninhibited, that she doesn't have a thousand emotional issues weighing her down all the time.

The sky is bright blue, the nearby playground packed full of kids and their parents yelling back and forth. On the rolling stretches of grass, concrete picnic tables are decorated with balloons for various after-school birthday parties, and a group of young kids is swinging a bat at a SpongeBob piñata strung from one of the oak trees.

Zoe digs around in the back of the Expedition and pulls out a black belt bag, which she now buckles around her hips.

"The tapes are in there?" I confirm.

She nods. "Remember, Eddie wipes them after every episode and reuses the same ones. I did some research, and I'm pretty sure the cops' forensics teams wouldn't be able to access any old footage that's been deleted."

I nod. "And Jacob's camera is . . . out there somewhere." Stolen by whoever stabbed him. *But why?*

We stand in silence for a moment, contemplating that loose end. The reason for his killer to steal the camera is obvious: He got a recording of them.

"Ready?" she prompts.

"Let's do it." I lead the way across the grass toward a wall of trees. When we get closer, a small trail widens and takes us through a gap in the forest to a new stretch of grass more expansive than a football field. On the left, cages and stone enclosures dating back to the Art Deco days stand abandoned, grates hanging open for exploration. We considered doing an episode here but decided it's been documented thoroughly enough. Besides, it's no fun if the spot's already open to the public.

"The trail I'm talking about picks up over there," I tell Zoe, pointing across the grass to the woods where a few trails branch out in different directions. The most popular path heads upward and has a view of the city, but I want the forested ones that wind deep into the crevices between the hills. Woodpeckers rattle merrily up in the trees, and we pass a handful of other hikers on our way to the trailhead.

My route takes us straight into the shade and follows a dry creek bed studded with crumbling concrete dams now spray-painted with murals. Griffith Park is full of these urban ruins, banal monuments of drainage channels and walkway bridges.

As we go, I tell Zoe what my library research uncovered. "So, the Valentini house has changed hands a bunch of times. It seems like everyone who inherits it dies."

"Who has it now?"

"The last owner died when his kids were little, and he wasn't married to their mom. I think it must be in trust waiting for those girls to become adults. I have no idea how this works. But my question is, who looks after the place? Maybe their mom? A lawyer?"

With extreme caution, she sidesteps a fern that's encroaching on the path as though it's a tentacled beast with a thirst for human blood. Safely out of the fern's reach, she muses, "Someone has to be taking care of that house. And that someone has access to the security system."

"Could you see the name on the alarm system account when you were in there?"

She purses her lips. "I can go back and check. I wasn't looking for that."

The path turns right and narrows. I tell her, "I was thinking we could bury the tapes down in that ditch." I point into the dried-up creek, now full of plant life.

She makes a disgusted face. "Fine. Let's do it."

"Why don't you be a lookout? I'll go down there."

"Perfect." I have to laugh at her relief.

She hands me the Ziploc containing our three tapes, and I extract a soup spoon from my backpack. We don't have any gardening tools, and the last thing I need is for us to get busted because I went to the hardware store to buy a trowel. Factoid: A large number of murderers get caught buying the supplies they needed for their killings. At least a dozen such cases spring to mind.

I climb down the rocky, spiky hill into the ditch, which turns out to be full of poison oak.

Avoiding the greasy leaves, I find a spot on the side of the bank, not completely at the bottom just in case this ever gets water in it, and dig out a recess. I stash the baggie, then scoop dirt back in. I search for something to mark the spot and end up making a little pyramid out of rocks, nothing you'd see from the trail but which I'd recognize if I got down here. I clamber back up the bank and find Zoe scrawling on a nearby tree with a pocketknife she must have brought in her fanny pack. She's carving a heart and the initials M+H. I look at her questioningly, and she says, "It stands for murder house." She snaps the knife shut and brushes shavings out of the inscription. "There. In case we forget exactly where this is."

As we walk back to the car, we strategize. Zoe has wiped all traces of *We'll Never Tell* from Jacob's laptop. She wants to check Eddie's today in case he missed anything. "At this point, I think we're as covered as we can be," she says, which makes me feel unsettled for reasons I can't quite put my finger on.

When we get to the Expedition, Zoe presses the button on the fob for the tailgate, which opens slowly. "Hang on a minute," she says. "This alarm thing is bugging me." She grabs her backpack and carries it around to the driver's seat.

We get in and she closes the door, starts the AC, and logs in to her laptop. She types fast, pulls up a file, reads through it, and says, "Okay, here we go. The alarm system account. Look." She turns the laptop toward me and points. "That's who the alarm is registered under."

The screen is all text, some kind of contract or details of a service agreement. There's an illegible signature and a typed name beside it. The name reads *C. Klein*. I point to it, excited. "Camila Klein. That's the girlfriend of the last owner who died. The mother of Dallas and Morrison."

"I thought she didn't inherit the house."

"Who knows. I mean, they weren't together long enough to be common-law married. But maybe there was something in the will."

She snaps the laptop closed. "You already know where to find her, don't you?"

"Of course."

She slips the laptop beside her and buckles her seat belt. "Tell me where to go. Let's check her out."

SIXTEEN

Tuesday, March 28

JACOB

I STOOD IN FRONT OF EDDIE'S BUILDING FOR A while after he went back upstairs. *You're a mess* would be on a loop inside my skull for a long time, I could already tell. My torso felt carved open, like he'd taken a surgical instrument and dissected me, leaving my guts splayed out, bloody and vulnerable.

I couldn't go home. My room was full of memories. We'd kissed for the first time on my bed, listening to music—Frank Ocean, his choice—when the air between us had been electric with desire for so long that we turned to each other and closed the distance with something like desperation. It felt like giving up, giving in, giving.

And now I was stuck facing the sushi restaurant across the street, his words pinballing around inside me: *Look at you. You're a mess.* I'd invented a whole narrative about us falling in love, while he was just getting off with the most convenient person in his life. How pathetic.

I turned away from Eddie's building and headed east. It wasn't until I'd been walking through the busy, cool night for a while that I realized I was nearing the Silver Lake house.

Just like Eddie, the house had had a hold on me lately. I found myself thinking about it every day, finding excuses to visit, spinning fantasies about what used to be, what could have been. It was lucky for me that the others agreed it would be a good location for our last episode of *We'll Never Tell*; otherwise, I didn't know what I'd have done. Break in by myself, I guess, but without Zoe's help, I'd have probably gotten caught.

I hopped on a bus at Vermont and got off a few stops later. I walked past rows of tents and barred-up businesses, then into the trendy neighborhoods where storefronts advertised CrossFit and doggie daycare. I didn't know what time it was exactly, but the city was winding down, traffic moving faster now, cars with more space between them.

And then up into the hills. After so much obsessive research, I didn't need a map. My breath came faster as I climbed, my old Converse slapping the pavement. I turned onto the footpath that snaked between properties, then went around the block to get at the house from the front. I wanted to see its face.

After some thoughtless, peaceful climbing through refreshing, floral-scented darkness, I turned left, went another half block, and there it was: a quiet giant behind a high, wrought-iron fence, set far back from the street. Spanish-style houses always seemed so quintessentially LA, and it made me homesick for all the parts of this city I'd never access, me and everyone else with no money.

The gates were chained shut, and a series of huge NO TRESPASSING signs were posted every twenty feet along the property line. I confirmed I was alone, gripped the wrought-iron bars above my head, toed off, did a pull-up, got my foot up on the top railing, and jumped down onto the lawn inside the fence. Crouching there, I forced my breath to settle and listened for any indication that I'd been caught.

The night remained silent, except now I could hear crickets chirping in the tangled, overgrown lawn. A pair of huge trees with wide-stretched, gnarled branches stood guard between me and the mansion. I'd learned the hard way that motion detector lights had been attached to the branches, so I stayed toward the periphery of the yard, wading through high grass and weeds, making my way past these two guardians. I tried to ignore thoughts of what might be in the brush (rats, ticks, snakes) until I was closer to the house, at which point I ran to a more open space, brushing myself off and shivering like I had things crawling up and down my legs.

The windows were dark eyes sleeping, curtains like eyelids visible behind the windowpanes in the faint moonlight. I sank down onto the dead grass and tucked my knees into my chest. This place was desolate, but it could be brought back to life if someone put their mind to it. I tried to picture living here. What if the lawn was mowed, the fountain trickling with water, the house repainted, new carpeting, new everything...? What would that be like? I wondered how much it would cost to fix up. Probably a lot.

It's what the property deserved, though, abandoned and lonely for so long. I imagined the house welcoming me like the one in *Beauty and the Beast*, relieved to have someone who saw past its curse. After all, homes never killed anybody; 29 Lakeview was an innocent bystander.

I pictured Rosalinda here, under a clear blue sky back when the grass was green. I'd seen a million photos of her, so blond and fabulous, and I could easily envision her stepping out of a white 1971 limousine in a lime-green, ankle-length maxi dress and a wide-brimmed hat. What an icon.

Something flickered behind the kitchen window—a flashlight? My heart skipped a beat. Did they have a night security guard? Good thing I was finding out now and not while we filmed our finale episode. I tensed, ready to spring up to my feet and run.

The light glowed again—a white flash—and I realized it wasn't in just the kitchen. Every window flickered simultaneously, like an attempt to strike a lighter, and then darkness. Just as quickly a new white light started low, slowly glowing brighter. While it bloomed, the curtains rustled as though a faint breeze were stirring throughout the house.

I got to my feet, eyes skipping from window to window. What was I witnessing? The curtains blew more violently now, like a tornado was moving through the house. That vicious white light pierced through every window, appearing neither natural nor electric.

Suddenly, I could no longer hear the crickets or the rustling overgrowth. The outside world had gone dead silent. Motion sensors be damned—I turned on my heels and ran.

SEVENTEEN

Wednesday, April 12

NEAR KOREATOWN, IN A DILAPIDATED NEIGH-borhood on a street lined with check-cashing businesses, barred-up windows, and liquor stores, Zoe slows down to peer out the window at a green-fronted shop with a cannabis leaf logo painted on it in white and yellow. The faded sign reads NATURE'S HEALING. "You sure this is the right place?" she asks skeptically.

"I mean, no. The internet could definitely be wrong."

She pulls up to the curb, turns off the car, and we hop out. She beeps the alarm, casting a worried glance back over her shoulder. "Don't get stolen," she mutters. I want to make a rich girl joke, but I understand her concern. A pair of guys leaning on the wall in front of the liquor store across the street are tracking us, languidly raising cigarettes to their lips.

A bell jangles on the glass door when we enter, and we're instantly immersed in a hotbox of incense and weed. The store is full of hanging rugs, shelves stocked with glass bongs, a huge painting of a buddha in the lotus position, hookahs, and every other piece of hippie-stoner paraphernalia you could imagine. The ceiling speakers play slow, gentle reggae. Behind the counter sits a woman in her forties with long, tangled blond hair smoking a clove cigarette. She watches us approach with hazy blue eyes. "Hey," she says, taking a drag.

"Hi," Zoe says. "Just looking. Thinking of buying a new pipe."

"Mmm." She blinks, contemplating that, and then gestures to the glass counter in front of her. "The price range is fifteen to a hundred dollars. Let me know if you want to see anything."

Her eyes trail off, and I notice she has a little vintage television set behind the counter that's playing *Scooby-Doo*. As she watches, her mouth opens a bit and stays that way. This chick is stoned out of her mind.

Zoe and I exchange a glance. "Can I see that pink one?" she asks. Slowly, painstakingly, the woman fumbles with a key chain, opens the display case, and pulls out the pipe with delicate fingers. She's attractive, I guess, with bright blue eyes, skin tanned from the sun, and a willowy figure. She's wearing bell-bottoms and a white tank top, like she made a lifelong commitment to this look in 1997.

As Zoe examines the pipe, pretending to consider it, I say, "I've never noticed this shop before, and I drive by here all the time. Have you guys been here long?"

"Oh, yeah. I bought it twenty years ago."

I keep my face blank. "Oh, you're the owner?"

She nods. "Bought it with my ex, and then he passed away. So it's just me." She smiles.

Zoe sets the pipe back down on the counter. "I'll take it." I shoot her a surprised look and she shrugs, sneaking me a little grin.

Back outside, I say, "She could be overseeing the alarm system at the murder house. After all, she has a security system for the store."

"How do you know?" Zoe asks.

"There's a sensor on the front door and by the windows." She beeps the fob, and we climb in. She sets her new toy down in the coin tray.

Zoe says, "I'd love to get into her personal computer. She's low tech. I bet I could get into her account. At least then I could see what triggered the alarm, if it was from inside the house or from something I forgot to disarm."

I nod, excited. "Can you look up her address from your laptop? Since our phones are off?"

"Of course!" She pulls the laptop out from beside her. "Let's see where Miss Klein lives."

✧

In less than an hour, we're parked across the street from Camila's apartment complex, which turns out to be a run-down, two-story building in North Hollywood a mile north of the Arts District. A painted logo across the front declares it to be The Palms.

"How many apartment buildings in LA do you think are called The Palms?" Zoe muses.

"At *least* a hundred." I'm dubious about the prospect of yet another break-in—although at this point, what's one more? "Okay, there's no intercom. But that front entrance is obviously locked." I point to the flaking, baby-blue wrought-iron gate that spans the entryway. Behind it, I glimpse a courtyard with cement walkways where all the apartments' front doors face out onto a central planter, similar to my building's layout.

Zoe already has her lock-picking kit in hand. She waves the little black case at me. "No problem."

As I get out of the car, I think about the difference between this neighborhood and the Silver Lake hills where the Valentinis resided before their deaths. How much money did the family have then versus now? Did the loser heirs waste all the money, or is there still more waiting for these girls when they reach adulthood?

We wait for a break in traffic and jog across the street. Three sofas and a rogue toilet are displayed in the median strip, clearly having been there for a while. At the front gate, we fall into our usual rhythm. Zoe picks the lock while I give her cover, nonchalantly pretending to check my turned-off phone. In thirty seconds, I hear a click, and she's got the door opened. Knob in hand, she grins. "I'm gonna miss this in college."

"I'm sure you'll find plenty of locked doors in Boston."

Inside, we pass a bank of mailboxes, pausing by one with Camila's name on it. I can tell Zoe wants to open it, but I shake my head at her. We need to be in and out quickly before anyone notices us.

The front doors are a dull shade of aged turquoise, and I realize this place is supposed to be beach-themed. Something about that makes me sad, picturing Camila gravitating toward this connection to a beach culture she can't afford to access. I remember her tousled hippie hair, and I imagine she thinks of herself as someone cool and bohemian, someone who would be right at home on a tropical island.

We find apartment 109 toward the back of the building. After a repeat performance with her lock-pick set, Zoe has 109 open and we're slipping in, closing and locking the door behind us. The messy front room is a living/dining room/kitchen combo, like my apartment, but the kitchen is on the right instead of the left, and no one is using the living room as a bedroom. Instead of windows, there's a sliding door out to a balcony, which I explore first to make sure no one can see us in here. It faces the side area next to the apartment building, where a mostly empty planter stretches the length of the building six feet below.

The furniture in here is worn and mismatched, and ashtrays sit on the coffee and dining tables, which are piled with mail, purses, a couple of pipes, and empty cigarette boxes.

"Let's check the bedrooms," Zoe says, her voice a low murmur. She heads left and I go right; bedrooms branch off both sides of this central space. I find myself in what must be the daughters' room. There are two twin beds, one on either side, and two desks shoved into the space at the beds' feet. The room is neater than I expect, both beds tightly made, books on the shelves arranged by color, no discarded clothes or papers anywhere in sight. An aging PC sits on one of the desks. I pull a pair of latex gloves out of my pocket, slip them on, and gently open it. The screen blinks to life, and the account name is Dallas Klein. It invites me to enter my username and password. I leave it for Zoe and notice this bedroom also has a slider out to the balcony. I unlock the door, sliding it open and peering out. Same view as the living room.

"Hey," Zoe says, entering the bedroom. "That mom's a mess. And there's no computer in there. She's, like, real obsessed with Bob Marley and has a thousand joints." She holds one up. "For a rainy day."

I point to the computer. "Maybe she uses her daughter's?"

"Maybe." She bends down and starts poking at it with gloved fingers.

My eyes have landed back on the bookshelf, where I stand fixated on something I hadn't noticed at first, a teddy bear sitting on the top shelf beside a jewelry box. It's not a Build-A-Bear, not from Disneyland, not themed in any way. It's just a typical brown bear like you'd see in a movie.

A clicking-jangling sound in the living room makes us straighten up and shoot panicked looks at each other. Keys jingle in the lock.

Zoe swiftly closes the bedroom door, and I fly to the balcony. Zoe follows me, sliding the door shut behind us. She's already over the railing, feet on the other side, and then she's leaping softly into the planter below. I follow suit, landing on the balls of my feet with a painful jolt to my ankles. She leads the way, walking quickly to the front of the building, always composed.

We pass the couches and toilet, head across the street, and

are back in the Expedition in a matter of seconds. Only when Zoe has her hands on the steering wheel do we allow ourselves to exhale shaky breaths. Pulling away from the curb, Zoe says, "That was close."

"Yeah, it was. And we learned nothing."

I'm quiet, thinking about the two girls our age and their neat, pristine room, an eye in the hurricane. I feel bad for them. My apartment is homey, full of the smells of baking bread and flower arrangements and art on the walls. Every time I walk in, my grandma smiles like she's glad to see me. Somehow I doubt that's what Dallas and Morrison come home to. A twinge of guilt and appreciation pinches me, and I want to go home and hug my grandma.

Zoe's getting into the exit lane. "Where are you going?" I ask.

"I thought we could swing by Eddie's and check on him. He's been MIA long enough."

I feel a rush of gratitude. She's so thoughtful, always one step ahead. "Good call." I reach out and put a hand on her shoulder, and she tosses me a surprised glance.

"I'm having a moment," I say. "That apartment felt...cold. I feel sorry for those girls."

She nods, squeezing my hand. "We're lucky."

Thinking about Jacob, I realize how right she is. It could have been any of us in that living room. Whoever was in that house probably didn't care who they stabbed; it's not like they targeted Jacob in particular, right? No one knew we were going to the house, so it couldn't have been premeditated. I shiver.

Somehow, I've gotten so caught up in figuring out who set off the alarm that I've pushed aside the greater question about who stabbed Jacob.

Maybe that's not an accident. Maybe my mind is running from that question on purpose. Sometimes I think I don't understand myself at all.

EIGHTEEN

Wednesday, March 29

JACOB

THE BUS RIDE BACK TO MY APARTMENT FROM Silver Lake was a blur. I stared out the window, eyes unseeing. What had I just witnessed? I remembered the flashing, glowing lights, like nothing I'd ever seen before. Maybe every room had lamps plugged into dimmer switches, controlled centrally? And the lamps had really high wattage bulbs? But no. I remembered how the lights had strobed, then flashed, then glowed brighter, then dimmed. I don't believe in ghosts, not even a little bit, but I could not explain what I'd seen.

Maybe the legends about the house were true. I trembled, cold in my T-shirt, then realized it was almost my stop. I stumbled to my feet and made my way to the exit. Hollywood at midnight wasn't so different from Hollywood at nine. It was bright, chaotic, and a little gross. A lot of my friends hated it and wished they lived somewhere more normal, somewhere you could go to Target without standing in line for ten hours with people in costumes for no reason. Not me. It made me feel punk rock, like I belonged to something weird and ridiculous and special. Still, I could do without the stench of piss everywhere.

I trudged off Vine onto Fountain, then turned left onto my little side street. I was almost in front of my building when I noticed Eddie sitting on the steps. His chin was in his hand, and the way he was slumped over, I got the feeling he'd been there for a while.

"Eddie?" I said, approaching warily.

He snapped his head up. "Where were you?"

My hackles rose. "What do you care?"

He stood, brushing himself off, looking clean and neat as always in joggers, spotless Nikes, and an immaculate white T-shirt. My heart lurched, and I had to swallow hard to clear my throat of a sudden lump.

He trotted down the steps and closed the distance between us. "I was worried."

I lifted my chin. "Well, don't be. I'm going to do a lot worse than wander around at night, and you're not going to be there to see it." Jesus, I sounded like a bitchy ex.

He took an audibly deep breath. "Jake, you know this isn't easy for me, either."

"I don't know a damn thing." My eyes burned and my chest throbbed. No wonder people wrote so many depressing songs about love.

He stepped forward so we were almost touching, which shocked all the thoughts out of me. One hand snaked around my waist, and he pressed his forehead to my shoulder. I didn't move, afraid I'd scare him away, like he was a butterfly that had landed on me by accident. I closed my eyes and breathed in his clean fragrance, certain it was the last time I'd be this close.

His voice rumbled in the space beside my neck. "I like to make plans."

I felt one of my hands lift and rest on the side of his face. "I know."

His other arm wrapped itself around me, and he squeezed me to him. "This isn't...I can't...This isn't what I *planned*." I suddenly understood exactly what he was feeling. I pictured his parents, never home; his Nikes, polished with a toothbrush; his T-shirt, ironed; his brows, furrowed with worry. I pictured his mom, breezy and beautiful, always blowing kisses from afar, and his dad, eternally on location. I pictured his empty fridge, those clean glass shelves, and the way his eyes lit up when my dad invited him to stay for dinner. My eyes stung; how many years had I watched him without seeing? He was contained, orderly, annoyingly perfect. But it came at a cost, didn't it?

"Eddie," I whispered. It's all I could say, all I could think. Tears were overflowing and dripping onto his shirt; I'd pressed my face into his shoulder and was clinging to him, dying for him to read my mind and know all the things I couldn't shape into spoken words.

He turned his face, and his lips met mine. A breath passed between us.

"You know I love you," he whispered, so quiet I wasn't sure I was supposed to hear it.

"It made more sense when you didn't."

He kissed me again, harder, the way he did when he was angry, and I was lost, drowning in it. We were on the sidewalk in front of my building, I realized through a haze. He didn't kiss me in public. This was a different Eddie, unhinged.

"I love you," he said again, the words like an incantation.

NINETEEN

Wednesday, April 12

NO ONE ANSWERS WHEN WE RING EDDIE'S apartment from the intercom, so Zoe picks the front door lock and charges through the lobby, full lips pressed into a stubborn line. "He's in there," she mumbles, pushing the elevator call button a million times. And sure enough, Eddie answers the door when she pounds on it for a solid minute. He's wearing rumpled sweats and a T-shirt and looks confused by our presence, like we woke him up.

"We came to check on you," I say as Zoe darts forward and gives him a hug.

"What the hell is wrong with you, we were worried," she says, squeezing hard.

He disentangles himself. "I'm fine."

"No, you're not," Zoe, the queen of tact, blurts out.

"I'm fine," he snaps, backing up a step. "I'm just tired. I want to go lie down. I'll call you later."

She looks hurt. "How's Jacob? Any news?"

He shakes his head, eyes on the floor. "They say the longer he stays in a coma, the more likely it is he won't wake up."

"God," Zoe whispers. "Eddie, are you okay?"

"I need to rest. I'll call you tomorrow." He glares at her like she's personally offended him. "Please. Go."

I try to soften the mood. "Zoe and I have been playing detective, trying to figure out who set off the alarm. We found the owner of the house."

He stares at me, face blank. I glance at Zoe, but she's fixated on him, her face full of hurt feelings. "When are you coming back to school?" I ask.

"Dunno. Not this week."

"Next week?"

Another shrug. He closes his eyes. "I'm going to take a nap. You guys can let yourselves out." He turns and leaves the room, slamming his bedroom door behind him.

"What—" Zoe starts after him, but I grab her forearm.

"He needs space," I say. "He's not mad at you. He's angry at the world and freaked out in general."

She meets my eyes. "I just want to help."

"Zoe, there's no helping him. His best friend is—" I stop myself. I can't believe I almost just said *is going to die*. I finish by saying, "Let's just leave him be."

The ride back to my apartment is quiet. She's clearly upset, and I don't intrude on her thoughts. We give each other a brief hug in front of my building, and I hop out and hurry across the street as she pulls away. It's almost dark now, around seven thirty, and I know my grandma is going to be mad. My phone's been off all day, and if she doesn't know where I am, she starts to panic. Honestly, parenting a teenager is too much for her. She already did this when my mom was growing up, and look how that turned out.

I wonder what these years would have been like if my mom had survived. My grandma would have just been my grandma, someone I visited for Sunday dinners and holidays. In my bones, I know it was supposed to be that way. She was never supposed to be my parent.

Sometimes, grief seizes me in a violent grip, and when it does, I almost double over in pain. I pause, breathe, try to release the image of how my life was meant to be. It doesn't matter what was destined; it only matters what actually happened. That's what I tell myself.

I'm so wrapped up in my thoughts that I don't notice the person sitting on the steps of my apartment building until I'm almost on top of her, keys in hand. She's my age, with dyed black hair cut into a shaggy bob, a short plaid skirt, black boots, and a baggy sweater. She stands, blue eyes blazing with hostility, and says, "Casey? Casey Costello?"

"Yeah," I reply, confused until I realize I know exactly who she is.

"I'm Dallas. You were in my room earlier?" She crosses her arms over her chest, chin raised, challenging.

And then I remember the teddy bear in her bedroom. I know where I've seen it before—at the murder house. In almost every room.

"Well?" she says.

I swallow. "Okay, yeah, I was in your house. And you know that because the teddy bear is a nanny cam."

She raises her eyebrows. "You're a genius. Yes. Obviously."

Rude. "Do you have a lot of those bears?"

"You mean, am I the one who put them in the Valentini house?" Before I can respond, she says, "It's my house. Creeps like you and your friends are constantly trying to come in and, like, hold séances and shoot up heroin and steal my family's stuff."

Like you and your friends? "So, wait..." I hold a hand up. "My friends? You were watching us?"

"Yes, I saw you guys. And I triggered the alarm. Do you think the house is set up to automatically flip the panic switch when someone gets stabbed? You think I have, like, anti-stabbing technology?"

I step closer so I can lower my voice. "Did you tell the police?"

She hesitates. "No." We stare at each other for a few seconds, each of us seeming to dare the other to speak.

I break the silence first. "I have to let my grandma know I'm home. I'm already super late. Can you just...come inside real quick? I'll say you're a friend from school, and we can come back outside and talk more."

She nods slowly. "Okay. Fine."

I get out my keys and open the glass front door. She follows me in, side-eyeing the courtyard, which is a bit eclectic and very eighties in its decor. Whatever. It's not like her place is so freaking nice.

I let myself in. "Grandma?"

My grandma looks up from the dishes, which she's washing in the sink. A big pot of soup is bubbling on the stove behind her, and the room smells like sage and chicken. "Oh, Casey. Thank god. I was—"

"I know, I'm sorry." I hurry to give her a kiss on the cheek. "This is my friend from school. Dallas. We ran into each other outside and we've been chatting."

"Oh." She's surprised, which is insulting but fair.

"Hello," Dallas says, giving her a nice smile I haven't seen yet.

I ask my grandma, "Is it cool if we keep talking? Maybe we'll go on a little walk or go get coffee or something. I'll eat when I get back."

"Um…" She glances at the partition, which I know means she's looking toward the window, wondering if it's dark outside.

"We'll stay away from Runyon and won't go farther south than Sunset," I promise.

"Take your phone. Be smart. Don't get in anyone's car—"

"Grandma, I know." I kiss her again. "See you in a bit."

I deposit my backpack on a chair, pocket my phone, keys, and a ten-dollar bill, then lead Dallas back outside. As we exit onto the sidewalk, she says, "How old are you? Twelve?"

I shoot her a defensive glare. "She's just protective, okay? Back off."

She huffs. "Jeez," she mutters. "You broke into my place. Both of my places. You'd think you'd be a little less of a dick about it."

I can't help but laugh. Touché. "You want to walk?" I ask, gesturing to the end of the street. It's a nice night out.

"Okay." She falls into step beside me.

"How did you find out where I live? And why didn't you tell the police about us? I thought the house wasn't yours yet; isn't it in some trust fund?"

"It's mine when I turn eighteen in a few months. I've been taking care of it for years. No one else is going to do it. I got them to upgrade the alarm system and do some maintenance." She stops. "I don't have to justify any of this to you. It's none of your business. Why don't you tell me why you keep breaking into my houses?"

I stuff my hands into my pockets, which is why I buy men's jeans—so my pockets have room for things like my hands when I'm nervous. "Fine. You've got a point. We were just . . . exploring. We weren't going to vandalize or anything."

"Why did you have those big honking movie cameras?"

"We were thinking of making a short film. Just for fun."

She shakes her head. "My family's problems are not your entertainment. You think this is so fun and edgy? I hate true crime people. You have no idea how much trauma ruins things for generations. . . ." She waves her hands. "You know what? Forget it. Maybe now that your friend got stabbed you won't be so entertained by other people's suffering."

I'm stunned by what she said; it's like she peeled my skin off. She thinks I'm one of the people I hate, the true crime junkies who sit around on Reddit arguing about cold cases all night long for sport.

Here's the thing, though. I hate those people—everyone knows I hate them—but I have a secret, like, obsession with them. I've spent countless hours on those Reddit threads. I've listened to the podcasts. I'm hate-consuming the true crime media, I tell myself, but then . . . at what point am I just one of them?

"So how's your friend?" she asks a little more gently.

"He's in a coma," I say. I realize my voice is tight, like I'm about to cry.

She sighs. "I'm sorry. I really am. But why were you in my apartment? It makes no sense."

"We were trying to figure out who tripped the alarm that night."

"Seriously? You could have just asked me. What were you going to do—hack into my computer?"

I shrug.

She snorts. "Wow. Airtight plan."

"Well, when you put it like that." We walk in silence for a few minutes. We've passed Hollywood Boulevard and are continuing south toward Sunset when I say, "You're right about us breaking in, filming the house. It was a dick move. I'm really sorry."

"At least you didn't steal anything."

A twinge of guilt—the letters I'd found. I'd intended to give them to whoever owned the house, but now I'm afraid to admit I'd taken them, but I need to get rid of them before the cops find them.

And then something occurs to me. "Hang on. Hang on." I put a hand on the arm of her sweater. "You have nanny cam footage from that night. Did you see who attacked Jacob?"

She shakes her head. "I didn't have an angle. I saw him stumble into the frame and collapse, but not who stabbed him."

"Can you show me the footage anyway? I might see something you're missing."

She doesn't meet my eyes. "No."

That's a surprise. "Why?"

"Why should I? I don't owe you anything."

"Why didn't you show the footage to the cops, then? I don't understand why you'd keep that from them."

"So you *want* me to tell them I saw you guys in there?"

"No." We're at a stalemate, facing off on the sidewalk.

"Here's the thing," she says. "All I want is for people to forget about the house. I just want to be able to sell it and help my mom get a better place. My sister's really smart. She should be able to go to a good college. I don't want police investigations, tourist buses, randos doing séances on the front lawn...." She rubs her arms. "So yeah, I'm not showing the footage to the cops. I..."

"What?" I prompt, sure she's on the verge of some revelation.

"Never mind."

"I can't repeat anything you tell me. You have me over a barrel, as my grandma says. You have footage of me and my friends breaking in. You could ruin our lives."

She looks up at the sky. "Everyone thinks the house is cursed, haunted, you know?"

I nod. "Everyone who inherits it dies within a few years."

"My family's full of drug addiction, so yeah, that tends to happen."

I lift my hands, defensive. "Hey, I'm with you. I don't believe in curses."

"Right! But, like…" She scuffs the toe of her boot on the sidewalk. "So, there's some weird stuff on my nanny cam footage sometimes. I think it's just lighting, artifacts on the recording, nothing important. There was some of that the night your friend was attacked. If the footage gets out, we'll never sell the house."

I'm trying to follow. "What kind of stuff? What do you mean, 'artifacts'?"

She sighs, then meets my eyes at last. Hers are a beautiful, clear blue rimmed with smudged black eyeliner. "Weird lights. Things that can't easily be explained."

I blink at her for a minute. "Okay, now you *have* to show me."

"No way."

"Come on. I'm not superstitious. I don't believe in ghosts. And I'm sure as hell not going to share the footage with anyone."

"This has nothing to do with your friend's attack."

"Yeah, but it could have something to do with what was going on downstairs at the time he was stabbed. For example, if there were creepy lights happening, maybe someone came inside to check it out, saw Jacob, and thought he was an intruder."

"He *was* an intruder," she points out dryly.

I ignore the dig. "Come on. We're going to look at the footage together, and we're going to figure this out. Do you have a car? Did you drive here?"

"I borrowed my mom's. It's next to your apartment."

"Okay, then, let's go." This is progress. This could be good.

We turn around and walk up the moderate incline heading back to my street at the foot of the hills. Dallas looks like she's deep in thought, eyebrows drawn together. At the light, as we're waiting to cross Hollywood, she says, "So, your friend Jacob. What do the doctors think is going to happen with him?"

I sigh. Cars flash by, but I barely see them. "We're in a holding pattern, waiting. I guess the doctors say there's a lower chance of him waking up the longer he stays in the coma."

"That really sucks. I'm sorry." Her eyes are full of empathy. "I told my mom to make sure the police know we want to keep this quiet. He shouldn't have to deal with any media vultures when he wakes up."

"Thanks. Yeah, so far, I haven't seen anything about his attack online. Which is weird if you think about it, since the alarm went off and the cops had to come. I'm sure it was a visibly active crime scene." The light turns green and we resume our uphill walk.

"The neighbors don't want the drama any more than we do. They hate all the tourists taking selfies and cameramen filming episodes of whatever stupid *Unsolved Mysteries* shows."

"Is that still on?"

She laughs. "I don't know. Rosalinda's murder was the subject of an episode back in the eighties. Which makes no sense because it wasn't unsolved, not really. Everyone knows Andrew did it."

"But they never closed the case," I can't help but point out. "There must have been evidence the police didn't share with the public." We've reached my street. She's just starting to argue when we both see the unmarked police car double-parked in front of my building. Our steps slow, then stop.

Someone gets out of the driver's-side door and approaches the front door. It's the detective I met at the hospital, Detective Adams.

My stomach drops. "What do you think he wants?"

No answer. I look to Dallas and realize she's gone. I spin, searching, and see her already halfway down the block, speed walking away.

"Nice," I mutter. Well, there's nowhere else for me to go. I clench my jaw, square my shoulders, and walk in. The detective is sitting at the dining room table, talking to my grandma, who is pale and drawn with worry. When I enter, they both look up at me. His expression is smooth; this is just another workday for him. My grandmother looks tormented, like she's walking through hell for the second time and knows what lies ahead.

"Casey," he says. "How are you this evening?"

"I'm okay." I sit in a third chair and look back and forth between them. "What's going on? Is Jacob—" I'm suddenly afraid this means Jacob has died, that Adams came to give us the bad news.

"He's still unconscious. I'm actually here to ask you to come down to the station for an interview."

I meet my grandma's eyes. "What kind of interview?" I ask.

"We need your witness statement on record."

As far as he's concerned, I'm not a witness. I don't have to feign confusion. "But I didn't witness anything...?"

His answer is smooth, but there's something sharp and cunning behind his eyes. "We need your account of where Jacob said he was that night. Everything you told us at the hospital."

I don't trust it, but I can't think of a way around it. "When would you like me to come down?"

"Now, if you don't mind. I can give you a lift in the—"

"I'll drive her," my grandma interrupts in her take-no-prisoners voice.

I wonder if Zoe and Eddie have already given their statements. I wonder if they'll catch us in a contradiction. *Here we go.*

TWENTY

Wednesday, April 12

THE POLICE STATION IS SURPRISINGLY MODERN, all glass and angles set prominently on a corner in Atwater Village. We park and enter the cavernous lobby through a set of glass doors. Detective Adams parks around back and comes to greet us. My grandma is holding my hand, which is infantilizing, but I allow it. She's super freaked out to be back in a police station after all these years, and I can't blame her.

He leads us through a locked door, and then we're in a cold, sanitized hallway with doors spaced out every twenty feet or so. He opens the third one, which turns out to be an interview room like I've seen in police shows.

"Please. Have a seat." He indicates two chairs together on one side of the table, and he sits across from them. "You ladies all right?" His eyes go from our hands, tightly interlaced, to my grandma's pale, lined face.

I feel fiercely protective, so of course I turn sarcastic. "My mother was murdered almost ten years ago, and her murder was never solved. So yeah, this is not our happy place."

"Shhh." My grandma pats my hand. She takes a visible deep breath, then lets it out slowly. "If you could please just ask what you need to ask so we can move on, that would be great."

"I'm sorry. I didn't realize." He studies me. "I need to know where Jacob said he was going to be on Saturday, where you were, and where your friends Zoe and Eddie were."

I pull away from Grandma and fold my hands in my lap, summoning everything I've read about witness statements. They're notoriously inaccurate; It will be more suspicious if Zoe, Eddie, and I all have the same exact memories of times and events. If we really were just hanging out, playing the night by ear, we wouldn't remember times or details with any precision.

Here goes nothing. "In the morning, I worked a shift at Sunset FroYo from ten to six. I work there after school a few days a week and on weekends."

"Okay. And then what did you do?"

"I went home and changed, then went to Zoe's for a while." All true.

"And what did you do at Zoe's?"

"Just hung out." Organized her lock picking tools, watched her check through the security system on her laptop, packed up our movie cameras, charged the burner phones.

"What does hanging out mean, specifically?"

"Her mom made us some snacks. We talked about this guy she likes." I'm careful not to reference anything online that could be checked, like watching YouTube or playing video games.

"What kind of snacks?" He says it pleasantly, but I know what he's doing: digging into details to test the strength of a story. I won't go down this way. Everything I'm telling him is true; it's what I'm not saying that matters.

"Grilled cheese sandwiches and fruit. Oh, and these little quail eggs. Zoe's mom is obsessed with them. She thinks we love them, but we all kind of, you know, pity-eat them." I flash my grandma a little smile. She knows about Maria's quail egg obsession.

He nods. "So then when did you go over to Eddie's house?"

I let a little frown flicker across my face and cock my head. "I mean, can I be honest? I'm not totally sure." This is still true.

"Can you give me your best guess?"

I consider for a long moment, thinking about how Zoe doctored the security footage... I'm pretty sure it was eight or nine o'clock. How can I not remember this?

I let my anxiety show so it doesn't look like I'm hiding anything. "I could be way off base, but maybe like, eight or nine? I'm sorry; I really didn't look."

"Did you have your phone with you? Did you get any calls or texts that might jog your memory?"

I shake my head. "I remember having to turn it on when we got to the hospital. I hadn't looked at it for a long time."

He furrows his brow. "Is it unusual for you to not use your phone for an entire evening?"

Yes, in fact. "Why, because I'm a teenager?"

He shrugs. "In my experience, yes."

A little defensive, I say, "I was already with Zoe. So it's not like I was waiting for anyone to hit me up."

"What about your grandma? Doesn't she like you to keep your phone on in case of emergency?"

I exchange a look with her. "Yeah. She gets annoyed with me because I always forget." True.

"Really?" He looks at my grandma. "She sometimes forgets to turn her phone on?"

Jaw tight, she says, "Yes." I can tell she doesn't like the way he's digging into my responses like I'm in some kind of trouble.

He cocks his head and leans forward, elbows on the table. "So you sometimes just...power off your phone? Why?"

I really wish he would stop. "I don't know. Sometimes it dies and I forget to charge it."

"Did it die that night? Did you have to plug it in before powering it on?"

I wince, then hope he didn't notice. "No. I don't think so."

"So you turned it off at some point during the day or night, but you don't remember when."

"I guess."

He leans back, and I get the distinct impression that he's enjoying this. "See, here's the thing. Zoe's phone was also off. Eddie's, too. Three teenagers, all with phones powered off at the same time their best friend was breaking into an exciting, cool, abandoned house all alone. Odd coincidence, don't you think?"

I don't answer. Panic is rocketing around my skull.

Testily, my grandma says, "Was there something else you wanted to ask her?"

He smiles at me. "Casey, how did you and Zoe coordinate your plans, and how did you know Eddie was home if no one had their phones on?"

I'm spitting panicked curse words inside my head, but I force myself to be calm. "We didn't need to. We thought Eddie and Jacob would be hanging out at his house."

A horrible, stomach-deep realization of a way we'd messed up: On the security tapes, Eddie was entering his building from the parking lot with us. Clearly, we'd been in his car together. All three of us, coming in at once. If none of us had our phones, how had we coordinated that?

My body feels cold with anxiety. I'm sure he can see something wrong on my face.

His scrutinizing eyes never leave me. "All right. You were at Eddie's house together. What did you do?"

We rehearsed this; I just pray I'll get it right. "We talked about college, Zoe's dorms at MIT, about whether Eddie's going to live at home to go to USC, that kind of thing. We talked about Jacob. He's having a hard time right now because his dad wants him to go to college and he wants to start working on set as a PA."

"And where are you going to school, Casey?"

"LA City College. I'm going to do two years there, then transfer to a four-year school."

"And what do you want to study?"

"I'm not sure. The first year or two are gen ed, so I have a little time to figure it out."

"What are you interested in?"

I splay my hands, confused about this line of questioning. "I mean, I like research. Maybe I'll go into law, or history, or library science. I really don't know."

"You like research? Like, digging things up on the internet?"

Now I'm worried. "I...guess."

"Do you like procedurals, cold cases? A girl like you, seems like that would be right up your alley."

He's a step ahead of me at every turn. I say, "I have a problem with crime as entertainment. I think the way our culture does this true crime thing is a huge violation to the families of victims, and the fact that we make murderers famous is just gross." My grandma puts her hand over mine and squeezes in solidarity.

He's nodding in agreement with me. "I hear you, Casey. That's why I do this. To get justice for victims."

I meet his deep, intelligent eyes. "Good. Find out who did this to Jacob."

"Let's talk about that. Picture an old place a lot of people like to break into, one that's been vacant for decades. You'd have a ton of footprints in the dust from years and years of intruders, visitors, and you'd have to date them all. A huge pain, right?"

"I can see that."

"But here's the thing. The footprints tell us that Jacob wasn't the only person recently in that house, and I mean very recently—within the last week. I'm finding between three and five other sets of distinct footprints from the same time period. What are you, a size eight? Eight and a half? And your friend Zoe is about a size seven?"

My grandma sucks in a breath. "Hold on one second. You said this was a witness statement."

"And it is." He holds a hand up. "Bear with me." To me, he says, "I want you to know something, Casey." He leans far forward, chest touching the table's edge. "There's such a thing as gut instinct. I'm twenty years into this job, and my gut is telling me Jacob wasn't alone in that house. I see the four of you, inseparable, and I see him, by himself in that creepy old house, and I think: This seems like something a group of kids would do together. I see you, with your family history. I see your friend Zoe, who's going to MIT, such a smart girl, and I think, these are kids who could cover their tracks if they wanted to. I see your cell phones, all turned off that night." He sits back. His eyes never leave mine. "You're a witness now, Casey, but you should start thinking about what it might feel like to be a suspect."

My grandma explodes out of her chair, knocking it over. "How dare you," she roars. "My daughter has been dead for nearly ten years, and LAPD hasn't done a goddamn thing. And now you have the nerve to accuse my granddaughter of—" She chokes, a wet sound. Tears are coursing down her cheeks. I can't bear to see her like this, but I can't look away.

Detective Adams rises slowly. "Ma'am, I'm truly sorry for your loss."

"You think Casey could do to Jacob what was done to her

mom? What is wrong with you?" It looks like she's struggling to breathe.

I can tell he wants to reach out for her, but instead, he says in a quiet, controlled voice, "Sometimes that's how it happens, ma'am, as much as we wish it didn't."

"Not Casey." She puts a hand on my arm. "Let's go. If they want to talk to you again, they can do it with a lawyer."

I follow her out into the hallway, heart pounding, thinking about how wrong she is about me and how right he is. I may not have stabbed Jacob, but I'm not the person she thinks I am.

Out in the parking lot, in the cool night air, she wraps her arms around me and squeezes too tight. I pat her back and say, "It's okay, Grandma. He was just trying to scare me. It's what they do."

"We can't afford a lawyer," she squeaks.

"I know. We won't need one." We stand there quietly, her arms wrapped so tight around me, it's like she's afraid I'll vanish if she lets go for even a moment.

"I'm sorry," I whisper. She doesn't know it, but this is really and truly all my fault.

✧

Back home, Grandma orders me to eat some chicken soup and shuts herself in the bathroom to get ready for bed. I escape to my bedroom, gratefully pulling the room divider closed behind me and collapsing on the bed. I get my phone out of my pocket and call Zoe.

It rings out to voice mail, and I hang up and check the time.

It's only nine; where is she? I call again, let it ring five times, hang up, then try FaceTiming. Nothing. Angry, I call one more time, and Maria picks up on the third ring.

"Hello?" She sounds irritated.

I'm surprised. Maria has never answered Zoe's phone before. "Sorry, Maria. I was looking for Zoe. Is she there?"

"She can't talk right now, Casey. You can see her at school tomorrow." She hangs up. I stare at the phone for a minute, then pull up our chat app, which I know Zoe can check from her laptop. **What's up with your mom? Did she confiscate your phone?**

No answer.

I'm assuming Zoe got called down to the station, too. Maybe her mom doesn't want us talking to each other. I try Eddie, who doesn't answer the phone or chat, and then I sit there for a minute, confused and scared.

I open the blinds and look out the window. I feel trapped, smothered. Maybe it's my grandma's grief, an ever-present substance in this house, hanging over us like smoke. Sometimes, I wish we could just... open a window.

Of course, I miss my mom every day. Her picture is smiling at me right now, urging me to never forget a single thing about her. But I have. I've forgotten a lot. I remember a few anecdotes, funny memories of her quirky sense of humor, but I don't know if what I'm remembering is real or if it's mutated over the years, formed from pictures and videos. Sometimes, I wish I could forget. How horrible is that? But what's the alternative—an entire life spent with a hole inside me?

It's different for my grandma. She lost her daughter. There's no forgetting, no moving on. That cloud of grief smoke will follow her around until the day she dies.

I grab my purse and slip my shoes on. I slide the partition open and listen. Faintly, I can hear her snoring. She's already asleep. My heart aches; she works incredibly hard, and she's just so, so tired. I scribble a note on the Post-its we keep on the kitchen counter.

Couldn't sleep. Be right back. Don't worry, I'm safe. I have my phone if you need me.

She'll be livid when she wakes up and finds this note, but she'd be angrier if I didn't leave one at all. I burst out of my apartment building, walking so fast it's almost a run. I'm making my way toward the Hollywood and Highland Metro Station, heading to North Hollywood; I'm going to Dallas's house.

I need to see that footage. If the cops are moving in on us, I need to find new evidence, something to protect us.

THE HOLLYWOOD REVIEW

ADRIAN WONDERS FOUND DEAD

MONDAY, JUNE 19, 1972

In a new and shocking development, medium Adrian Wonders was found dead in his home in the Hollywood Hills on Sunday, June 18. His body was discovered by a housekeeper, who arrived early to prepare for a brunch Mr. Wonders was scheduled to host.

The LAPD confirms that Mr. Wonders's death appears to be self-inflicted but has so far refused to comment on the cause of death. That said, the housekeeper has been talking to publications and claims she found him hanging by the wooden beams in his 1920s home's vaulted ceilings.

Suicide strikes a truly wretched chord for someone so attuned to the spirit world. One would hope such an enlightened man would be immune to the woes that plague us common folk. However, close friends of Adrian Wonders have often commented on his tempestuous nature, emphasizing the burden his gift has proven itself to be.

Mr. Wonders's obituary will be penned by none other than Kal Lindthrop, screenwriter and director known for his Academy Award–winning *On the Water*, in which Rosalinda Valentini played Lela, a young blond with an end as tragic as Mr. Wonders's. There is something gruesomely poetic about this connection. One can't help but

contemplate its tidy symme-
try and recall the dramatic
recent séance at the Valentini
mansion.

Services will be public
at Forest Lawn, hosted this
Thursday, June 22, by the
deceased's mother, Lydia Wonders, and officiated by Oscar
nominee Marilyn Struthers.
It is destined to be quite the
affair.

TWENTY-ONE

Wednesday, April 12

I WAIT IN FRONT OF THE APARTMENT BUILDING, then hit the buzzer for the third time. I'm about to give up when a crackly voice bursts through the old speaker. "Who is it?"

"It's, um...Is this Dallas? It's Casey."

A pause.

"Hold on."

I fidget, waiting for her to buzz me in, thinking about how upset my grandma would be that I took the Metro to North Hollywood alone at night and then walked on barely lit streets to get to here.

Anger flares up. For god's sake, when Grandma was my age, she had already gotten her GED and was living in San Francisco with her boyfriend. But here I am, worried she'll freak out because I took public transportation. It's not fair. I need to be able to *live*.

I squash down the resentment. There's no point in it. Life is always unfair.

The door clicks, unlocking, and I grab the handle and yank it open. It clanks behind me, and I make my way sheepishly to the apartment I remember from my little illegal visit. Dallas opens her front door as I approach, poking her head out. "What are you doing here?"

"Sorry, I know it's getting late. I was hoping we could look at that footage together."

She glances behind her and steps out into the walkway. She's wearing black sweats and a white Blondie T-shirt with the sleeves cut off. "So, my mom and sister don't know about any of this." She gestures to the air beside us.

"They don't know about the palm trees here in the courtyard?"

She rolls her eyes. "Don't be cute."

"They don't know you have creepy teddy-bear nanny cams in the murder house," I clarify. She nods. "Do they know you have control of the alarm system?"

"Not so much." She looks embarrassed now. "I may or may not have used my mom's information to set some things up."

I consider this. "So I'm a friend from school. We're in drama together or something."

"How do you know I do drama?"

"I googled you." Duh.

"Hmph." She's cranky by nature, I realize. Kind of like an

old man. "Fine. Come in." She turns, and I follow her into the apartment. It smells like fast food—burgers and fries. The TV in the living room is on, and her younger sister is sprawled out on the couch, watching a nature documentary while texting. She's pretty, with long, silky blond hair and glasses. She looks up at me with curiosity.

"Morrison, this is my friend Casey. She's from school. We're going to finish a drama assignment real quick."

She's clearly surprised, but she doesn't say anything except, "Cool."

"My mom's in the shower," Dallas mutters, leading me to her bedroom. Once inside, she shuts the door behind us. "Nice room," I say, again needling her without understanding why.

"Like you've never seen it." She flops into the spindly desk chair, which squeaks in protest.

I perch on the bed beside her, which is just a mattress and box spring with no frame. "How old is Morrison?" I ask.

She darts her eyes sideways at me. "That wasn't part of your stalking?"

I sigh. "Fine. She's sixteen."

A snort, and the eyes return to the screen. It's a desktop PC that's seen better days, but when she boots it up, it starts quickly, like a much newer computer. I wonder if she fixed it up herself.

"So how'd it go with the cops?" Dallas asks, clicking on an icon that looks like a circle surrounding an eye.

"Um..." I readjust my position, crossing my ankles.

"That good, huh?" She turns to face me. "What happened?"

I consider withholding, but what the hell? She's in this,

too. "They're pretty sure the three of us were there with Jacob that night. They...suspect me. Us. I haven't heard from Zoe or Eddie. I don't know if they've had the same conversation with each of us."

She's studying me as I say this, analyzing my facial expressions. When she stops being snarky, she has a pretty, open face, with crystal-clear blue eyes set far apart and sculpted, arched brows. I find myself studying her lips for a moment too long, blush, and redirect my attention to the screen. "So is that the software that goes with the nanny cams?"

"Yeah. Let me pull up the—" She bites her lip, and I notice her cheeks are flushed. "Keep in mind these are cheap cameras. They aren't reliable. They're clearly malfunctioning; there's something going on with the lenses or..."

"In all of them, or just one?"

"I've seen this on all of them. It's probably the batch of cameras, something like that. You promise you won't freak out and call a reporter or something?"

"Should I go ahead and cuff myself, too, to save the cops the trouble?"

"Fair." She maximizes a window and says, "This is the live feed right now." It's got six windows tiled together, each with a different view of the inside of the vacant house. Since it's night, they're all in shadow, only the outlines of walls and furniture visible. The living room is the best lit thanks to the huge picture windows. Looking at the screen, I feel a chill sweep through me as I'm mentally transported back to that night.

Dallas searches through menu items and pulls up a new

window, this one paused on a night view of the living room. She keeps searching and pulls up five more, one each from the kitchen, hallway, dining room, and two other rooms I don't recognize.

"These are all the rooms downstairs," she explains. "I don't keep cameras upstairs because there's no point. No one's going to Spider-Man up the side of the house and climb in through a second-floor window."

"Have you had a lot of break-ins?"

"A handful." She rubs her forehead. "It's exhausting. This one group likes to hold witchy rituals on the property. Tarot readings, séances, candles, chanting. They broke in once, got busted, and now they do them in the backyard."

"Do you have a camera out there?"

"No. I installed motion-sensor lights, but they don't care. And the cops don't want me to call every time someone trespasses onto the property. They'd be there all the time. I wish I had the money for a private security patrol." For the first time I realize how weird this must be for her, managing such a legendary, infamous place.

She searches through footage for a few minutes, and I fiddle with the zipper on my sweatshirt. "Here," she says at last. "This is you guys breaking into the kitchen." She shows me a camera view where, sure enough, we file in through the back door, our camera lights illuminating everything in the room. There's Zoe, then Eddie and Jacob, then me. Even with ski masks on, I can tell us apart. Zoe is shorter and curvier than I am; Eddie and Jacob, though almost identical in outline, move differently.

Eddie is more stiff and athletic, while Jacob has a natural slinkiness to his movements. He could have been a dancer.

I scoot closer, almost shoulder to shoulder with her so I can see the screen up close. "Here you are rummaging through my family's stuff," she says as the guys open the cabinets and remove cans and jars.

"We really had no idea—"

"Whatever." She pulls up another view. "Here are you and your friend Zoe." This is the living room camera. Again, we're lighting up the room as we explore. "There you are, super excited to see the place my family members were murdered. So fun."

I bite my tongue. I'm going to have to endure her commentary.

"And there you and Zoe go upstairs, to defile the bedrooms. Now the guys start searching around downstairs, looking for other things to mess with. They split up. Jacob is in the front room, Eddie in the kitchen."

"How can you tell them apart?" I ask. "I mean, I can, but I've known them for years."

"I dunno. They move differently; Eddie's more athletic. And besides, I've rewatched this a thousand times. In the moment, I was trying to figure out why the alarm system didn't go off."

I look down at my lap, embarrassed.

"Yeah, you guys apparently disarmed it somehow. But here's the thing." While she talks, on screen, Eddie and Jacob come in and out of the view of the cameras, slowly walking around the kitchen, opening cabinets, peeking inside, picking things up and setting them down. "Even though the alarm was turned off, I can still see ins and outs. Entries and exits. You know what I mean? I can see a log of when someone opened and closed a door or window, even if the alarm is disarmed."

I glance up at her, processing what she's saying. "So..."

"No one came in before or after you."

I frown. "Zoe says she left the back door partway open. How can you tell if—"

She shakes her head. "No. The door was closed behind you, and no one opened it again until after the alarm went off."

My eyes are fixed on hers, and then something on screen catches my attention. It's the living room camera. No one's visible; it's just the darkened room with the fireplace, couch, and end tables, all from the point of view of the teddy bear I remember seeing on the grand piano.

A flicker of light unlike that coming from our cameras illuminates the screen, then fades. It's like someone turned on overhead lights, then turned them right off. There, again—a flash of light revealing the whole room, then darkness.

"What is that?" I ask, leaning in. When the light blazes, I can see all the furniture, pictures on the walls I hadn't noticed, a hanging curtain above the fireplace.

"That's what I was saying. It has to be some glitch with the cameras."

"But, no. That doesn't make sense. If it was something with the cameras, the screen would turn white—it wouldn't illuminate everything in the room. The source of light is *inside* the room."

"So maybe one of your friends' camera lights is malfunctioning."

"Maybe," I murmur, watching as the room strobes intermittently. "But then...where's the camera? Where are the guys when this is happening?"

She toggles through the other camera views, each in its own window. "One is in the kitchen. Eddie, I think. See, this is Jacob, out in the hallway."

"He's looking into the living room," I cry. "He sees it! He's holding his camera by his side." It's not easy to make it out; the hallway is dark, and Jacob is just a flat shape, his camera a distorted blob by his leg. The light flickers over his profile, a strobe highlighting the black-on-black of his clothing.

The living room light show is intensifying. Jacob walks out of view, and I frantically search, trying to see where he went. Eddie is still in the kitchen, pulling things out of cupboards, placing them on the table, and getting footage of them.

"He's about to come in," Dallas says, pointing at the time stamp. Sure enough, Jacob staggers through the door of the living room, no camera in hand. As the light strobes and pulses around him, he collapses onto the carpet. Blood spreads out in a viscous, liquid stain. The lights go out. Darkness.

The darkness is inside me, along with the searing image of Jacob, stabbed, bleeding out on the carpet, and shock—what could have caused the light show we just witnessed? My stomach is full of ice. I shiver, a whole-body shudder that ends in a wave of nausea. I haven't pictured the stabbing—the wounds, Eddie's blood-soaked hands, the stain slowly spreading on the carpet—since that night. Somehow, I've had the sensory memory of Jacob's attack locked away, my brain efficiently sweeping it into a hole and covering it with a rug. Maybe there's a lot more under that rug.

"This is when I hit the panic setting on the alarm," Dallas says. I realize one hand is pressed to my mouth and tears are running down my cheeks.

And then—"Wait," I choke. "I just saw something. Rewind. Can you do slo-mo?"

"Yeah, hang on." She backs up the footage. "What are we looking at? Living room?"

I nod, shoving my glasses up to wipe my face on the sleeve of my sweatshirt.

She rewinds, searches settings, and slows it down. Again, Jacob staggers into the room. "There. Stop." I point at the space behind Jacob in the doorway, briefly lit by the mysterious light source. It's a shadow, just a faint, blurry shape. "*There*," I whisper.

"Someone's behind him in the doorway," Dallas breathes, leaning in so we're almost cheek-to-cheek. "Damn. That's a person. Only visible in one or two frames. How did you spot that?"

"I'm used to looking at footage." I stop. I can't believe I said that. I'm not feeling well. The edges of my vision are dark, like we're under a spotlight.

She doesn't react. "Right. From the YouTube channel." I stare at her, aghast, and she shrugs. "It didn't take a lot of research to figure you out."

"How?" I ask, horrified to have been found out, wondering if anyone else has made the connection.

She shrugs. "There are four of you. My house is the perfect place for one of your episodes. It just makes sense."

I'm a little relieved that she doesn't have hard evidence, but it's still unsettling. I return my attention to the shape on the monitor. "The resolution is too low. I can't tell..." I'm going to say I can't tell if the shape is human, but I stop the words from coming out.

"Here's the thing." She leans back in her chair and faces me full-on. "You and your friend Zoe were together upstairs, right? Eddie is on camera down in the kitchen this whole time. No one came in or out all week except for you guys. So who the hell is that?"

Together, we stare at the dark shape—just a blurry shadow, nothing more. And now the memory hole overflows, and I'm back in the house, the alarm screaming around me. Jacob is splayed out on the carpet, which soaks up his blood like an offering, evil like a fog clouding the room with darkness instead of smoke.

I stand, bumping against Dallas, who looks at me in surprise. "I'm sorry," I mutter. I turn and hurry for the door before I dissolve completely.

TWENTY-TWO

Wednesday, April 12

I BURST THROUGH THE FRONT GATE OF DALLAS'S apartment building and falter on the sidewalk, panting. My stomach is roiling. When did I last eat—is there any food in there? I'm drawing a blank. It's scary, the emptiness where memory should be. I search back through the day and can't conjure anything up. It's just Jacob, bleeding, and I realize I never saw the wounds, because his shirt was black. I'm not even sure where exactly he was stabbed. Eddie had already pulled the knife out. I picture it—the image of the knife embedded in Jacob, the sound it would have made being withdrawn—

My breathing is too fast. It's not good. My eyes are stuck on the collection of discarded items in the median strip. Couch, couch, toilet, couch.

I look up at the cloudless sky. The moon is almost full, blazing down white light that mixes with the streetlight. The door bangs open and Dallas jogs out, flip-flops slapping against the cement. "What's going on?" She stands beside me and follows my gaze up at the moon. I don't look at her face, but I sense her confusion. I take deep breaths, trying to calm my heart, which is racing like I'm the one fighting for my life.

"Casey?" A warm hand rests on my shoulder. "You're hyperventilating."

I need to walk. I need to go home. I need to curl up in bed, pull the covers tight over me, and then I'll be able to breathe, once I'm safe in that little cocoon. I start walking, steps hesitant, and then gaining speed, Dallas at my elbow.

"Casey?" she repeats. "What're you doing? Where are you going?"

"Home," I say. I can speak; that's good. Walking gives my body something to do.

"If you're heading for the Metro station, you're going the wrong way. This is north." She points ahead of us.

I stop, disoriented. She grips my upper arms. "You're having a panic attack. You need to try to calm your central nervous system. I'm going to hug you. Okay? It will help." It's a complete non sequitur. Before I can answer or even understand the statement, she wraps her arms around me so mine are trapped at my sides and squeezes me hard. I want to struggle against it, but then I feel a sort of warmth running through me from scalp to tailbone, and something in my chest unlocks.

"See, it's working," she says, squeezing tighter. "I saw it on *Grey's Anatomy* and started using it on my sister. She has anxiety." Her chin is on my shoulder; we're pretty much the same height. She's wiry and strong, and I feel my muscles loosen in a whoosh. A gust of pent-up air escapes my lungs, and my legs turn into jelly. I rest my forehead on her shoulder, embarrassment beginning to take hold where panic left off.

"I'm sorry," I mumble.

"What was the trigger? The lights? Are you afraid of ghosts?"

"No. It was Jacob." The image of him staggering into the frame replays on a loop, and I beg my mind to return the memory to its place under the rug.

"I didn't think the footage would upset you so much. I figured you'd watched your own footage a million times, that this wouldn't be the first time you were seeing...I should stop talking."

I pat her arm to indicate it's okay to let me go, and she pulls away, keeping hold of my shoulders. She studies my face, concern and pity written across hers, as I straighten my bangs and glasses. I'm sure my eyeliner is a mess.

I may as well tell her.

"My mom died that way. Stabbed. Murdered." I can't meet her eyes. "Anyway, I hadn't really let myself picture it. I haven't even visited him in the hospital."

"Whoa," she breathes. "Casey, I had no idea."

"It's bad luck, right?" A dry laugh ends that statement. "I hate that you think I'm one of those true crime tourists. My mom's story was on one of those murder podcasts, and it was the worst."

Her brows draw together. "Are you serious? Casey, that's so messed up." It's her turn to look up at the moon. "You know, sometimes this world is just..."

"I know."

She turns to me. "I'm really sorry. I had no idea."

I smile weakly. "It's not your fault." There are a few awkward moments, and then I say, "Well, I should get home. If my grandma wakes up and finds me gone, I'll be on house arrest until graduation."

"This is why she's so protective," she says, just understanding.

"Yep."

"Well, I'm driving you home. You're not taking the Metro at this time of night."

I almost protest, but then I swallow my pride and nod. "Okay. Thanks."

She runs inside, and I wait until she reemerges with our bags and a set of keys. "My mom's car is down the block."

It turns out to be an aging Ford Taurus. The inside smells like incense and cigarettes, and she adjusts the mirrors before pulling away from the curb. She's a safe driver, both hands on the wheel, profile meditative in the streetlight as she navigates toward the 170 freeway.

"You can't tell anyone about the lights and stuff," she says after a few minutes. "Not even your friends. Promise?"

"I promise." I hesitate. "But why are you so..."

"If I'm going to sell the house, I need it to not be, like, completely haunted?" She says it like a joke, but the tone falls flat, and I think she's being more serious than she lets on.

"There was something in there," I say, watching the lights of the city fly by.

"I know." She says it quietly.

I've never believed in the supernatural, but I can't think of another explanation for what we saw. I've heard of places having bad energy, which always sounded fake. But can it be possible that the murder house is some kind of evil vortex, attracting murders like a black hole pulls in stars and devours them?

The ride is peaceful; without traffic, our houses are only fifteen minutes apart. When she double-parks in front of my building, she turns toward me. "I really am sorry."

"It's fine. Thank you so much for the ride."

I have a hand on the door and am about to get out when she says, "Hey, um, Casey? Would you . . . Do you want to go out sometime?"

I blink at her, uncomprehending.

"It's weird to ask like that, I know, but it's not like we're going to see each other in school." She shrugs. "Maybe we could, I don't know. What do people do? Go to a movie? A graveyard?"

My heart is pounding again, but this is different. I look down at her hands; one is clutching the wheel, the other resting on her knee, fingers tapping nervously.

I meet her eyes again and clear my throat. "Sure."

She smiles. "Good. Okay. Then I can text you?"

I nod stupidly.

"I don't have your number," she points out.

I fumble my phone out of my pocket and unlock it. I pass it to her so she can enter her number, and then I text her: **This is Casey.**

She examines my face. "You okay? Did I make it weird?"

"No, I—" I'm confused by the sensations inside my chest. "I'm happy. Text me when you get home?" I instantly regret the clinginess of the request.

She smiles. "Sure."

Out on the street, the world is spinning around me. I let myself into my building and stare at the palm trees in the courtyard, feeling blank and empty when I should be all kinds of things.

She asked me out? I stare at my front door, trying to process. Why? No one has ever been interested before. I'm glowing. My chest feels warm. I could almost smile.

I refocus on the last few hours. I don't know what I think about the strange lights on the footage. Could I ever believe in ghosts? I guess, but the idea that a ghost stabbed Jacob seems intensely stupid. It was done with a knife. Someone took his camera. This is the work of a human. But...the footage. Eddie was in the kitchen at the time of the attack. Zoe and I were upstairs. No one else came in or out all week.

Wait.

Was Zoe upstairs?

A rush of dread fills me from head to toe. I want to push the thought back into the darkness it came from, but it's too late. It's out. I try to remember every detail. When Zoe and I reunited in the hall, how long had it been since we'd seen each other? Five minutes? Ten? We'd met in the upstairs hall, then had run down together, but…I didn't have any way of knowing where she was in those minutes leading up to Jacob's stabbing.

I remember her reaction after the attack, how collected she'd been, how she'd insisted on doctoring the security camera time stamps. And she hadn't let me see the footage before we buried the tapes.

"Oh my god," I whisper, a shiver running through me. It doesn't make sense. What motive could she possibly have to hurt Jacob? They're friends. She loves him.

A breeze swishes past me, raising my hair off my neck and sending a chill through my veins. Maybe ghosts are real.

I don't buy it. Humans are worse than anything we dream up.

TWENTY-THREE

Wednesday, March 29

JACOB

IT ALWAYS FELT WEIRD GOING TO SCHOOL AFTER ditching for a few days, but I wanted to see Eddie. After last night, I was light on my feet, springy with the knowledge that he loved me.

He loved me, and we were going to be together, and he was going to think about how to tell his parents. He wasn't ready to be out at school and with friends yet, but that was okay. He needed time. I respected that. I'd told him I probably wasn't coming to school today, but then I hadn't slept more than a few hours, too excited and happy to close my eyes. At six, I figured I might as well go. Maybe I could convince him to skip his last period and go get naked while my dad was at work.

Was I whistling? Jesus Christ. Someone needed to come along and slap me in the face.

There he was! He and Zoe were tucked into a recess in the building beside the steps, deep in conversation. I raised a hand to wave, but then I sucked in a breath. Zoe was lifting her arms and winding them around his neck. My steps faltered.

She got onto her tiptoes and kissed his cheek. He tilted his head back, still talking to her, and then he gripped her hands and pulled them off. This seemed to upset her; she held a finger up, pointing at him. He retorted and then she stepped back as though in shock.

His posture was pleading now; he reached for her, put his hands on her waist, lips moving quickly. She pulled away, wiped her eyes, and hurried toward the stairs. He leaned against the building and shoved his hands in his pockets, looking down at his feet. I realized I was stunned, frozen into place like an ice sculpture.

I turned and walked fast, getting away from school as quick as I could, trying to wrap my head around whatever the hell I had just seen.

It was mind-boggling; Eddie and Zoe weren't super close. Now that I considered it, I had noticed them bonding here and there over being ambitious in ways Casey and I weren't. They were stressing out over college applications and tests I didn't even remember the names for, studying together...

Zoe was perfect for him, wasn't she? She had her life in order. She was beautiful. Her family was wealthy. She had everything. But then, why had he kissed me on the sidewalk and told me he loved me?

My feet took me back home, where I let myself into my

apartment and stood for a long moment, staring into the dimly lit living room. In my room, I reached under my bed and dug out a binder, opened it, and flipped through it. It was full of newspaper articles and printed research about the Valentini house.

I pictured what it would have been like before the crime, paging past a series of photographs of Rosalinda taken during her career. She was so divine; she never looked real. And these were the days before Photoshop. I'd studied this binder a hundred times. It made me feel hopeful. Soon I'd be in there, touching things with my very own hands.

If only Eddie knew what was about to happen. Things were about to change in a big way. And now the satisfaction of sharing that with him had been stolen from me.

TWENTY-FOUR

Thursday, April 13

THE MORNING IS COOL, THE SUN BLASTING ME with eye-splitting brightness. It's ten a.m. and I've been on the bus and on foot for two hours, crossing the five miles from my neighborhood to Griffith Park and the trail Zoe and I walked a day ago. I barely slept last night, trying to make everything make sense.

I follow the path under a lacy canopy of trees, keeping an eye on the series of concrete ruins. Maybe this was some kind of aqueduct or drainage. According to my research, this area was developed in the early 1900s; the original LA Zoo was named the Griffith Park Zoo, opening in 1912. It closed in 1966 when the zoo moved into its current, huge location, leaving the old zoo and its surrounding infrastructure to dissolve slowly back into the land. It's interesting how nature takes things back, eating away at concrete and steel with slow, tiny teeth.

At last, I come to the spot where we'd buried the tapes. There's the tree, with the markings Zoe had carved into the bark. I run my finger over the M+H. The letters are already fading. I silently apologize to the tree for wounding it.

I turn off the path and climb down into the creek bed, wary of poison oak just like I had been last time. There's the mural I'd used as my landmark, and—wait.

I don't even have to search for where I'd buried the tapes. There's an open hole spilling over with dark earth. I dig around in the loose soil, frantic. The tapes are gone.

I brush my hands off on my jeans and stand, getting my phone out of my back pocket. Anger rockets through me. Why would Zoe do this? I call her, but of course it goes straight to voice mail; she's probably in school, and she's actually good about turning her phone off during class.

I think for a minute, absently watching a pair of squirrels dart from ground to tree and back again. I scroll through my contacts and call Eddie. We never talk on the phone, but I can't text him about this, and I certainly can't drop it into our group chat. He doesn't answer, but a text buzzes, and I hang up to see it's from him.

Can't talk. At the hospital.

I consider my response. **I really need to talk to you.**

Sorry.

I huff, frustrated. I don't know how to convey the urgency via text without putting something incriminating in writing. I guess I'll have to go to the hospital and talk to him in person. My stomach turns over at the prospect. I don't want to see Jacob, don't want this to become any more real than it already is.

A memory surfaces—Zoe grinning at me, eyes twinkling, as she picked a lock. "It's hard, but we can do hard things." She was quoting our eleventh-grade English teacher, who had sent us into silent hysterics with that expression.

Is it possible that all this time my best friend was a potential killer and I never had a clue? What does that say about me? Could I have spent years analyzing what happened to my mom, reading up on a million other cases, and never developed a single ounce of self-preservation instinct?

Maybe my mom was naive, too. Maybe we were born to be prey.

I gnaw on a hangnail, stalling on the sidewalk outside the hospital, having been deposited right out front by the bus. Traffic noise flows like water, punctuated by the occasional honk or screech of brakes. People bustle past me, all in a hurry—in scrubs, in wheelchairs, propping up pregnant family members, holding babies. The hospital is a monolith, towering above me. I look down at my feet. It's too raw, too real, all this dealing with mortal bodies. I can't imagine how medical professionals do it.

Go in there, an inner voice urges. *Enough already.*

Fine. I square my shoulders and march through the sliding

glass doors. The intensive care unit is through a maze that takes me a while to figure out. I remember Zoe being able to navigate it easily, and I feel a fresh pang of resentment.

The elevator lets me off in front of a door that requires me to be buzzed in, and then I'm signing in to the visitor log at a nurse's station. It's an interesting layout in here, the rooms built in a rough circle so the doors all open onto a central space manned by nurses. I don't see Eddie anywhere. Maybe he's in Jacob's room.

"Third door down," I'm told by a nurse who's absorbed by his computer screen. I close the distance slowly, clenching and unclenching my hands. A lump in my throat, I pause outside the doorway.

All at once, a thousand gallons of liquid sadness splash down on me like a monsoon. This is *Jacob*. Of the four of us, he's the only other one who doesn't have money, who's queer, who doesn't know what his future holds, who can't afford to go to a fancy college or live in a dorm or... or anything. He's the only person I know who's also lost his mom. No one understands what it means to lose your mom unless they've experienced it. He's the only one, and now he's—I can't go in there.

I *have* to go in there.

I cross the threshold. The room is darkened, the blinds closed. A curtain runs across the space, hiding the bed, and I blink against the change in light, halted by the realization that I'm not alone in here. A low voice comes from behind the curtain, murmuring. It must be his dad, I realize, from the intimacy of the speech patterns. I cringe; are those tears I hear? I'm about to leave when something catches my eye.

Under the curtain, the visitor's shoes are visible—spotless, high-top Nikes. That's not like Jacob's dad. He's more of a beat-up Docs kind of guy. Drawn forward, I step around the curtain to peek, and what I see freezes me solid.

Eddie, slumped across the bed, one hand tangled in Jacob's hair, one gripping his hand, fingers laced through Jacob's. His face is buried in Jacob's arm; it's as close to an embrace as he seems to be able to get with Jacob's chest covered in bandages.

Jacob is deathly pale, face relaxed in sleep. Tubes snake from his nose, mouth, and arm, connecting him to a machine that beeps quietly in the semidarkness. As I stand there, fixed in place, Eddie mumbles again, something I can barely hear despite the tomblike stillness. I'm almost certain it contains the words, "I love you."

Holy shit. They're together. Like, *together* together. I have to recalculate everything.

"Eddie?" I murmur.

He startles, jumps, spins to face me while removing his hands from Jacob like he's been caught shoplifting. His face is wet with tears and blank with shock.

"I'm sorry I scared you." I step forward with exaggerated slowness as though to show him I'm not a threat.

He runs his hands over his face, his hair, glances down at Jacob, then up at me. He looks gaunt and exhausted, eyes sunken into shadow. I pull the blinds open halfway. "Let's get some light in here, okay? It's a nice day outside."

He sinks back into his chair and stares at Jacob's face, eyes searching, maybe hoping for a reaction to the change in light. I pull another chair over and pick up one of Jacob's limp hands. It's cold and dry. "Eddie, are you guys a couple?"

His eyes are fixed on his hands, clasped in his lap. "Not really." He looks up at me. "You can't say anything. To anyone. Not his dad, the cops, Zoe, no one."

"I'd never do that." The fact that he thinks I'd out him hurts. He knows I'm queer. It reminds me how little I actually know Eddie. He plays his cards very close to the vest. Jacob's always been the one who helps him open up around us, who can access the funny parts of him. But now...

I squeeze Jacob's hand and lay it back at his side. This is obviously not the time to bring up my suspicions about Zoe. "How are your parents doing?" I ask, but what I'm really asking is if they're even home, or if Eddie is dealing with this completely alone.

He shrugs. "Dad's filming something in Atlanta. Mom is casting a few shows right now. Haven't seen her much this week."

Of course. "Dude. Sweetie. You're not okay."

He covers his face with his hands and folds forward, coming to rest with his head on Jacob's leg. "I was so awful to him," he says, voice breaking and muffled. "You don't even know."

My heart wrenches, and I feel tears prick the backs of my eyes. "You guys were in a fight, right? I remember things were off between you."

"He wanted to..." He quiets, and I count twenty seconds

before he finishes the sentence. "He wanted to be out, to just be together. I wouldn't let him."

"That's not so bad. It's a whole process. I'm sure he understood."

"It's worse. There's more. I can't..." I can see his ribs through his T-shirt.

"You and Jacob have been friends for how many years—ten? That's a bond that can survive a lot. And Jacob isn't fragile. I didn't know what you had—have—is romantic, but that doesn't matter. He loves you. You're the most important person in his life."

It's pretty rich, me giving him this advice. When my mom died, I had been mad that she took away my iPad for not finishing my chores. I'd been furious and had said mean things to her. I've been mad at myself about it for a decade; I don't think I'll ever forgive myself.

Almost inaudibly, he says, "You know my parents are all about, like, being special. Doing something big. They always act like Jacob's this... distraction. Like I should be friends with more important people. They like Zoe. She's somebody."

My heart twists with empathetic pain. "That's not right. Jacob's special. Of course he is."

"He's not *somebody*," he whispers. "He's just Jacob."

I protest, "That's all any of us are." He shakes his head like he's unable to say anything else.

"Come on," I say, standing up. "We're going to get you something to eat."

"I'm not hungry."

"Jacob would want me to make sure you were taken care of. So those are the rules." I come around to his side of the bed and tug on his arm. Reluctantly, he stands. Before we exit the room, I cast a glance down at Jacob. *You need to wake up.* It's a prayer and a plea all in one.

In the hallway, I ask Eddie, "Did the cops interview you?"

He looks surprised, like he'd forgotten. "Yeah. I had to go down to the station."

"Did you tell your parents?"

He shakes his head.

"How'd it go? The detective was pretty intense with me. And Zoe's mom isn't even letting her answer my calls. This is bad."

The whites of his are bloodshot. "Maybe so." This level of exhausted apathy unsettles me, and I worry he forgot all our planning and told the police something completely out of bounds.

✧

By two o'clock, I'm leaving Eddie's apartment, having forced him to eat and to take a nap in his own bed. Inside the soft, silent privacy of the elevator, I rub my temples. I couldn't press him further about the police, and I couldn't share my suspicions about Zoe. He's too fragile right now. What am I going to do? Should I call his parents? I vow to ask my grandma.

My phone buzzes in my back pocket, and a rush of adrenaline passes through me as I get it out, worrying it's Zoe, no idea what to say to her. Instead, it's Dallas.

Yeah yeah, I have no chill. Texting you less than a day later. What are you doing tonight?

I smile a little despite my dark mood. The doors ding open, and I step out into the building foyer.

Working until 7, I reply.

Where do you work?

I wince. **Frozen yogurt shop.**

She produces a thinking emoji, and then says, **Want to do something after?**

I consider whether my grandma will have feelings about that, but I decide I can't worry about it. I'm almost eighteen. I say, **Sure. What do you have in mind?**

I actually hadn't thought that far?? Let me figure something out.

I shake my head. I can't believe I'm going on a date. It's epically bad timing. But a part of me feels like even though we've only met twice, Dallas might understand me better than Zoe, Eddie, or Jacob ever have. So much for best friends.

TWENTY-FIVE

Thursday, April 13

I'M IN THE BACK ROOM OF SUNSET FROYO, UP TO
my elbows in the sink scrubbing topping bins when Raul sticks
his head in. "Someone's here to see you."

Cold stress washes through me. I've been worrying about my
date with Dallas this entire shift, to the point where I'm barely
functional. "Who is it?" I ask, superstitiously convinced she's
going to stand me up.

He shrugs. "Kinda cute. Goth but not." Raul's also a senior
at my school, but I never see him there because he's way into
sports. He has practice almost every night of the week and usually only works weekends; today he's covering for the owner's
daughter, who's filming a car commercial downtown.

"I'll be right out," I tell him.

He does a little dance, popping his butt. "Casey's getting some ass tonight...," he sings in a falsetto, fake R & B voice.

"Shut up!" I hiss, flicking soapy water at him. He gives me an evil grin and slithers out. He's always like this except when Zoe visits the shop, at which point he turns into a sweet angel of free frozen yogurt.

I hurry to get the containers in the dishwasher, worried about what he's telling Dallas in my absence. I take off my apron, straighten my bangs, pull my hair out of its bun, and smooth out the vintage dress it took me an hour to pick out. When I emerge, wiping my hands on a white bar towel, she's sitting in the farthest corner away from him, scowling at her phone, legs crossed tight like she's trying to be as small as possible, while Raul watches her with open curiosity from behind the register where he rings up a gaggle of post-yoga thirty-five-year-olds. As I push the swinging door aside and step into the customer area, Raul hums his little song at me, and I wave him off, which makes him chuckle.

"Hey," I tell her, approaching. "Sorry to keep you waiting."

She looks up. I forgot how blue her eyes are; maybe it's the eyeliner or the fluorescent light, but they're neon tonight. "You're fine. I was a little early." She stands and shoves her phone in her pocket, and we share an awkward moment where neither of us knows how to greet the other. She's wearing black jeans and boots with a cropped white sweater that shows her belly button, something I'm going to have to avoid looking at.

"So what do you want to do?" I ask.

"I have a plan. You ready?"

I indicate the purse I'm carrying. "Yeah, I've got my things."

As we pass by the register, Raul says, "Have a good night, Casey," in a singsong falsetto, and I shoot him a glare that delights him even more.

Dallas looks amused and holds the door open for me. "Friend or foe?" she asks.

"Friend—kind of."

"I'm parked up there," she says, indicating a side street. We walk in silence for a minute, and then she breaks it with a fast string of words. "I'm sorry. I feel like I'm the most awkward person ever. If I don't have a script in my hands, I don't know what to say. I've always been like this."

Some of my nervousness melts away. "Oh, same. Except without the script, so I never know what to say."

She smiles faintly. "It's not like we're strangers."

"Yeah, but…" I try to put my hands in my pockets and discover I'm wearing a dress.

She turns to me and touches my shoulder. I stop walking and face her. "I thought we could go up to my favorite spot," she says. "I brought coffee and doughnuts. We can just hang out? Is that okay?"

I'm so relieved, I can't help smiling. "That's great. I was worried we'd be, like…"

"Eating dinner at Olive Garden?" I crack up. We start walking again, the tension broken. "I made it weird," she confesses. "I just didn't want to never see you again. I didn't know how to…" She gestures back and forth between us.

I swallow down nerves. "You did the right thing. I'm just… I don't…"

She casts me a glance, and it looks fond or something adjacent to it. "We're a hell of a pair. Maybe one of us will finish a sentence sometime tonight." I like the way she talks. She kind of sounds like an old movie. She gets a set of keys out of her pocket and presses a button on the fob. Her mom's car beeps at us from across the street.

✧

Dallas's favorite spot turns out to be an overlook up on Mulholland, past the crowded one all the tourists find on Tripadvisor. Instead of the Hollywood sign and Downtown, it has a view of the valley, where the streets extend in perfect, perpendicular gridlines toward the hills. She pulls onto the shoulder at an angle she's clearly practiced a thousand times. From the back seat, she grabs a tote bag. "Come on," she says.

Outside, she pulls a blanket from the bag and throws it over the closed trunk, then indicates that I should climb up and sit beside her. We settle in, leaning back against the rear windshield, and prop our heads in our hands as we look out at the city. Tiny pinprick headlights and taillights are sparkling like Christmas lights, blinking in time to an unheard metronome. A soft breeze floats by, and cars make whooshing sounds, like waves, as they fly behind us on Mulholland.

"This is much better than I expected," I say, glancing at her. Her profile is sharp as she looks up at the sky instead of out at the lights.

She turns her head to face me. "I'm glad. How's everything with your friends? Is...Jacob? Is he okay?"

"Still in a coma. I was there today. Eddie is a mess, and Zoe—" I cut myself off, unwilling to voice my doubts to Dallas.

"I'm sorry," she says softly. "Can I do anything?"

"No. But thanks."

"Can I ask you something?" She sounds a bit more timid than usual, which piques my curiosity.

"Of course."

"Why do you guys do this? The YouTube channel. What's your reason for wanting to break into all these secret places?"

I'm surprised by the question. I consider it, looking out at the lights. "I guess we each have our own reasons," I answer truthfully. "Eddie is, like, a true artist. He's in it for the production. I think Jacob sort of pulled him into the idea in the first place. But then he got obsessed on his own. The footage he gets is really beautiful. He's talented."

"He is. I've watched a few episodes."

I smile, a little surprised and flattered.

"What about your other friends?" she asks.

"Well, Jacob just likes to do bad things. So he was originally in it for that. But then he discovered Avid, which he says is a perfect outlet for his hyperfocus. And he does the voice-over work. He should be an actor, honestly. I bet he ends up doing that someday—" My throat closes up. For a moment, I'd forgotten. He might not have a someday.

"And Zoe?" she prompts.

I swallow. "She's all about the puzzle, the unlocking and figuring out. Her brain never rests. It's like a hamster wheel in there. She needs puzzles the way some people need to go running. You know?"

She nods. "So what about you, kid? Your grandma is so protective. This is, like, the last thing she'd want you to do, right? Is it a rebellion thing?"

I start to answer and then realize I don't know. After some deliberation, I say, "I like the research aspect, I guess. I love to dig into things. So maybe that's why."

"You could research places without breaking into them," she points out.

"I... You're right. I'm not sure why I do it."

She cocks her head, sparkly eyes examining me closely. "I think I know."

"Do you mind sharing?"

"You're kind of diving in. After what happened to your mom, being in danger is a bit like a stove to a kid. You know it's going to be hot, but you need to touch the flame. Right?"

I mull it over. "I guess that makes sense."

"So, are you super freaked out by what you saw on the footage from that night? I mean, since you see creepy stuff all the time, I thought you might have some theory about the lights...." I get the feeling she's been patiently storing that question for a while. Maybe our whole conversation has been leading up to this question.

I consider my answer. "I mean, yeah. Maybe the house is haunted. I don't think a ghost could hurt us, though. It's not a ghost who stabbed Jacob. So, who cares? It doesn't change what happened to him."

She closes her eyes and nods. Her mouth twitches like she's holding back some strong emotion, trying to keep her face neutral. "I hate that house. I can't wait to get rid of it. Let someone tear it down and build a bunch of condos, I don't care. But what I *don't* want is someone turning it into a museum, some morbid theme park where visitors try to summon the ghost of Rosalinda. You know? That's my biggest fear."

"I can understand that."

"You didn't see any of the lights and stuff while you were there, right?"

I shake my head. "Nope. Nothing."

"What rooms were you in when you went upstairs?"

I pause, remembering the letters. I really need to tell her. It's only going to get worse if I don't. I have them with me in preparation, waiting for an opening in the conversation, and I don't think it's going to get better than this. I gather my courage and say, "I was up in the guest room. The one with the armchair that faces the backyard."

She nods.

I sit up and swivel to face her. "There's a little table beside the armchair. I sat in the chair and thought it would be a great place to read a book or write a letter. I..." I swallow. "I opened the drawer. There was a stack of letters in there."

She sits straight up and stares at me with wide eyes. "I didn't know there was a drawer in that table."

"It's kind of hidden. You have to pull the underside."

"How did you know to open it?"

"It just seemed logical that there would be one."

"Did you read the letters?"

"No. I..." My voice cuts out, throat going dry. I clear my throat. "I was worried, actually. They seemed like the kind of thing someone might steal, and I thought it would be better if I found out who owned the house and mailed the letters to them anonymously."

Her blue eyes are huge, shocked. "You took them?"

"I didn't know it wasn't abandoned. I didn't know you had access and were in there regularly."

She flings an arm out. "The security system didn't give you a clue?"

"I assumed it was just, you know, alarmed but not cared for. I mean, the bloodstain is still on the carpet! The cans are still in the cabinets!"

We're facing off, her expression both angry and hurt. At last, she asks, "Where are they?"

"I brought them with me tonight. I thought you might want..."

"Give them to me." Her tone is flat. I'm afraid I might have ruined everything.

I get my purse out of the back seat and bring it to her. She's standing by the trunk, wringing her hands. I pull out the sheaf of letters. She accepts them, examining them closely. They're smaller than the kind of envelope you'd use to mail a greeting card. She murmurs, "These were all delivered during the last two years of her life, 1970 through 1972." She lays them out on the trunk and counts them. "Eleven. One every few months." She starts putting them in order, older on top. "Mostly from Indiana, which makes sense. Her family was out there. She moved to Hollywood as a teenager." She picks up the top envelope and opens it with great care. "You really didn't read these?" She shoots me a suspicious look.

I hold my hands up. "I didn't even read the envelopes."

Dallas unfolds the letter. "This is from her cousin Mary. Wow." She reads quietly.

"When I found them, I kept thinking, what if these were my mom's? I'd want someone to send them to me, to keep them safe. I wouldn't want them to stay lost. I really wasn't trying to violate anything. I was trying to, I don't know, be respectful. I'm so sorry if I did the wrong thing."

She looks up. Her lips are parted slightly, as though I've said something that has shaken her. She sets the letter on top of the pile of envelopes and holds a hand there so they don't blow away. She leans forward and brushes her lips against my cheek. It sends a shiver down my spine.

"You did the right thing," she whispers. Pulling back, she clears her throat. She hands me the letter she just finished reading. "Look. Nothing scandalous. Just her cousin saying hi after a visit."

I accept the letter and glance through it. It's so interesting that people used to mail letters all the time. It's kind of nice, actually.

Having flipped through a few more, she hands me another one. "Same cousin. I guess they were friends. Imagine growing up in a small town in Indiana, then coming out here, and a year later, you're one of the biggest movie stars in Hollywood."

"That would be very weird," I agree, scanning the text. Same handwriting, different pen, longer letter this time. It looks like a roundup of family, kids, personal thoughts.

I hand it back to her. "How are you feeling about the house right now? Are the cops done in there?"

She sighs. "Yeah, they're done. I need to go pick up the teddy bear cameras, see if I can figure out if it's something wrong with them or if…"

I know where the rest of that sentence is going. *Or if it's really haunted.*

"But, um…" She clears her throat. "I'm only going to say this once, and you will take it to the grave."

I wait, curious.

"I'm scared to go in there by myself," she says fast, words stringing together.

I almost smile. It's clear how hard that was for her to admit, which is sort of charming. The fact that she feels embarrassed to be afraid says a lot about her—a lot of things I really like.

"I can go with you," I tell her. "Would that help?"

She nods, cheeks flushing.

Nervous but remembering her kiss, I reach for her hand and take it gently, thumb rubbing across her knuckles. "Let's go," I suggest. "Be done with it."

"Okay."

January 4, 1970

Dear Rosie,

I hope this finds you well and that your beau Andrew is as glad to see you as we all were when you came home. Everyone in town is still giving us a hard time for keeping you all to ourselves, but that's just because they wanted to get their picture taken with the famous Rosalinda West. How quickly they've forgotten skinny little Rosie, falling in the pool with all her clothes on at summer camp.

Can you believe that was only a few years ago? It feels like a century. So much has happened, and so much has changed.

I know you'll want to hear how everyone is doing. My momma is fine, but you know that already, I'm sure. I hear she calls collect every Sunday and spills all the town gossip, so you no doubt also heard about our recent blessing. It's too bad you had to leave before Christmas or you'd have witnessed enough drama to inspire a whole Hollywood movie! We're going to be featured in the Gazette. I promise to send you a copy of the article when it gets printed.

Little Jonathan is doing well, as healthy as a horse, and we love him so much. All the other cousins say hello, and I'm supposed to relay a message from a gentleman caller. If you ever want to settle back down in Culver, Hank says he's eager to make you Mrs. Worthington Hardware. I'm sure it will be a difficult choice between dreamy movie producer Andrew Valentini and hardware store owner and amateur pig farmer Hank Worthington, but alas, a young lady's life is full of difficult decisions.

Love always,
Mary

TWENTY-SIX

Thursday, April 13

DALLAS PARKS AROUND THE CORNER FROM the Valentini mansion, pulling into a shrouded curve in the road sheltered by a bank of hedges. As I get out and shut the car door gently behind me, a whole-body chill shivers through me. I don't like being on this street again; it's too quiet, the curvy wooded lanes too dark. It's too easy to imagine that anything could happen out of view of the city's millions of prying eyes.

She pockets the keys. "You okay?"

"Yeah. Of course." I brush imaginary cobwebs off my arms.

"You sure you don't mind coming inside?"

"I'm good." I'm barely able to get the words out. She's closer now, and I can imagine what she'd feel like if I reached for her, pulled her in, kissed her. I shake the images off, my own inexperience screaming insecurities at me.

"Okay." She squares her shoulders and takes an audible breath. "Let's do it, then."

We walk in the middle of the narrow street around the corner to the front gate of the mansion. I've only ever seen this view of the house in photos online. The entry barrier is a huge, wrought-iron gate across the wide driveway, chained and padlocked twice over, the thick steel links wrapping around the center opening like mechanical snakes. Dallas bypasses this and heads for a human-sized gate to the left. She pulls out her key chain and unlocks the handle, a deadbolt, and a padlock attached to what looks like a heavy metal bike lock. A moment later, she's securing the gate behind us, and we're facing the mansion, which sits at the top of the steep driveway, looking down on us with spooky serenity. In the dark, you almost can't tell it's starting to fall apart: the Spanish-style white stucco looks pristine from down here, the gaps between terra-cotta roof tiles the only visible hints of decay.

She heads up the driveway and I follow, eyes on the peripheral tangles of wild bushes and grass, my brain conjuring up images of humans or animals hiding out there, watching us from the cover of darkness.

We're a little out of breath by the time we get to the front steps, and I have to recalibrate; the house is even bigger than I remember. Seeing it from the front like this, with its deep patio and huge, empty picture windows, I realize how rich the Valentinis must have been. Dallas goes straight for the front door, where she unlocks the knob, the deadbolt, and a third, heavy-duty steel contraption like something from a jail. The door creaks open, and an alarm beeps in the foyer, steady drips of sound warning us it's about to start screaming. A stale breeze swooshes out, like even the air wants to escape.

She beckons me after her, going straight to the alarm panel in the front hall. She types a combination of numbers too fast for me to catch, and the beeping stops. She closes the front door, fastening the deadbolt, and the house swallows us up.

I pull my phone out from where I'd stashed it in my bra strap to use its flashlight. In the glow, Dallas's features are distorted and blue. She follows suit, and we shine our lights around the hallway. Each time we swing our phones in a new direction, a vortex of darkness pools in the void where the light had been.

My breathing is speeding up, and I'm intensely aware of all the little stars and sparkles in my vision, geometric and strange, blinding me from anything that might be lurking in the black.

"You okay?" Dallas whispers.

"Yeah," I reply, which is probably a lie.

It's disorienting, entering the house opposite from where I'd come in last Saturday, and I need a moment to flip my mental map of the space around. The living room is ahead, past the hallway to the left. The stairs are in front of us, and then the kitchen, beyond the stretch of hall so wide you could drive a car through it. How did I not remember how big the house is? I guess being with my usual group made everything feel cozier, smaller, more under control.

A squeak, echoing from high above. We both jerk, shining our phones up at the ceiling. Nothing.

"Just the house settling," Dallas says. She's ghostly white—an illusion, not a premonition. "I have teddy bears in the living room, dining room, and kitchen. Let's just grab them and leave."

"Yeah," I reply, eyes still on the ceiling.

She heads left, through the arched doorway into the living room. Following her to the grand piano, I can't help shining my light down onto the carpet. A large new spot darkens the rug just a few feet from Rosalinda's—Jacob's blood.

It occurs to me that this is a crime scene, but I haven't noticed any evidence of the police. "Hey, are the cops going to get mad that we're in here?" I ask in a hushed, low murmur.

"I don't think so. They said they were done." She grabs the bear off the piano. "Come on. Kitchen next, then across to the dining room."

I follow her into the hall. Our footsteps creak noisily on the old floorboards. I'm tiptoeing, I realize, which makes no sense. There's no one here to disturb.

In the kitchen, as she grabs the teddy bear off its perch on the counter, my phone flashlight catches a darkness in the corner that stops me in my tracks. "Hang on," I say, caught in a wave of memory. "I just remembered something from that night."

Dallas whips around to face me, blue eyes translucent. "What?"

"The alarm was going off. It was unbearable. I ran back through here, looking for Jacob and Eddie." I point my phone in the direction of the dark, hollow space. There in the corner, the door I'm remembering lies ajar. "I thought that was a garage door, and that I weirdly hadn't noticed it when we'd come in. But I forgot all about it once we found Jacob." I take a few steps toward the door, then a few more. "I don't think this was open when we entered. I really don't."

She's at my side, shining her flashlight in the same direction. Behind the doorway lies only darkness. "That's not the door to the garage," she murmurs.

"I realize now—the garage is detached. I should have known; I'd memorized the floor plan. So where does that go?"

She puts a hand on my arm as though to still my progress. "To the basement."

I stop in my tracks. "Well, that sucks."

She snorts, a half-laugh she does a lot that I'm growing to like.

"LA houses aren't supposed to have basements," I whisper. There's an urban legend that California doesn't have basements because of earthquakes, but it's more about the frost line and the rush to build houses out here. The factoid flits through my brain like a text message. "You think the cops opened that door?" I ask.

She hesitates. "I mean, there's really nothing down there. An old TV, couches, a pool table. But it was definitely closed when they left. We locked everything up. I didn't take the bears because I didn't want them to ask for the footage, you know..."

My eyes are glued to that gaping, pitch-black doorway. "If this were a movie, the audience would be screaming at us to get out."

She says, "This is ridiculous." She turns and marches toward the alarm panel by the back door. She punches in some numbers, then pushes a few things on the touchscreen. "I'm setting this to Away. We have ninety seconds to get out or punch in my code before the alarm goes off. If anyone—I mean, if anything…"

She doesn't finish the sentence. She examines the panel and presses a final button. It beeps, then again three seconds later. She grabs my arm. "Come on. Ninety seconds."

We hurry toward the basement door. She's determined now, emboldened, ready to fight against fear. She pulls me through the doorway, where our phones illuminate a set of stairs. "We're coming in!" she calls into the emptiness, which makes me want to grab her and pull her back. "Come on, Casey, eighty seconds."

I hurry to follow, almost eating it on the carpeted steps, and then we're in a room with a fireplace and cushy, dust-blanketed couches in front of a massive vintage cabinet television. As promised, a pool table is set up in the corner next to a floor-to-ceiling bookshelf.

She stumbles abruptly, like she's tripped over something. I shine my phone on the ground by her feet. It takes me a moment to process; at first it seems like trash or leaves and sticks spread out over the carpet. She squats down, examining it with her phone, and I lower myself beside her. The sticks are organized in a circular pattern five feet in diameter, with little triangles and stars of clustered branches oriented around the circle's center. She grips my shoulder hard, gasping.

I see what scares her in the same instant—the sticks are

small, delicate bones. The star-shaped clusters here and there are made of small skulls surrounded by tiny spikes of bone.

"Oh my god," I hear myself whisper. Above us, the alarm beeps, beeps, and then goes silent. Our eyes meet. In that instant, the room blinks with sudden white-blue light. It flashes, then goes out, leaving us blinded in the dark.

TWENTY-SEVEN

Thursday, April 13

THE LIGHTS BLINK ON, THEN FADE, BLINK, FADE. I shriek, terror and surprise pounding my skull. "Dallas!" I scream. "What's wrong with the lights?"

"There are no lights!" Her voice is as panicked and shrill as mine. "There's not a single freaking lightbulb down here!"

I grab the sleeve of her sweater and yank her toward the stairs. Lights strobe around us as our feet pound a frantic rhythm on the steps. Vaguely, a corner of my brain registers that the lights don't seem to be coming from a single point of origin; they're evenly distributed around the room, a laser-bright shade of bluish white materializing out of thin air.

We burst into the kitchen, which is pitch-black and silent.

Our hoarse breath rips through the stillness. "Out the front," Dallas pants.

Fear is squeezing my chest like a vise, pressing into my lungs, a cancer metastasizing in my brain. I follow the ghost of her sweater, sneakers pounding the floorboards, then the carpet of the living room, and then we're exploding onto the porch. She slams the door shut behind us, struggling to lock the deadbolt with shaking hands while I search every corner of the darkness with desperate eyes still blinded by the light show.

And then we're sprinting down the driveway, gravity increasing our speed; if we stumble, we'll break a nose or a wrist, for sure, and the thought sticks with me, images of blood and crunching bone.

Through the gate, our clumsy hands working together to fumble the bike lock thing around the wrought-iron spokes, and then down the narrow street to her car, where we throw ourselves into the seats and compulsively lock the doors, twice, three times.

The car screeches as she pulls away from the curb, and for the first mile she drives too fast, flying through a couple of stop signs, and I don't say a word because all I can think is *faster, faster.*

Out on Glendale Boulevard, she joins the flow of traffic. The streetlights and headlights are bright around us, illuminating our pale, scared faces.

What if whatever was in there is following us? The superstition gets its hooks into me, and I can't banish it. "Don't drive home," I say. When a freeway on-ramp appears to the right, she gets on. I realize I'm still shaking, deep inside my core.

I don't know how many exits we've passed when she says, "I'm heading for the beach."

I nod. It sounds like a good idea. We're quiet until she gets off on Ocean and turns right, then pulls into a public lot for a beach just north of Santa Monica.

I find myself stumbling out, slamming the door shut behind me and running for the sand. It isn't until I've blundered across the cool, clumsy dunes and am standing on wet sand, sucking in lungfuls of cold, salty air, that I feel the thick mental fog of panic begin to clear.

Dallas is near me. I hadn't heard her approach. She seems to notice me at the same moment, and our eyes meet. She opens and closes her mouth, like she's searching for words.

"I know," I say. "It's just..."

"It has to be a ghost," she bursts out, flinging an arm for emphasis. "That's what it is, right? The house is haunted, it's..." She laughs, almost maniacal. "Sometimes I lie awake wondering if it's possible to commit a crime so horrible that the place it happened is cursed forever."

"Like a black hole," I murmur, fresh goose bumps pimpling my arms and legs because I've wondered the same exact thing a hundred times.

She grips the sides of her head. "I just want to sell it and be rid of this...legacy...or..." She presses her hands to her face and folds forward, then crumples until she's squatting on her heels, a huddled, small figure against the nighttime oceanscape.

"Come here." I grab her arm and pull her up, then indicate that we should sit on the drier sand a few feet behind us. We settle in, surrounded by the whoosh of waves and the light breeze that whips our hair together. The skirt of my dress ruffles across my skin, and it occurs to me that this dress was around when Rosalinda was still alive.

"What was all that stuff on the floor?" I ask. "The bones, the shapes."

"I don't know. It wasn't there before."

"Dallas." I squeeze her arm to get her attention. "That means someone else has access to the house. Can you think who that could be? Remember those witchy people who used to break in? Maybe them."

She lifts her hands, helpless. "They can't get in. You saw the security."

"What about your mom? She seems kind of spiritual. Do you think—"

She shakes her head. "She's not exactly on top of her life, okay? She would never be able to figure out how to get past all those locks, the alarm. And my sister is just a kid, she's busy with school. She doesn't know about any of this. It's *my* job." She pounds her chest with a fist, and it dawns on me how thin she is, how stressed she looks.

My heart aches for her, and my fear seems far away now. I take her fist and wrap my hands around it. I have no words, so I hold this hand. It's all I can think to do.

She turns her head to face me, and her blue eyes are liquid in the night. "I wonder if it's Rosalinda. Sometimes I think she's angry that no one figured out what happened to her. Or maybe it's Andrew, and he's mad he got blamed. You know the police thought it might be someone else? They did, Casey. I read part of the police report. One of the detectives thought a third person was there that night. There were too many dishes in the sink for two people."

"Did they have any ideas for who it could have been?"

"I don't know." She shakes her head almost like she's clearing water out of her ears, and then she faces me, legs crossed. "I'm sorry. It's my fault we were in there."

I gasp with a sudden realization. "You didn't get your teddy bears!"

She sighs. "What am I going to do? I can't go back there, but I can't *not* go back there." She reaches for my hands, rubs them between hers, and meets my eyes, hers earnest and huge. "I'm trying to say thank you. And I'm really sorry. Worst date ever."

I'm suddenly nervous. We're so close. Just as I think that, she reaches for my neck and rests her fingertips against it.

"Can I kiss you?" she asks. Adrenaline responds for me, and I feel myself nod, just a bit, and then her lips are on mine, her hands in my hair, and I'm breathless again, but in the best way.

TWENTY-EIGHT

Friday, April 14

MY ALARM GOES OFF TOO EARLY, AND I GROAN, fumbling in the sheets for my phone. I whine internally—it's still dark outside, it's not right, why do I have to be awake—but then I realize it's not the alarm, it's my phone. I'm getting a call.

I sit straight up in bed, immediately thinking *Jacob*, but no, it's Dallas, FaceTiming.

I blink sleep out of my eyes and answer. Dallas's face swims into focus, pale and intense, eyes ringed in dark circles. "Sorry sorry sorry," she says. "Please don't kill me."

"What time is it?" I turn on the bedside lamp, and my own face joins hers on the screen, my eyes bleary, hair messy. If I weren't so tired, I'd be embarrassed to be seen this way, but she looks as disheveled as I am, black hair tangled and shoved behind her ears.

"It's five thirty. I'm so sorry. Can you forgive me for waking you up so I can tell you what I called about?" She's jittery with either excitement or anxiety.

I can't help smiling. "You're forgiven. Tell me."

She blinks. "I'm just—you're not wearing your glasses."

I cover my face with my free hand. "I was sleeping!"

"No, you look—" She clears her throat. "Sorry. Distracted. Okay, so, after I dropped you off, I started thinking about what we were talking about, about how the detectives investigating Rosalinda's murder thought there was a third person in the house with them. Remember?"

I nod, gesturing that she should continue.

"I got out my files, found the names of the detectives on the case, and I started looking them up. I knew they were Guzman and Schmidt, but those names are pretty common. I've been digging around all night. I haven't slept. I've had like two liters of coffee."

"That explains a lot," I deadpan, and she issues her now-familiar snorting half-laugh.

"Shut up. Sorry. Okay. So. Detective Schmidt, he was older at the time of the murders. He died in the nineties of natural causes. But the other one, Guzman, was younger. He's seventy-eight now. Retired." She's bouncing up and down with excitement. "Casey, I found his address. I had to use those people finder sites, and it was not easy. I mean, the man's name is Robert Guzman. There are about ten thousand Robert Guzmans in

LA. But I found him. He lives in Los Feliz." She stops, grinning, clearly waiting to be praised.

"Wow," I say fuzzily, not understanding why she would want to track him down. "So, what...do you...why?"

"I'm going to go talk to him. I'm going to ask him what their theories were, what they knew but couldn't prove. I'm going to go see him today."

I rub my eyes with my free hand. "That's cool."

"You don't understand. My whole life, I've been told over and over that my ancestor was a murderer. I just don't want it to be true...you know?"

I'm finally awake. "You should definitely go get some closure. Get answers. If I had that option, I'd totally do it." The detectives on my mother's case didn't have a secret theory. They didn't have any theories. She'd been killed by a stranger, without a doubt, and they had not a single suspect.

"Will you come with me?" she asks. "I'm going first thing this morning."

Another day of ditching? At this point, what difference does it make? Plus, it will save me from seeing Zoe. "Sure," I agree.

"I'll drop my mom off at work at eight, and then I'll pick you up."

"But wait. If you drop your mom off at work, won't she know you're ditching?"

She waves that off. "She doesn't care what I do."

We hang up, and I feel a twinge of sorrow for her. My grandma cares too much, but the alternative is sort of sad.

Robert Guzman lives in a slightly run-down bungalow a couple of blocks off Vermont in Los Feliz, just a few miles from me. When we walk up from our parking spot down the street, I'm struck with the impression of staleness: The paint is peeling, the front lawn brown, and the car in the driveway is an ancient Toyota. Despite everything being worn around the edges, it's clean, the car sparkling, the brown grass neatly trimmed.

I follow Dallas up the front steps and let her ring the doorbell. A handwritten NO SOLICITING sign hangs above it, and I wonder what kind of weirdos he gets. Around here, the standards for weird are awesomely high.

A little metal window at the top of the front door slides open, and a brown eye peers out at us. "What do you want?"

Dallas says, "Detective Guzman? I'm Dallas. I want to talk to you about the Valentini case."

He coughs out a wheezy laugh. "Get lost, kid. I'm not interested."

He's sliding the metal window shut when she says, "I'm Rudolph Valentini's great-granddaughter. I own the house. I need to talk to you."

The window opens, and he peers out again. "Let's see some ID," he says, sounding very cop-like.

She fumbles in her purse and gets out her license, then presses it to the window. He examines it, metallic sounds of unlocking come from the door, and it swings inward. The man standing before us is tall, with broad shoulders and stick-straight posture. It's only nine o'clock, but he's fully dressed in a tucked-in button-down shirt and ironed jeans. His white hair is cut short, his face is clean-shaven, and his dark eyes are every bit as piercing as they must have been when he interrogated suspects for however many years on the job.

"What do you want?" he asks.

Dallas seems to take a deep, nervous breath. "I've seen part of the case file. It sounded like you thought there was a third person with them that night. I'm about to turn eighteen and inherit the house. I want—I have to know."

He shakes his head, lips pursed. "That's a hell of an inheritance for a kid your age."

"Tell me about it."

They lock eyes, and they share a silent smirk while I awkwardly toe the floor with the old Vans I've been wearing every day since I got rid of my favorite Converse.

"Come on in." He backs up, inviting us into the living room, a bright, clean room sparsely furnished. As I enter, he looks me over, frowning at my green and orange paisley shirt from the sixties and cutoff jean shorts. "And you are?"

"Casey," I answer. "Her friend."

"Good that you brought a friend," he tells Dallas. "It would be stupid of you to come to a strange man's house alone."

"I mean, you're a cop," she says, and he and I both make cynical shapes with our mouths.

He gestures toward the worn plaid couch, and we settle on

it across from him. He sits straight in a wooden chair and examines us. "So what are you hoping to find out?"

She asks, "Did you think there was a third person? I read there were too many dishes in the sink."

He counts things off on his fingers. "Too many wineglasses. Too many cocktail glasses. Three dinner plates, three of everything. They'd had someone over for dinner. We knew that from day one."

"But did you have any suspects? Anyone you questioned? Anyone who had a motive?"

He leans forward to rest his elbows on his knees, then buries one fist in his other hand. "Gah, what the hell. This is your family. If you had known these characters, met them in person." He looks up at her, flicks his eyes to me, then back at her. "We had no solid evidence. You understand? No witnesses, nothing. That house is isolated now, but you should've seen it then. No neighbors on either side for a quarter mile. Complete privacy."

Visibly disappointed, Dallas nods.

"But on the other end, we can look at who benefitted from these deaths. You have a beautiful young actress, a sex symbol. You can understand why someone would target her, but she wasn't assaulted. Not a mark on her except the stab wounds. Not a single stitch of clothing out of place. So the crime wasn't sexual. And you have Andrew, a studio exec, lots of enemies, but someone who wanted to kill Andrew would have no motive against the wife. So the question is, who benefits if *both* of them are dead? Or are we chasing our tails, and they just had someone over for dinner, got into an argument, and later on that night,

Andrew spiraled?" He pounds his fist into his hand. "So those were our two possible killers. He was either a dinner guest with an appetite for murder, or Andrew himself, set off by something that happened at dinner."

"Or she," I point out. "The killer could have been a woman."

"Sure, fine, but the arm strength involved in those stab wounds made us think a man. Unless the circus was in town. In those days, you didn't have women pumping iron like you do now. Women looked like women."

"Got it," I say, ready for him to move on from this little rant. Dallas crooks an eyebrow at me, and her lips twitch like she's holding back a smile.

He gets back to the point. "So then you have to wonder. If someone ate dinner with them that night, and later they heard that Andrew had gone off his rocker and committed this horrible murder-suicide, why didn't that person come forward? Wouldn't any innocent person come tell us, 'Hey, I saw them that night,' and answer questions about how they were behaving? Wouldn't they give interviews to the press? It was a media frenzy. Everyone was talking to the press. The dinner guest's silence was suspicious."

"That does sound suspicious," I concede. "So did you go through all their friends and family to see who didn't have an alibi?"

"That's what we did. Every single one. Every girl Rosalinda got to be friends with on set. Every one of the male costars she was rumored to be connected to. Everyone Andrew knew. Every ex-girlfriend who might've had a catty vendetta against his new girl. Every friend, relative, and potential enemy."

Dallas asks, "And what did you find?"

He sits back and settles his arms on the armrests. "We found lots of folks with no alibi. But only one person we really liked for the crime. Andrew's brother, Rudolph. Rudy."

"Why?" Dallas asks, voice sharp.

He ticks the reasons off on his fingers again. "He lived in New York and was not seen at his apartment for a week on either side of the crime, before and after." He ticks a second finger. "His car had a ton of miles put on it between oil changes that year. An extra ten thousand miles from the year before. But this was all circumstantial. We worked that angle for years. Never got anything solid enough to take to the DA. But I'm sorry to say, he's the guy. It goes down like that a lot, where we know who did it, but we can't gather enough evidence to prove it."

"What about fingerprints?" I ask.

He shakes his head. "Nothing. But I will tell you this. There were a lot of clean surfaces in that house. Doorknobs with no prints on them. Silverware without a single damn print, impossible unless it was wiped." He looks at Dallas. "He's the guy. It was him."

Dallas looks like she's been punched in the gut. "He was my great-grandfather."

He shakes his head, face creased with regret. "I'm sorry, honey. But if I can give you some advice? Get rid of that house. Sell it for whatever someone will offer, walk away, and don't look back. That place is pure evil." And then he does something completely unexpected. He lifts his hand and crosses himself.

TWENTY-NINE

Friday, April 14

DALLAS DRIVES ME HOME IN BROODING SILENCE. I keep my eyes out the window, giving her space. I can imagine what she's thinking. She's worse off now than she had been before this conversation, and she's still stuck with the house and the legacy and everything that goes with it. So yeah, it makes sense that her jaw is clenched tightly shut.

She double-parks across from my apartment and leans her head back against the seat. Eyes closed, she says, "That was pointless. I shouldn't have dragged you along."

"It's fine." Not sure if it's okay, I gently place a hand on her shoulder.

She opens her eyes. In the light coming through the windshield, they're like sapphires, full of mutable kaleidoscope shapes.

"Sometimes it all feels so . . . fated. Like we're born to be who we are. Like we never had a choice."

I'm not sure what to say. I don't think she's completely talking to me.

She shakes herself minutely, and the sapphires fix on me. "Sorry, Casey. I'm really tired."

"Go home and get some sleep. You were up all night."

She brushes a hand to my cheek. "I promise, next time we hang out, it won't get all dark."

My cheek thrums where she'd touched it. "I really didn't mind coming with you."

The corners of her mouth tweak into an almost-smile. "We'll go to an art exhibit or something."

As I get out and watch her drive away, I marvel at the weirdness of the world. This week has been the second darkest in my life, but somehow, I also met someone real. It's like she and I have some deeper connection, like the things we've gone through separately were actually experienced together.

I check for oncoming cars and cross the street, digging my keys out of my purse. It's too late to salvage the school day. Maybe I'll go see Jacob at the hospital, or maybe I'll hide in my room and dissociate on YouTube all day. That sounds amazing.

I let myself into my apartment, close the door behind me, and stop short. Sitting on the couch, watching TV, is Zoe.

"Case!" She jumps to her feet and engulfs me in one of her attack hugs. Words rush out of her. "I'm so sorry I haven't been answering my phone. My parents took it away; they've basically been holding me prisoner. Why haven't you been at school?" She pulls back and holds me at arm's length, like a grandma studying her grandkid after not seeing them for a while. "When you weren't there today, I was like, that's it, I'm going to her house, and I'm going to find out what's going on. I took the bus here! Can you believe it? By myself."

I'm overwhelmed with different emotions—confused by how normal she's acting, bewildered by the knowledge that she dug up the tapes, that she's been lying to me, that she might have been the one who stabbed Jacob, but doubtful now, looking at her earnest face, feeling the warmth that radiates off her like light. She can't be a killer. She just can't. Wouldn't I have known after all this time together? And what motive can she possibly have had?

"Casey? Hello? Why are you standing there like you've seen a ghost?"

I force myself to smile. "I'm sorry. You just startled me. How did you get in—Oh, wait. Stupid question."

"Right. So come on, tell me, did you get questioned by the detectives, too? Did they make it all threatening? They scared the crap out of my parents. My dad called in lawyers, it's a whole thing." She takes my hand and drags me to the couch, where she pulls me down to sit beside her. The remote is on the coffee table, and I turn off the reality show she was watching.

"They did," I told her. "It really freaked out my grandma. Me too, honestly. They clearly suspect that we were there that night."

"I know. But, like, all they seem to have is footprints, and even those aren't conclusive. My dad's lawyers say the footprints are circumstantial."

"They are. But I think the real problem is, they have us in their minds. And now they'll be looking at the case from that angle instead of searching for the person who actually did this." I watch her closely, looking for a sign that she's guilty, but she just nods.

"That's exactly what I've been thinking."

It occurs to me that I may not be safe alone with her. Is there any chance she'd want to hurt me? After a moment of calculation, I ask, "Is it cool if I tell my grandma that you're here? She won't tell your parents. I'll say it's a mental health day."

She shrugs. "That's fine. And even if she does, I'd tell them to suck it. They need to chill. The cops aren't going to arrest me for going to my best friend's house. The fact that we're not talking looks worse than if we were. But, you know, lawyers." She puts a hand on mine. "Case, I can tell you're mad. I'm so, so sorry for ghosting you. How've you been holding up? This can't be easy for you or your grandma. Talk to me."

I feel something welling up inside me, something reacting to her sympathy and the weight of her hand on mine. I have to look down, blink hard, fight against tears. "I'm fine. I just...Eddie's not doing too good. I saw him at the hospital. He's not holding up great."

Her hazel eyes are deep with empathy. "I bet. Plus he's not in school—of course he's not—but I wonder if that makes it worse, being alone with no distractions. I was thinking." She leans back into the cushions, drawing her feet up underneath her. A pair of purple Docs is lined up neatly by the front door.

"You know how I have Jacob's laptop? Remember, Eddie gave it to me to wipe?"

I shrug. I vaguely remember a discussion around this in Eddie's room.

"I need to get it back into Jacob's room. I think my dad's lawyers will kill me if the cops find it on me. Will you go over there with me?"

I consider this, examining the expression on her face. She can't be a psychopath; I've seen her experience empathy many times over the years. If she stabbed Jacob, it was a crime of passion, but why?

"Well?" She pokes at me. "Will you?"

Why did you dig up the tapes? I want to ask her. *What didn't you want me to see?*

Instead, I nod slowly. "Okay. Let's go."

✧

She has the door to Jacob's apartment open in three seconds flat, scoffing under her breath about how easy apartments are to break into. It's dark inside and has the aura of somewhere abandoned: dishes piled in the sink, clean but not put away, windows and blinds closed, mail strewn across the dining table.

Zoe leads the way to Jacob's room, backpack slung over one shoulder. I follow her, silent and nervous, though I tell myself to relax. She's not going to start stabbing me out of nowhere. It's a ridiculous thought.

She closes his bedroom door behind us. It's daylight, but his blackout curtains keep almost all the light out. I flip the switch, and the ceiling light flicks on, illuminating his messy, comfortable space. The bed is unmade, the dresser drawers all in various stages of being pulled out. The walls are hung with posters old and new, some of bands like the Clash, one of *The Nightmare Before Christmas*. On top of the dresser, a series of photos in frames draw my attention. I've never really looked at them. I pick one up, then another. They're of Eddie and him, one at Disneyland as kids, their limbs awkward and gangly, another from last summer when they went to San Diego. The images send my heart twisting in a new direction given what I know now.

Zoe has her backpack open and is sitting at the desk, pulling out Jacob's laptop. "Wipe it down, make sure your prints aren't on it," I advise her.

"Yes, ma'am." She grabs a T-shirt off the floor.

Just like the fingerprint-free silverware at the Valentini dinner party, a spotless, print-free laptop in the midst of all this chaos will be suspicious, but at least it won't incriminate us directly.

I sit on the bed, eyes drifting to the clothes on the floor. The contrast between Jacob's messiness and Eddie's neatness is comical. My eyes land on a plain black binder, half shoved under the bed. I pick it up and flip it open, expecting schoolwork, but instead I find an eight-by-ten color photograph of Rosalinda Valentini.

Why does he have this? I page through the binder slowly, finding printed articles about the murder house neatly stowed in clear paper protectors, photos of Rosalinda, handwritten notes on lined paper. I realize there's a whole research collection here, easily a hundred pages. I stop at an article from September 20, 1969.

ROSALINDA WEST FLIES EAST FOR THE WINTER

The stunning Rosalinda West abruptly bowed out of her publicity events for *Kiss Me Deadly* after reportedly being summoned home to Indiana to care for an ailing relative. Some whispered about the curious timing (Wasn't she just spotted arguing with beau Andrew Valentini, majority owner of Sunset Studios?), but representatives assure us it's an untimely, if unrelated, family illness that called her off the publicity trail.

In any case, filming for *On the Water* begins in April 1970, and we're assured she'll be on set in Malibu and more glamorous than ever.

What is all this? Why was Jacob doing his own research on the murder house? That's my territory, and I'd done plenty of research for this episode, more than enough. If he was working on this, too, why didn't he tell me?

I flip forward to a notebook paper at the end filled with Jacob's familiar handwriting, a messy printed scrawl in mostly all caps. It's Rosalinda's and Andrew's family tree. Apparently he'd done the same research I had, except he'd also looked into Rosalinda's family. But why?

FAMILY TREE

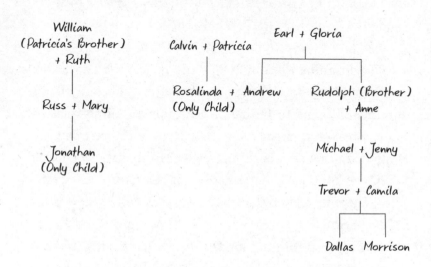

"What are you looking at?" Zoe asks, flinging Jacob's shirt back onto the pile, having finished wiping down the laptop.

"Oh, it's just...research materials about the murder house."

Her eyebrows shoot up. "You left stuff here in Jacob's room? Good thing we came back. If the cops had found that...I don't know. Seems bad."

"Yeah," I reply emptily.

"Well, grab it. Did you leave anything else here?"

"I don't think so. No."

"Good. Okay, let's get out of here."

We're on the bus on the way home, binder thumping against my spine inside my backpack, when I turn my phone back on. Text messages from Eddie pop up, a whole string of them.

"Zoe, look," I tell her. She's standing with her hands fisted in her armpits, shoulders hunched, like she can curl into a germ-repelling Pokémon if she tries hard enough. We read the messages from Eddie together. They're to both Zoe and me.

You guys have to get to the hospital.

Jacob isn't doing good.

Something's wrong.

December 25, 1970

Dear Rosie,

Merry Christmas, my favorite cousin. Of course, you won't get this until the New Year, and you'll be out frolicking in fancy gowns with your Los Angeles folks by then, ringing in 1971. But I'll be picturing my Rosie celebrating New Year's with me in our spot in the woods, drinking something stolen, freezing our tails off. Those are the holidays I miss.

Speaking of holidays! Little Jonathan just celebrated his first birthday. He's such a joy. We got the family together over at my daddy's house—you know it's much bigger than my own—and I baked a two-layer chocolate cake. Russ got after me for spoiling the boy with too many decorations and presents. You know what a grump he can be! He kept saying, "For God's sake, Mary, the kid won't remember any of this!" And then I'd say, "But I'll remember! And we'll take pictures to show him later." Jonathan is never fussy, always smiling and laughing, such an adorable little towhead. I'll enclose a photo for you, and you'll forgive my going on and on like the doting momma that I am. I love him dearly, and I thank God for him daily. He's brought so much light and life into our house. Even Russ can be found throwing him up in the air or crawling around on hands and knees, chasing him around the living room. It's a happy life.

We all miss you, Rosie. You're loved and thought of constantly. I'm so proud of you, don't get me wrong, but when I look at photos of you now, in magazines or in the newspaper, I worry. Are you happy? I remember a hometown girl who liked simple things: swimming, catching fireflies, running around barefoot. You liked baking, bowling, boating, fishing. Do you get to do those things anymore? And please, honey, eat something! You're so thin.

Come home soon so I can feed you my famous brownies, and so you can play with little Jonathan.

Love you lots,
Mary

THIRTY

Friday, April 14

IN TOO BIG A RUSH TO TAKE THE BUS, WE UBER to the hospital on Zoe's dime. I read and reread Eddie's texts as we sit in restless silence in the back of the lemon-scented Prius, trying to imagine what Zoe might be thinking. Could she be hoping Jacob dies so he can't tell anyone she stabbed him? Is it possible she would try to silence him forever before he can wake up? It feels wrong, suspecting these horrible things of her, and yet...

When the Uber pulls up to the hospital, we burst out and run across the wide stretch of concrete to the building. We arrive, out of breath, in the ICU waiting room, where Eddie is pacing back and forth in front of the picture windows.

"Eddie," Zoe says, closing a hand on his wrist.

He startles, rips his arm away from her, and then calms. "Sorry. I'm jumpy."

"What happened?" I ask.

I don't know if I've ever seen someone look this tired. "He was fine, everything was normal, JJ and I were just in there, both of us were napping a little, and then his monitors started beeping like crazy, and the nurses rushed in, and I had to leave. That's when I texted you. JJ is still in there. I don't know—" He chokes and can't finish the sentence.

Zoe rubs his arm. "We're here with you now. It's okay." She shoots me a worried look. If she is guilty, she's a hell of an actress.

"Let's sit down," I suggest, indicating a few empty chairs. A smattering of people are waiting in this room, reading magazines, messing with their phones, napping. None of them looks at us. After all, this is the ICU. Nobody is here for happy reasons.

Eddie slumps into a chair, legs extended in front of him, and Zoe and I sit on either side, holding his hands. After a few minutes of silence, I say, "It hasn't even been a week. Think about how much can change in that time."

Zoe stirs, patting at her hair. The blue is fading out, and she has it tied in an uncharacteristically messy bun. Maybe trying to murder people is stressful. She says, "I feel like an asteroid hit us. Like we were just walking along and a piece of space garbage fell out of the sky."

Eddie makes a snorting noise that reminds me of Dallas, which reminds me of the letters, which remind me of Jacob's binder. I stew on that, wondering why he was researching the house, why he had pictures of Rosalinda. Why the family tree?

The double doors open, and JJ comes out. A nurse walks beside him, and they're deep in conversation. He spots Eddie and waves him over. Eddie jumps up and hurries to join JJ, and Zoe and I quickly follow.

"Hey, guys," JJ says. He tries to smile, but the corners of his mouth twitch downward. I take back my thought about Eddie looking more tired than anyone I've ever seen. JJ looks like he shouldn't even have the strength to stand upright.

"What's going on?" Eddie asks.

"I wanted to give you an update because it looks like—" The words choke to a stop.

The nurse, an older woman with sharp, kind eyes, finishes for him. "Jacob won't be able to have visitors right now. He's experiencing some new symptoms. We're doing a number of tests."

JJ takes over. "Eddie, you should go home." The pity in his eyes is agonizing; it's clear what he's saying. Jacob might not make it, and he doesn't want Eddie here to watch. He's protecting Eddie even as he's dealing with the loss of his son.

"But what happened?" I ask, unable to compute what could have changed so quickly. "He was fine."

The nurse glances at JJ, silently asking permission to speak. JJ nods. "Go ahead, tell them. They're his best friends."

To us, she says, "His blood pressure dropped, and there's some fluid in his lungs. We're running tests, but we're worried about his kidneys, and..." She looks sympathetically at JJ. "We're doing everything that can be done."

He puts his face in his hands, and his shoulders quake once, twice. Eddie and I freeze, no idea how to handle a crying father, but Zoe puts an arm around his waist and hugs him, resting her head on his arm. "He's going to be okay," she murmurs. "He's alive. There's still hope."

He squeezes her in return, and we stand there in silence as the nurse leaves. JJ wipes his face, takes a breath, and says, "I'm going to set up camp here. Girls, will you take Eddie home with you? I don't want any of you to be alone."

"He can come to mine," I offer. "My grandma won't mind."

"Aren't you working tonight?" Zoe asks.

"Oh my god, I forgot. I'm so getting fired."

"He's coming to mine," she says, decisive. "And we're going to feed him, and he's going to take a nap, and there will be no arguing."

Eddie's been silent, staring at the floor. Not meeting anyone's eyes, he says, "I'm going home. I want to be alone." He turns and walks out, slamming the waiting room door open so hard it bangs against the wall.

JJ puts a hand on Zoe's arm to stop her from following him. "If he wants space, give it to him. Just make sure he gets home safe." Defeated, Zoe turns to leave, and I follow right behind her. But something is brewing in the back of my mind, something that slows my feet and forces me to stop. I turn to JJ.

"When did the new symptoms start?" I ask him.

He's settling into a chair. "A couple of hours ago. Why?"

"All at once?"

"Mostly. There was a spike early this morning, which they thought was related to something else and treated, and then his numbers started bottoming out—" He chokes and can't finish the sentence.

Like a puzzle, the scenario starts to fit together, truths clarifying with each piece that falls into place. His sudden symptoms are one piece. Another piece is Zoe. She didn't go to school today. Would Zoe try to silence Jacob forever just to clear her name? Zoe is smart. She's as good at research as I am when she wants to be.

I step slowly toward the double doors, then a little faster until I'm almost jogging. I have to be buzzed through, and I wait impatiently for someone to open the doors. I approach the nurse's station I remember from earlier, feeling shaky and unsure.

"Can I help you?" a young man in scrubs asks.

"I'm…" I hesitate, uncertain. "Who's in charge of Jacob Anderson? He's the guy in a coma, in room—"

The double doors slam open, and Detective Adams bursts through, Martinez a pace behind him. His eyes flick over me, and a nurse calls out, "May I help you?"

He flashes his badge. "Need to talk to the doctor working on the kid in room 415. Now, please."

I realize I'm standing with my mouth hanging open, because I think I know why they're here. He meets my eyes. "Where are your friends?"

"They left." I point with a shaking finger to the door. "Going home."

"Why are you still here?"

"Jacob's symptoms…" I swallow hard. "Is it poison?"

Detective Adams's face is grim. "Martinez, stay with the doctor. Casey, let's go try to catch up with your friends."

She nods, and he puts a hand on my back and hurries me

through the double doors. JJ is in the waiting room, having a rattled conversation with a uniformed cop. "Be right back, sir," Adams calls to him as he rushes me out. We're almost jogging through the hallways.

"Why is it so important to find Eddie and Zoe?" I ask. Does he have the same suspicions I do? Has he uncovered something in his investigation that points to Zoe?

In the elevator, he presses the lobby button. When the doors close, he says, "We know you kids were filming in the house. We found your cameras. They're Edward's, right? You took them from his dad?"

I don't say a word. The elevator doors ding open, and he leads the way. "Visitor parking lot, you think?"

"I don't know. I assume they were either taking Eddie's car or calling an Uber."

"Main entrance, then." Almost jogging through the crowded lobby, he says, "We found Jacob's camera, though it's clear someone didn't want us to. It's a match with the others. All of y'alls prints are on all four cameras. You're going to have to start telling the truth. Where's the film from the rest of them, the other three?"

I'm blown away by this revelation: I have no idea how to answer while trying not to bump into strangers. The sliding glass doors let us out into the nuclear sunshine, and there are Zoe and Eddie, standing on the curb. His posture is defeated, the picture of misery. My chest floods with adrenaline as I realize—I almost sent Zoe back to Eddie's house alone with him.

"Hey!" Adams calls. A cop car pulls up to the curb, and

Zoe and Eddie look around, confused. Two uniformed police officers jump out and jog toward the detective. Adams closes the distance and pulls Zoe away from Eddie. I clap my hands to my mouth. It's real. She did it.

He turns to Eddie and says, "Edward Yu? You're under arrest for the attempted murder of Jacob Anderson. You have the right to remain silent." He's got Eddie's hands cuffed already. Eddie cries out, a scared, surprised sound that goes right to my stomach, and a lightning bolt of shock strikes me.

"Hey," I cry, breaking out of my frozen moment. I hurry toward Adams. "You have the wrong person. Eddie didn't do anything. He wasn't even in the same room as Jacob."

The detective glares at me. "You need to step away."

"But—"

"We found Jacob's camera," Adams says. "I won't say it again—Step away."

It takes the fight out of me. He found the camera, and he found Jacob's footage. Eddie is in that footage, but Zoe and I aren't. They were filming downstairs, and we weren't in any of the shots. I watch, numb and horrified, as he leads Eddie to the cop car. Eddie glances back at me, eyes full of despair.

I turn on Zoe. "You have to tell them."

Tears are running down her cheeks, taking no mascara with them. For the first time, I realize she isn't wearing makeup. "Tell them what?"

I advance upon her. "Tell them what you did."

The cops drive away, and Adams hurries toward the parking

lot, probably to get his car so he can go book Eddie for a crime he didn't commit.

"What did I do?" Zoe asks.

"Where are the tapes?" I almost yell the words, furious, indignant on Eddie's behalf.

"What tapes?"

"The ones we buried. I know you dug them up. Where are they?"

Fire comes into her eyes. "What are you talking about, Casey? Have you lost your mind?"

"You did this! Just admit it! Are you going to let Eddie get blamed? Is that really who you are?"

Her jaw drops. "Are you kidding me right now?"

"Admit it," I demand. "Tell them or I will."

"Tell them what?" She crosses her arms. "Say it."

"You tried to kill Jacob that night. All this cover-up stuff was your idea. Where are the tapes? Who wiped the computers? Who doctored the security camera footage?"

She levels me with a glare. "Fuck you for accusing me of that, for even *thinking* that. Go to hell, Casey." She turns and walks away.

I'm left alone in the blinding sunshine, my body cold despite the heat.

CULVER GAZETTE

CHRISTMAS MIRACLE

DECEMBER 28, 1969

What a winter wonderland for our little town: Record snowfall, a visit from local prom queen turned Hollywood celebrity, and a Christmas miracle for a childless couple.

The heartwarming story takes place on Christmas Eve. Russ and Mary Anderson, married five years, had all but given up on a bundle of joy and instead filled their lives with friends, family, and service at the Methodist church. Per their usual tradition, they were dropping off baked goods at the church for the Christmas morning charity breakfast. After setting their donations down in the kitchen, they heard a noise coming from the sanctuary. They hurried to investigate, and they found a newborn baby in a basket on the steps of the altar, crying his little head off.

After a round of consultation with local authorities, it was determined that the baby had been abandoned. As God clearly intended, he went home that night with Russ and Mary. Their church rallied around them, and they were gifted all the baby supplies and furniture they could ever need. Baby Jonathan, as he was named, slept that night warm and cozy under the roof of his new parents.

It's with a tender heart that the town of Culver wishes these fine people a happy New Year with their little Christmas blessing. For all the readers wondering if miracles really do happen, take note.

THIRTY-ONE

Friday, April 14

ZOE STORMS OFF TO CATCH AN UBER, LEAVING me standing on the concrete walkway in front of the hospital, people flowing around me like water around river rocks. Two things spring to my mind, crystal clear.

First, enough is enough. Eddie got arrested. I need to start telling the truth, even if it means getting in serious trouble.

Second, Zoe's protests of innocence were convincing. Could I be wrong?

I'm about to turn my feet toward the bus stop when I realize I left my backpack upstairs in the waiting room of the ICU. As I head to the entrance, I wonder if I look like a patient sleepwalking, but then of course, that's a narcissistic thought. Everyone here has their own problems to worry about.

The maze of corridors takes me to the elevator, and I find myself pushing through the door into the room where JJ sits in a corner chair, bearded face buried in his hands. Nearby, a pair of frightened-looking elderly women in neat, floral outfits sits holding hands.

I find my backpack on the floor where I'd left it. I consider my options. I could go in and find Detective Martinez, tell her everything. That's probably what I should do.

Do I tell her about Dallas? The police will demand to see her nanny cam footage. Would that be so bad? I really don't think the cops would stir up some big media storm about the house being haunted. Dallas is kind of paranoid about that. And her footage proves without a doubt that Eddie was in the kitchen when Jacob was attacked. Right?

My backpack is heavier than usual, and I remember—the binder. Jacob's research. I unzip the bag and pull out the binder, opening the front cover. The first page is a photo of Rosalinda Valentini, long legged and glowing blond. I try to picture Jacob, printing this out at...school? The library?

I flip to the next page, which is a newspaper article from the *Culver Gazette* about a couple finding a baby in a church. I read through it, frowning. What this has to do with Rosalinda, I can't imagine.

Then I remember the letters I'd glanced through with Dallas. Rosalinda's cousin had been named Mary. Could she be the same Mary Anderson who'd found the baby?

Something washes over me like cold, drenching rain. I look up at JJ, who sits slumped across the room, buried alive in grief.

Oh my god. The letters—the article from the *Culver Gazette*.

I shove the binder back in my bag. I'm shaking. I think I know why someone stabbed Jacob.

The door to the ICU opens, and a woman in scrubs says, "JJ?"

He looks up.

"Honey, he's awake. Come on, hurry." She beckons him in.

He leaps up and jogs across the room. "Marta, are you serious? Don't tease me."

"Come on, come on." She puts a hand on his back and hurries him through the door. I'm already out of my seat, following them, backpack bumping against my hips. JJ glances back at me, nods, and I take that as permission to follow. Inside Jacob's room, a flurry of doctors and nurses are rushing back and forth with equipment. A few scrub-clad people shift position, and I catch a glimpse of Jacob lying on his back while they listen to his chest, mess with his IV, inject something into his arm. Jacob looks confused, and when his eyes land on his dad, his face screws up like he's going to cry.

"What's going on?" he croaks, and JJ grabs one of Jacob's hands and sobs quietly into it.

Jacob sees me, frozen in the doorway. "Case," he half-whispers.

I approach, weaving past a pair of nurses examining something on an iPad. "Hey, Jacob. You scared us really bad."

Groggily, his eyes swim up to the ceiling, and then he closes them. He takes a ragged breath. "We were at the house."

Detective Martinez pushes past me. "Jacob, I need to ask you a few questions."

A doctor holds up a hand to stop her. "I'm sorry, but you're going to have to wait. We'll let you know when he's ready." Martinez turns on him to argue, and I slip past them and stand by Jacob's bed. JJ is smoothing Jacob's hair, whispering things in his ear. Jacob looks up at me, and I try for a smile that probably looks like a grimace.

"How long was I out?" He starts coughing, and the nurses shove an oxygen mask in his face, telling him to breathe slowly and deeply.

"Days," JJ says. "God, you scared us."

"Jacob, who did this to you? Do you remember?" I ask, voice low so no one will hear.

He pulls the oxygen mask away from his mouth a little. "You won't believe me if I tell you."

This is not what I was expecting. JJ and I glance at each other. "Who, Jake?" JJ asks.

Jacob's eyes meet mine. "It was Rosalinda. I swear to God."

I feel like I've stepped into another dimension. "Wait, what?"

The doctor puts a hand on my shoulder. "What are you doing in here? We need to examine him and run tests. He's not being questioned by anyone. Out, please. Family only."

Nurses guide me, and I'm in the corridor again where Detective Martinez is talking angrily on her cell phone right under a NO CELL PHONES sign. A pair of uniformed cops is stationed at the double doors to the waiting room, which brings it home for me in a new way: Jacob is in danger. Someone tried to poison him. Someone didn't want him to wake up. *Rosalinda?*

He's been in a coma. He has to be confusing a dream with reality. He probably got stabbed by someone he didn't see in the dark, and then while he was lying there unconscious he dreamed that Rosalinda did it. He knew what she looked like; he'd collected photos of her. She was fresh in his mind.

Wait. My stomach drops, and I feel my blood go cold in my veins. The whole picture is swimming into focus.

I head for the nurse's station and find the sign-in book tucked neatly into its spot on the counter. Pulling it toward me, I ask the nurse at the computer, "Everyone who comes in here has to sign this, right?"

She barely glances up at me. "Yes."

I scan through today's names. Nothing jumps out at me. I flip back to yesterday and read down the list. There's Eddie, there's...

Oh my god. I'd been right. Clear as day, the name I'd been looking for stares back at me.

Morrison Klein. She's young and pretty. She has long blond hair, and in a dark, terrified moment, Jacob had mistaken her for Rosalinda Valentini.

THIRTY-TWO

Friday, April 14

I FIND MYSELF BACK OUT ON THE CURB IN front of the hospital with no memory of getting here. My head is swimming, and I'm not sure what to do next. Do I go down to the police station and tell Detective Adams my suspicions? Do I call my grandma? Do I...

The answer pops into my head, so obvious I feel chastened for not having thought of it first. I have to tell Dallas. Of course. Her sister is a would-be murderer.

I check my phone. It's two thirty. How weird, that so much could have happened since this morning when Dallas woke me up. Cringing in anticipation, I text her. **Are you at home?**

She replies right away. **Yeah. How's your friend?**

I'd texted her earlier when Zoe and I were en route to the

hospital. **He's okay. I have to tell you something, actually. Can I come by?**

Sure.

I hesitate, thumbs floating over the screen. **Is your mom or Morrison home?**

No. Mom's working and Morrison has some debate club thing after school today.

Sure she does.

Be there soon, I text, and I speed walk across the street to catch the Metro.

An old man in a brown suit with a bow tie and cane accompanies me the entire way to North Hollywood, posture straight in the plastic chair, cane clutched across his lap. I'm a little worried about him; he's small and thin, and his hands on his cane are shaky. I follow him off the train and up the escalator, matching my steps to his painfully slow gait. He limps heavily past the chaos of skaters, people selling sodas out of coolers, and guys milling around smoking weed, to the crosswalk, where he presses the button and waits for his turn to cross, leaning neatly on his cane.

Irrationally, I want to follow him all the way home, wherever that is, and make sure he gets to his front door safely. I force myself to turn in the opposite direction and hurry toward Dallas's building.

The front door of her building is propped open for a set of movers, who are taking boxes out of a truck double-parked out front. I slip between them, my steps slowing as I approach her door. I lift a hand, take a deep, shaky breath, and knock.

She pulls the door open, and I'm filled with the now-familiar, stomach-fluttering crush feeling. She's in black jeans and a baggy T-shirt with Mickey Mouse on it, and her hair is tucked behind her ears. "You okay?" she asks, beckoning me inside.

I set my backpack on the small dining table beside an empty, flung-open pizza box. "I'm all right," I reply, but I can hear the dissonance in my own voice, so I'm not surprised she isn't fooled.

"Let's go to my room. It's a mess out here." She casts a disgusted look at the piles of mail, the kitchen sink full of dishes.

I grab my backpack and follow. Inside her tidy bedroom, she visibly relaxes, throwing herself onto the tightly made bed. "What's going on?"

"I'm going to go in order," I say, having decided how I want to tell her. "First, I'm going to show you something." I get the binder out of my backpack and sit beside her. "I found this in Jacob's room today. He's apparently been collecting stuff." I flip it open. "It's full of documents about Rosalinda, about the house." I show her a few articles.

"Was this for your YouTube channel?" she asks, glancing over an article about one of Rosalinda's movies. "It seems excessive."

"My thoughts exactly. Look at this." I flip to the end, where his hand-drawn family tree occupies the last page. "And there you are," I tell her, pointing to her and Morrison's names.

"That's a little weird," she murmurs, tracing the names with a fingertip.

"More than a little." I flip to the article about Mary and the baby boy abandoned at a church. "Read this," I tell her, and then I hold my breath while she does. She looks up at me, eyes full of questions. "Jacob's name is Jacob Anderson," I tell her. "His father is Jonathan Jacob Anderson."

She still looks blank.

"Remember the letters from Rosalinda's cousin?" I prompt her. "The cousin was named—"

"Mary," she says, voice cautious.

"Jacob's dad moved here from somewhere in the Midwest back in the nineties. He wanted to be a musician. His family was super against him moving to LA. He isn't close with them anymore, and it's always been a thing." I pause to collect my thoughts. "Dallas, JJ is adopted. I don't know what his adoptive mom's name is, but I bet it's Mary."

She holds a hand up to stop me. "Wait. So you're saying you think Jacob's dad is the baby who was found in the church, the son of this Mary Anderson?"

I nod, searching her eyes, waiting for it to sink in.

At last, she shakes her head. "But . . . so what? I don't get it."

"Rosalinda's cousin was named Mary."

"No, I got that." She waves a hand. "I mean, I guess you're saying that Jacob is some long-lost tenth cousin of mine or something, that JJ's the adopted son of Rosalinda's cousin? It's a weird coincidence, but I'm not biologically related to Rosalinda, remember? So we're not actually cousins."

"Wait." I flip through the binder, then tilt it toward her. The article I'm showing her is short, entitled "Rosalinda West Flies East for the Winter." "Rosalinda was in Indiana with her family right before this mystery baby was found. And remember the letter. Don't you get it?"

She bites her lip. "You're saying Rosalinda...like...knew JJ before she died or something? How would that—"

"No. I'm saying I think Rosalinda was JJ's biological mom."

She stares at me, eyes wide, mouth hanging open.

"Think about it." I'm warming up. "Rosalinda was a budding star. She was dating Andrew Valentini. But then she got pregnant. She couldn't let people know. So she went home to have the baby, and she left it with her cousin, who pretended to find it at church once Rosalinda was back in California."

She looks doubtful. "Who's supposed to be the father?"

"I don't know. Andrew? Someone else, and she was afraid Andrew would find out? I have no idea. But JJ is Rosalinda's son. And that's why Jacob was attacked."

"Wait, hold on. Why would someone try to kill him for that?"

I put a hand on hers. "It's not just someone. I'm so sorry. It's Morrison."

She stares at me, unblinking, eyes flitting back and forth, and then her face relaxes. She says, "You're joking. But why? I don't get it."

I get my phone out of my back pocket and open the Photos app. I pull up the most recent one, a shot of the hospital visitor log. I show it to her. "She went to the hospital yesterday. She poisoned Jacob. He almost died of organ failure, and the experience woke him out of the coma. He's up now, and he thinks Rosalinda is the one who stabbed him that night. Don't you get it? Rosalinda and Morrison both have long blond hair."

"It could have been anybody," she protests.

"But it wasn't anybody." I point to the screen again, reminding her of the signature. "It was Morrison. Because if Jacob is Rosalinda's grandson, he's a closer relative than you guys are. He could have rights to the estate, to the inheritance."

"That's ridiculous," she declares, jumping up and staring down at me. "That is the most ridiculous and...irrational—" She stops, eyes on the wall, and seems to be thinking about something. "Oh my god." She slumps onto the bed beside me. "What time was Jacob poisoned?"

"I don't know."

"Morrison did have to do some errand for school last night. She borrowed Mom's car after I got home. I offered to go for her because she isn't supposed to drive at night, but she refused." She rakes her hands through her hair. "I can't believe it."

"I'm so sorry." Timid, I touch her arm. I expect her to yank away, but she puts a hand on mine and closes her eyes. A few seconds tick by like that, and when she opens her eyes, they're wet and shining.

"We've both been worried about our mom," she says, voice low and gravelly, like she wishes she weren't saying the words. "She has this stupid smoke shop, but it makes, like, no money. We're constantly struggling. There are days we have nothing to eat."

I had no idea things were so tight for them. I try to come up with something to say, but I've got nothing.

She puts her face in her hands. "I've been so busy sneaking around with my stupid nanny cams, trying to keep people out of the house, trying to hold it all together. I do random jobs, mow lawns, wash cars, babysit, anything. I have a secret stash of Top Ramen and instant oatmeal under the bed so Morrison never has to go hungry."

It's so piercingly sad, tears prick up behind my eyes, imagining her stowing away food.

She whispers, "I thought I had sheltered her from all this. She's always in her own little world, doing her Academic Decathlon and debate club and chess. She's just a happy little nerd. But then she has these panic attacks..." Her shoulders rise and fall. "Maybe that place is cursed. Maybe Morrison was always destined to be exactly like our great-grandfather."

After an interminable silence, I whisper, "Can I hug you?"

She nods. I scoot closer and wrap my arms around her, and she rests her head on my shoulder. We sit there for a while, thinking our private thoughts. Personally, I'm thinking about my mom, about ghosts, about whether she still haunts the parking lot she died in. What if she's been there all this time and I, in my fear of seeing that horrible place, have been missing her?

THIRTY-THREE

Friday, April 14

DALLAS PULLS AWAY FROM ME AND WIPES HER eyes with the back of her hand. "Did you tell the cops about Morrison?"

"No. I wanted to talk to you first."

She takes a deep breath and blows it out through her mouth. She rubs her hands on her thighs. "Okay, then. I guess I should call Adams." She grabs her phone off the desk.

"Are you—" I stop myself from asking if she's okay. I'm sure it's hard, and I'm sure she's not okay.

She's already found the contact, and she has the phone to her ear. "Hi, yeah, I need to talk to Detective Adams. This is Dallas Klein. It's important. He'll want to hear from me." A pause. "Yeah." She rolls her eyes. "Hold music," she whispers.

I get my own phone out and flip through stuff while she waits. I wonder what's happening to Eddie right now. He's eighteen and in the hands of the LAPD. He's sensitive, soft, a sweet person. He's not built to be tormented like this.

"Detective Adams?" Dallas says. "It's me, Dallas. I have… I don't know how to say this. I think…" She grimaces. "This is weird and hard, so I'm just going to say it straight. I think my sister, Morrison, might be behind what happened to that guy Jacob." She stops, listens. "Yeah. Exactly. She signed the visitor log at the hospital. You should go look at it." After a moment, she casts me a sudden, worried look. "Hang on," she says, then puts a hand over the phone. "I'm going to have to tell him that we've been hanging out. Otherwise, it doesn't make sense how I'd know about the visitor log."

"I know." I pat her knee. "Just tell the truth."

She returns to the call. "Hi. Yeah. So, you know Casey Costello? She and I have been talking this week. She saw Morrison's name on the log. She took a photo. And…" She grimaces. "I didn't tell you this, but I have nanny cams in the house. They're in the teddy bears. Anyway, we've been looking at footage from that night. I—" She stops, clearly having been interrupted. "Yeah. They're still at the house. I wanted to get them, but…" This time, she trails off on her own. She starts nodding. "Yes, they're still there." After a long minute, she says, "I have my mom's car today, so we don't need a ride. Maybe half an hour? All right. See you then." She puts the phone in her back pocket and shakes her head. "He wants both of us to meet him at the house. He needs to retrieve those cameras and wants a statement from us. His partner is going to look into the records at the hospital."

I take a deep, frightened breath, anxiety flooding my body, making my hands cold at the thought of returning to the house. "I'm not going back in there without Adams."

"Same." She shudders visibly. She starts gathering her things, putting her wallet in a black canvas purse. "Give me a few minutes. I've got to get some of my mom's things out of her car and pull it around. Be right back."

I watch her leave and find myself opening the binder again and flipping through the articles. I find one about a séance at the house, and another about the death of the medium who conducted the séance, just a short time later.

I remember our planning sessions when we were first considering the murder house for our last episode. We had some other ideas as well—a famously haunted hotel downtown that's now under construction after another murder; an abandoned hangar on the south side that supposedly houses a UFO; the oil rigs in San Pedro. But Jacob had made a compelling argument for the Valentini mansion, and Eddie and Zoe had quickly gotten on board.

I close the binder and return it to my backpack. Jacob is awake now. Eddie will be released as soon as we give this evidence to Adams. Everything will be okay soon.

"Casey?" Dallas calls. "You ready?"

I join her in the living room. She locks the door behind us and leads me to the car, which is parked illegally in the alley behind her building. We're quiet on our way to Silver Lake, both

lost in our own thoughts as she navigates the freeway, then surface streets, and finally the narrow, wooded lanes that make my
heart pump fast and loud. She pulls up to the gate and gets out
to unlock it, pushes it open, then comes back to drive us up the
long driveway and around the side of the house, where she tucks
the car into a discreet corner.

She says, "He's not here yet, I guess. We beat him."

"Let's wait for him in the car. It's safer." My heart is going
double-time, a drummer on caffeine pills having taken up residence in my chest.

"Agreed. Let me just grab something." She comes around to
my side and gets into the back seat behind me. "I have a water
bottle back here," she explains. I keep my eyes on the tinted windows, on the blue sky beyond. Nothing bad can happen to us in
broad daylight, can it? It's too quiet here, too private. I wish we'd
waited for Detective Adams on the street.

Something clamps around my neck. A rope? A belt?

I struggle, try to get my fingers underneath it. I can't draw a
breath. Panic screams inside my head, my vision red with terror.

I open my mouth in a silent shriek, but there's no air. My
lungs are burning, my head spinning. A piercing memory—it
takes fifteen seconds to knock someone out in a choke hold. Fuzzily, my limbs tingling, I wonder how many seconds I have left.

Thoughts blur into colors, colors fade into black, and then
I'm floating away like a bubble blown into the open air.

THIRTY-FOUR

Friday, April 14

I WAKE UP SLOWLY, ONE BODY PART AT A TIME.
My feet first, then my hands, which throb with a painful numb-
ness. It's dark, but that's because I'm sleeping. I'm in such an
uncomfortable position, though. I try to readjust, to get the pil
low under my head to fix the crick in my neck, but there's no
pillow, and I'm sitting upright. I blink my eyes open, resentfully
grumpy about having been awakened, and then I gasp, sucking
in a startled breath.

I'm on an old carpet, my back pressed uncomfortably to a
wooden railing. My hands are trapped behind me; I'm trussed
like an animal. A figure squats on the floor, a long, graceful
hand tinkering with something as though trying to get it just
right. Candles occupy every surface: the side table next to an

armchair, the floor, a bookshelf. There are tall tapers in delicate holders and squat pillars sitting directly on the carpet, the dim room flickering with the glow from dozens of golden lights.

The figure looks up at me. In the half light, I think it's a demon, a spirit, but then it resolves into the shape of a very human girl. Dallas.

"You're up," she says, tilting sideways. The floor seems wrong, wobbly somehow.

"What's happening?" I whisper, unable to raise my voice to full volume.

"Ketamine," she replies, sitting cross-legged in front of me. "Ketamine is happening."

Nausea roils in my gut, and I try to clamp a hand to my stomach, but my arms are trapped behind me. Right. The railing. "Where are we?"

"The upstairs landing." She points behind me. "Down there is the living room."

Through the brain fog, I vaguely recall this landing. I squirm, something sharp digging into my wrists. This slouched position is killing my back. My whole body is sore, like I've been through the washing machine. How long have I been here? I can't turn around to see the windows, but the light on the walls is a dark purple-gray, the last remnants of day before night swallows it whole.

"What's happening?" I repeat, claustrophobia like a vice around my throat.

"Ketamine is horrible, right? It's one of my mom's go-tos when she's really digging in for a bad night." Her cerulean eyes, glinting in the candlelight, are tight on mine. The air swells around me, and I feel that the house is a sentient being drawing breath.

"You're pretty sharp," she says. "You were so close. Right idea, wrong sister."

I sort back through the information from the day, and at last I land on the point. My stomach clenches against another wave of nausea. "It's not Morrison. It's you, pretending to be Morrison."

She nods slowly, languidly.

"That's really messed up," I mumble. "Framing your own sister for murder? What did she ever do to you?"

She grins. "You're funny on drugs."

I don't understand what could possibly be funny. I open my mouth to ask again, but she speaks before I can get the words out.

"Let me tell you a little bit about my family." She draws her knees up and hooks her arms around them. "My dad was a piece of human garbage, high all the time, violent, just, like, a hurricane of bad energy. Then you have my mom. I don't think she's been sober a day in my life."

I slur my words as I reply. "So what? Look at the rest of us. No one's had it easy. But we don't go around stabbing and, like, poisoning people." For the first time, my brain wonders what her plans are for me. A chill passes through my chest.

She falls silent, eyes drifting from candle to candle. "Do you believe this house is haunted?"

"We saw it together," I remind her.

She waves that off. "I'm not talking about the light show.

257

That's something I came up with to keep people from trespassing. It's stage lighting, LEDs I got from Ikea. Theater kid, remember?" I gape at her for a second as everything swings into focus, the clarity bringing with it a ripping headache.

She says, "I'm talking about this house, the legacy. Do you understand what people have done for it? My great-grandfather literally killed for it, and he never even got to enjoy it. His son, my grandfather, was a loser. My dad didn't deserve it. Maybe it wanted to be mine. Maybe it saw me coming generations before I was born."

"What about Morrison?" I ask. "Doesn't she deserve the inheritance as much as you do?"

She frowns. "Morrison hasn't done a single thing to earn it. And Jacob? He gets to just come in out of nowhere?" She's rigid, voice loud and echoing around the cavernous ceilings. "He emailed my mom. He wanted us to take a DNA test with him before he told his dad. He used to visit the house. Did you know that? He'd stand outside, looking in the windows, hanging out in the yard. I'd watch him through the security cameras, wishing I could…" Her face has gone faraway, remembering, and then she refocuses on me. "And then he broke in—brought a team with him—unbelievable. But I was here, taking care of the house. You see how this is all meant to be?"

I don't want her to go on. I can picture what happened that night—her here alone in the dark, playing dress-up as Rosalinda. I wonder if Dallas liked to try on her clothes, and I realize, for the first time, there's a reason she never emptied the closets.

"What's your plan, then?" I ask, afraid to know.

"Picture me a year from now. I'll be a famous actress. You know from personal experience that I can act. That night here— that was a great performance. You see?"

Our first kiss. I'm such a fool.

She goes on. "Picture me, living alone in this house. It's only a few months until I turn eighteen. That's when the renovations will start. It'll be restored to its former glory, a monument to old Hollywood. I'll be Rosalinda but better. I'm not anyone's bride, anyone's victim. People will come from all over to photograph the house, and me in it. You haven't seen me as a blond. You don't realize how much I look like Rosalinda. The story is iconic. It's the stuff of Hollywood history. I'll get cast in *everything.*" Her voice is fervent, almost religious. "Marilyn Monroe, Jayne Mansfield, Rosalinda Valentini, *Dallas* Valentini."

What a narcissist. "And your sister? Your mom? What about them?"

She waves that off. "Whatever. They're not part of it. And obviously Jacob will, you know. I still have some loose ends to tie up. I'm honestly so frustrated about that. How many lives does that guy have?" A hand flicks out, an annoyed gesture, as though his life is an inconvenience on par with getting the wrong drink at Starbucks. "Oh, well. Third time's the charm, right? Maybe you poisoned all the food in his kitchen before you came here. That's an idea." Her eyes go unfocused, and she pauses to think.

The thought of Jacob and his dad finally getting home from the hospital only to be poisoned in their apartment is so horrifying, I find myself frozen, staring at her with my heart pounding and my mind blank for an uncounted number of seconds. When I find my voice, it's small and scared. "And what about me?"

Her eyes refocus, and she seems to regard me with amusement and a little anger. "Your obsession with this house is going to be all over the internet. You hate true crime? Wait until they learn about you. Murdered mother, obsessed with the Valentini mansion, attacked your friend out of jealousy after learning he was set to inherit it—"

"Jealousy?" I protest.

She ignores me. "Tried to kill him again to keep him quiet, came back here when you realized your second attempt was a failure, set up this whole shrine." She gestures behind her to the candles, the thing on the ground. I see now that it's another intricate display of bones. "You built a religion around this house. It's sick, really. You manipulated your way into a relationship with me. Anything to get closer to the house, to the family you were obsessed with. Poor Casey, so broken, looking for belonging, looking for love." She adopts a concerned expression that, contrary to her claims to being a great actress, looks completely fake—sloppy acting. "You'll take your own life. It will be sad, but also really *interesting*. So many TV episodes, Casey. So many. I'll do interviews about it. I'll do you justice. I'll say you lit up a room." She snort-laughs. "Don't you hate that expression? What are women, human flashlights?"

And now, my eyes land on a circular shape on the carpet by

the armchair, one I hadn't registered with my brain floating in a ketamine haze. It's a coil of rope, one tail trailing slightly aside.

I remember the newspaper article about the Hollywood medium who'd hung himself. "Dallas, did your great-grandfather kill the medium? Adrian Wonders? Because he was drawing too much publicity to that part of the case?"

"Not bad." She smiles, tilting her head, and a beam of light glints through her talismanic eyes. She's right. She will be famous.

"Remember what I said in the car about fate after we went to that old detective's house? When I learned for sure it was my great-grandfather, that was a big moment. It's like, there's no use fighting it. It always had to be this way. History repeats itself. That gave me so much peace."

Now I understand why we're on the landing. She's staging a fake suicide. She's going to hang me from the railing, where I'll die overlooking the bloodstains on the living room carpet.

THIRTY-FIVE

Friday, April 14

MENTALLY, I FEEL CLEAR, BUT A PIERCING HEADACHE is slicing through my skull. I try to ignore it, and then I realize it's radiating up from my back, a muscle spasm. I adjust my position, the thing she has me cuffed with digging into my wrists. It's sharp, narrow. I feel around for it with numbing fingers. I'm pretty sure it's a zip tie. Not good. There's no getting out of a zip tie.

How did she even get me up here? No wonder I'm sore; she must have found a way to drag me up the stairs.

Dallas has lost interest in me and is arranging something on the carpet, pulling slender objects out of a bag and setting them carefully in a circle. I realize with a start that everything is still blurry because I don't have my glasses. I guess they fell off somewhere between the car and here.

"More bones?" I can't help asking.

She holds one up. "These are chicken."

"But why? For what?"

She returns her attention to her project. "I'm not going to say I believe in all this spooky stuff. But there's something I like about the pageantry. I hope the spirits do live here. Anyway, the story is that you've been breaking in, leaving these. Remember, you're obsessed with the house."

"You're leaving prints everywhere," I point out dryly.

She holds her hands up and wiggles the fingers. "Gloves, bitch." It's dark so I hadn't noticed, but she's wearing the same kind of latex gloves we usually use during our break-ins.

Desperate, I look for other loopholes in her plan. "No one will believe this narrative you're creating. There's zero evidence that I'm obsessed with the house. In fact, all my friends will say that's not true. They know I didn't even want to come here in the first place."

She doesn't even spare me a glance. "Right. Your friends who are such reliable witnesses."

I'm stumped by that, and then I remember something, a whoosh of excitement rushing through me. "Wait! The cops have the footage from Jacob's camera. They're going to see you on there. You can't do anything to me. It will just make it worse."

She crooks an eyebrow at me, disdainful. "I gave them that camera; I turned it in anonymously after I checked the footage. He didn't get anything. His camera was pointed at the floor."

I sag, discouraged. Of course she's the one who gave the cops Jacob's camera. She's the one who stole it in the first place.

Done with the bones, she tosses the bag aside and grabs the

rope off the ground. "You like this little altar? I'm picturing you building it as a sort of final offering. You're, like, 'Here I am, Rosalinda, take me to the afterlife, I want to see my mom.'"

I struggle against the zip tie, hoping to loosen it, to rip out the banister, anything. She starts looping the rope. "You know, it's actually not easy to tie a hangman's knot," she mutters. I thrash and kick out, trying to strike her, but she ignores me. I stop struggling against the zip tie and picture the mechanism. *It's tiny little teeth, right? They grip forward. Can you push them backward and loosen their grip?* I try it, heartbeat moving past pounding into vibrating—or maybe that's my muscles, all quaking with terror.

Dallas makes a satisfied noise and tests the strength of the noose she's constructed. She pulls on the rope, widening the loop, then tugs it back, shrinking it.

She grins at me. "All right. Party time."

"Dallas, no. Stop." I'm backing up now, pressing myself into the banister, drawing my knees up so I can kick her in the face.

She seems to be calculating her best approach. "I feel like you're going to be difficult about this."

"I am. Extremely. You should just let me go."

She snort-laughs. I can't believe I thought that was cute. It's gross. Who snorts?

And then she rushes me, face going grim. I squirm, try to kick, try to bite, but the rope is already around my neck, and she's pulling it tight with both hands. She steps back, panting a little, gripping the rope like a leash. I'm crying, I realize, tears pouring down my cheeks.

"Grandma." It's an apology. She's going to think I did this. It's going to destroy her.

Dallas frowns as though I'm annoying her. I want to scream obscenities, rebellious words that will make her stop, but all that comes out is a roar of pure pain and rage.

She yanks the rope, mouth twisting into an ugly scar across her pretty face. I hear myself choke, and the panicky, throat-closing claustrophobia of asphyxiation assaults me again, like in the car but worse because this time I know exactly what's happening. She's close enough that I can see the sheen of sweat on her brow, the rise and fall of her chest as she cinches the rope tighter. Her face is set into a grim, pitiless expression, like she's killing a cockroach.

A breeze sweeps into the landing, whispering through the candles, whose flames dance in response. Dallas doesn't register it, but then the breeze intensifies, becoming a wind. She sputters, almost drops the rope, her hair whipping into her eyes and mouth. A few of the taper candles topple over onto the carpet, flames extinguishing in puddles of wax.

Dallas's grip on the rope has loosened, and I fill up my lungs and try to kick the rope out of her hands, hoping she's too distracted to maintain her grip. The wind picks up again, and I wonder if this is part of her fake-haunting theatrics. But her expression, frustrated and afraid, tells me it's not. A window must have come open; the Santa Anas must be picking up. All these thoughts blink through my mind as I thrash and kick.

And then something clicks; my hands come free.

I collapse sideways. I must have snapped the zip tie. It takes a tenth of a second to realize what happened, and then I have the rope in my hands, and I'm using her strength and the resistance to pull myself up to standing. She screams, the sound filled with fury. I respond with a wordless grunt, and then we're wrestling with the rope. *She's going to win*, I think, but I wrench it away from her, stumbling and surprised. I yank it off my neck, hurl it to the ground, and launch myself at her, desperate, ready to beat her to a pulp to keep her from hurting me.

Instead of fighting, she turns and runs, sprinting across the landing, knocking candles over, and then she's thundering down the stairs.

THIRTY-SIX

Friday, April 14

HER FOOTSTEPS FADE, AND THE HOUSE FALLS silent. Candlelight flickers on the walls. The wind has evaporated; it's as still as the grave. Somewhere downstairs, a creak—she's still in the house.

My heartbeat seems to have relocated to my head; it's pounding in my ears, my sinuses. My knees are mushy and weak, and I wonder if the ketamine could still be messing me up.

I can't just stand here. My eyes land on the rope. I do some quick calculations, grab the rope, loosely coil it, and hurry into the hallway toward the bedrooms. No way am I going downstairs, where she's probably waiting to jump out and surprise me. Absolutely not. I may have the floor plan memorized, but she has it written in her DNA.

It's pitch-black in here, and my phone is no longer in my pocket—stolen by Dallas—so I have to fumble around in darkness. Trying to be quiet and not trip over furniture, I seek out the guest room where I found the letters. A plan is forming. I'm breathing too hard, too fast.

Here, this room. The armchair is positioned by the window beside a queen-sized bed, just as I remember it. I head straight for the window. It's old, the kind that cranks open, and when I turn the crank, I realize it's locked. I fumble, hands so shaky it's like I'm wearing oven mitts, and find the latch. I grind it open four inches, and then it sticks.

I almost start crying. I shove my shoulder against the window and it finally budges another few inches, just enough for me to slip out. I tie one end of the rope to the leg of the bed, stretch it to the window, and dangle it out, measuring its length. It seems like I'll still have a good ten feet or more to fall once I get to the end of it.

I've climbed a lot of rope ladders for *We'll Never Tell*, but they've always been, you know, ladders, not solitary ropes dangling over some haunted darkness where I might break a leg only to be brutally murdered. *Get it together*, I command myself.

I press against the window, seeing if I can get it open any farther, and something snaps. The window detaches from the pane and goes crashing to the ground far below, where it smashes into a million pieces, as loud as if I'd shot off a glass-filled cannon.

The door behind me slams open. Dallas rages through it, eyes and teeth all but glowing in the dark. I shriek, a stupid noise, and clutch the rope, my only weapon. She snatches it, tries to wrench it from my hands, and we struggle. I fake her out, release it, and she goes stumbling backward. I dart past her, out the door, into the hallway, and sprint for the landing, hoping to beat her down the stairs and out the front door. She's fast, though, and she clutches the back of my shirt, pulling me to the floor before I can make it to the stairs. I turn as I fall, grabbing her leg, and she goes down, too, scattering a row of candles along the carpet. I try to get up, but she claws at my shirt, and I trip over a pillar candle, spraying a puddle of hot wax up my leg. Somehow, she still has the rope; it's around my neck again, and she's behind me, pulling it tight.

Before she can get me in a firm hold, I spin, slip beneath her, and do a roll, which kicks her off and sends her spiraling to the railing. She pulls herself up, and a scent—a whiff of smoke—catches my attention. Nearby, part of the carpet is burning from the fallen candles. A river of flame is carving a slippery path across the floor, and I cry out as it snakes past, licking at my feet.

Dallas sees it and shouts out a string of curses, turning to stomp it out with her boots. I take advantage of this new crisis and make a break for the stairs, but she catches my arm, yanking me back. I twist away, and we're wrestling by the banister, her trying to get the rope around my neck, me gripping the slick wood, pulling away from her.

Wind whips past us, and fire spreads like spilled water, rippling in waves across the carpet, up the walls. Dallas screams, turns, and I make one more break for the stairs. She grabs my shirt and pulls, but I whirl around, and the momentum throws her off balance, sending her staggering backward into the banister.

It cracks against her weight, perhaps weakened by my struggles. She cries out with surprise and fear. Her panic pierces me, and I reach out to help her, but the railing gives way and she crashes into empty air, a trail of her own screams chasing her down to the ground floor, where she lands with a dull thud.

Silence except for the crackling of fire. The walls are alight now, and when I look up, the ceiling above me ripples with flames and smoke.

I run for the stairs, almost tripping over my own feet. In the foyer, the walls and ceiling crack and groan, and pieces of the ceiling start to rain down, fiery hail birthing flames on the living room carpet. In the smoky moon- and firelight, Dallas is a quiet lump on the bloodstained carpet. I try to run for the door, but my legs won't go.

She's a human being, a girl my age. I can't just leave her. I turn to help. She's crumpled into an unnatural fetal position, back twisted ninety degrees so she stares straight up.

She's not dead, I realize with a shock. Her beautiful eyes focus on the space above me, a tropical sea reflecting sparks of wild orange firelight. She opens her mouth to speak. A trickle of blood leaks out.

"You," she whispers to someone I can't see.

Her eyes freeze, fixed on the ceiling, and her face goes still. This is what death looks like. All these years, I've pictured it. Here it is, facing me at last.

The ceiling sends a fresh load of ash and plaster raining down onto us.

"Dallas!" I yell, shaking her by the shoulders. Her eyes don't move, don't blink.

I cry out, terrified, and then the shrill sound is cut off by my coughing. Another shower of ash and burning ceiling pours down on us, and I know I won't be able to drag her all the way to the front door.

Her eyes are cloudy, her face coated with a fine layer of ash. She looks like a marble sculpture, a monument to the tragedy and injustice of death. I choke and cough violently, backing away from the horror of her and trying to find the front door. Every breath I draw is more smoke than air, and I've forgotten where I am. When I look down at my feet, they're strangely clear. I realize there's a little bit of fresh air down there, so I drop down onto my hands and knees and suck in a breath between coughing fits. I crawl for the entrance, for the hall. I shuffle madly, pleading for my life, praying to God and Rosalinda and the house and whatever other spirits care to help me.

Wind sweeps through again, bringing clear air with it. And there—I see the front entry. I croak with excitement, push to my feet, hold my breath, and run. While the house groans in protest as it burns around me, I fumble with the locks and yank the door open, letting in a blissful whoosh of clean night air.

Outside, firelight casts demonic, undulating shadows across the overgrown lawn. I sprint through the tall grass, but I feel the house calling me, pulling me back. My steps slow and I turn, gasping ragged breaths. The windows are inferno orange, flames licking through broken glass, blackening the white stucco. The

271

open front door yawns, glowing with hellish light. A groan comes from within, and something crashes, shaking the walls.

"Goodbye," I whisper.

I walk away, leaving the house to consume itself and the last person who loved it with the dark passion it deserved.

THIRTY-SEVEN

Friday, April 14

JACOB

ONCE THE DOCTORS WERE CONVINCED I WAS awake for real and the cops had a chance to ask me every question they could imagine, the flurry of activity in my hospital room died down. My dad and I were left alone, and he had a chance to bawl about the miracle of my resurrection, snotting up my sheets.

"Hey, kid," he said when he was done sobbing. "Tell me the truth. You weren't alone in the house. Your friends went with you, right? You're just trying to keep them out of trouble?"

I met his eyes and didn't answer.

"It's fine," he said. "I'm not going to tell the cops. I just want to make sure you're not stupid enough to break into a place like that by yourself."

I couldn't help smiling, but I still didn't answer.

"But here's what I really want to know, okay, son? This story you're selling the cops, about Rosalinda Valentini stabbing you—that can't be true. You're covering up for one of your friends. Right? But, Jake, I don't know why you'd do that if one of them tried to kill you."

"No," I protested, trying to sit up. I was hit with a wave of pain, a reminder of my stab wounds, and I relaxed into the pillows. "I told the truth. She had long blond hair and these insane blue eyes."

I tried to figure out how to describe those eyes. They were piercing, and they caught every bit of light, like crystals or gems. They were beautiful, but also cold and full of malice. When she stabbed me, she was methodical, like she was slaughtering an animal. I shivered.

"It wasn't a ghost," my dad said. "It had to just...be a blond woman, then."

I shook my head. "She was Rosalinda." I closed my eyes and started floating, drifting through the darkness behind my eyelids. I snapped them open, suddenly terrified. "I'm afraid of falling back into a coma. What if I don't wake up?"

He pressed his lips together like the words hurt him, and his red-rimmed eyes looked wet. "The doctors say that isn't going to happen."

"But they can't know," I protested. "They didn't expect me to be in a coma the first time."

He squeezed my hand. "How about this? I'll go talk to them. I'll ask what the chances are of a relapse. You need to get some sleep, and I don't want you feeling scared every time you close your eyes."

I nodded. "Okay. Good. Thanks."

He squeezed my hand one last time and released it, and I lay there alone for a while, staring out the window at the darkening sky, examining my memory of the blond stabbing me. She'd looked at me with those ice-blue eyes, and then her hand had snapped forward, and she'd stabbed me quick—one, two, three. It felt like getting punched until the pain set in.

Had I been attacked by a ghost? That was stupid. What next—ghosts with guns? Maybe she was an obsessed fan who dressed up like Rosalinda and hung around the house, recreating Rosalinda's death. That also sounded ridiculous, but it was the only explanation I could come up with.

The curtain rustled, and I assumed my dad was returning, but then the cloth parted to reveal Eddie. He stared down at me, eyes huge with shock, like he couldn't believe I was real.

"I'm awake," I said stupidly.

He pulled the curtain shut and approached the bed. I'd never seen him like this—skinny, cheeks drawn, eyes burning with something I couldn't quite name. I couldn't believe I'd been unconscious long enough for him to look this horrible.

He sat in the chair my dad had just vacated. His mouth opened and closed, and then he seemed to give up on talking and just stared at me.

"So, I've been stabbed *and* poisoned," I said. "I'm a cockroach. Can't kill me."

His head dropped, and he leaned his elbows on his knees and looked down at his lap. He was crying silently, his mouth stretched into a grimace of pure pain. "Hey, no, it's okay, I was just messing around. I'm going to be okay." I had no idea if this was true. "Please look at me. I can't lean over, and you're going to make me rip some stitches trying."

He wiped his face. "Don't do that."

I reached for him, and he gave me his hand. "I want to know what's going on with you and Zoe," I said, surprising myself with the words. *Really, Jacob? You almost died and you're worried about* this? *Actually, yeah, I am.*

He bit his lip. "She and I hooked up a few times. And then you wanted to—and then—" He cleared his throat. "It was vindictive. I think I was mad at you."

"For what? We weren't even fighting yet."

"I felt like, how did I get to this point where my entire life is tied up in this one person? If you and I decide to be together and then we break up, I don't just lose you. I lose your dad. I lose my place to go that isn't my empty house. I'll have to hide all our stuff in a box, shut my memories of you away." He took a shaky breath. "So I was like, let's make sure this is just casual. We can mess around and still be Jake and Eddie. It doesn't have to mean anything more. See—I can hook up with Zoe, too. This is not a big deal. I don't have to worry about losing everything." His voice broke, and he stopped talking.

"It's a risk," I murmured, understanding at last. "Because if we break up, we lose our friendship, too. And my dad is like a second dad to you. You have more to lose than I do. Is that what you're saying?"

He scowled. "I guess I just care more."

"You don't care more. You're a lot smarter than me. And you're not as impulsive. You think things through." I scooted over in the bed, clenching my teeth against the pain it caused. "Come here."

"I don't want to hurt you."

"I need a hug, and I can't get up, so you're going to have to come here." I patted the narrow space beside me.

Carefully, he sat on the edge and then settled back, barely moving the mattress. I wasn't capable of that level of care. I wasn't gentle, wasn't cautious. Once he was settled and we were squished together, he rolled onto his side and buried his face in my neck. An arm snaked around and laid itself across my waist, below my injuries.

"Here's the thing," I said. "I hear all your worries. And you're right. But I can't help being in love with you. So I have to let them go. I've got to accept things as they come. You've never lost anybody like I've lost my mom. I didn't lose her all at once. She was there, then not, then back, then gone."

"I remember."

"When something like that happens, you realize how temporary everything is. Our friendship could get broken up by you going to college, us growing apart. You could get into a car accident tomorrow. I could get stabbed in a freaking murder house. But no matter what happens with me and you, as long as my dad is alive and you want him in your life, he's going to be there. You won't lose him. And I'd never keep him from you out of spite."

He nodded.

I was sleepy, floating again, and I snapped my eyes open. "Eddie, I'm terrified I might go back into the coma. I need to make sure everything is all wrapped up in case I do. Are we okay?"

He propped himself up on his forearm and looked down at me. Cupping my cheek, he said, "That's up to you."

I sighed, relieved. "We're okay."

The curtain slid open, and my dad stepped through. He stopped mid-step, and Eddie jerked to a sitting position, eyes huge.

My dad broke the silence first, closing the curtain and sinking into the chair. "Hey, Eddie." He smiled. "Everybody relax. I already know about this." He gestured back and forth between us.

"You do?" I asked. "How?"

His mouth pinched into a smirk behind the beard. "Come on. You think I was born yesterday?"

"Well, no. You're, like, super old."

He reached out to playfully swat my arm. His eyes landed on Eddie. "Poor Ed looks like he's having a heart attack. Come here." He half-stood and dropped a kiss onto Eddie's head. "You're a good kid, and you've been worrying yourself sick. Jake is going to be fine. You can relax, okay? Just be yourself." He patted Eddie's back. To me, he said, "The doctors say you're out of the woods. No more risk of coma. No swelling in the brain, no new trauma. They caught the poison early, were able to counteract it, your organs are functioning well. You're a resilient little guy."

"Like a cockroach."

He laughed. "Like a cockroach."

I was so tired. Relief was a soft, warm blanket, and I couldn't keep my eyes open any longer.

"Come on," I heard my dad tell Eddie. "Let's go get some food and let him sleep. Everyone's had a long day."

I didn't see them leave. I was already sinking into dreams.

THIRTY-EIGHT

Saturday, April 15

I WAKE UP COUGHING FROM A RESTLESS SLEEP. My grandma instantly has my hand in hers. "Casey? You okay?"

I rub my eyes with my free hand. I'm in the hospital room I'd been checked into last night. From the quality of the light out the window, I assume it's late morning. My throat is aching and burning, the flesh sore and blistered from the rope.

"I'm okay," I reply, my voice hoarse and unrecognizable. I cough again, which hurts less than I expect, and then I realize—I'm on a lot of meds. I remember being given them last night by a nurse after a doctor told me I'd need to stay in the hospital at least twenty-four hours for observation.

Someone says, "Here. Drink water."

I turn toward the voice. It's Zoe, hair pulled up, face blotchy like she's been crying. She hands me a glass of water with a lid and a straw, and I accept it. "When did you—" I can't finish the sentence for coughing.

"Drink," my grandma orders. She looks exhausted, hair messy, makeup worn off, but her energy is calm. Before the pain meds set in last night, while she held my hand as I gave the cops an abbreviated version of what had happened with Dallas, I'd been worried she wouldn't be able to handle this. But she stayed strong, back straight, mouth set like a soldier. Sometimes I forget how strong she is; sometimes I really don't give her enough credit.

I end up finishing the whole cup of water in one go. My grandma says, "I'll get you some more," grabs the empty cup, and leaves.

Zoe leans forward in her chair, pushing my hair off my face. "How you doing?"

I grip her hand, press it to my cheek. "Zoe, I'm so sorry."

She forces a smile. It doesn't reach her eyes. "For what? Accusing me of trying to kill our friend?"

The words are barbed, but I deserve them. I can't believe how off-base I was. "Forgive me. Please. I promise, even in the moment, I couldn't believe I was thinking it."

"You're going to pay," she whispers theatrically.

Relief. If she's joking, she doesn't hate me. "Anything," I agree. "How's Jacob? Did the police let Eddie go?" I ask, clearing my throat. It feels like someone is sitting on my chest.

She nods. "Once Jacob woke up and started talking, it was obvious Eddie had nothing to do with stabbing him. They let him go before they even booked him."

"Oh, thank god." Last night, they'd been so focused on

grilling me, and then they'd zonked me out with meds, and no one had given me any updates.

Zoe says, "And you were, like, dating Dallas? And you didn't tell me?"

I grimace. "Maybe a little bit. Wait." I half-sit up as something occurs to me. "Do the cops know about our YouTube channel? Do they know we were with Jacob that night? Are we facing criminal charges? I just told them the bare minimum because I didn't have a chance to talk to you guys first."

She glances toward the door. "No, they don't know about our channel. They think we were just teenagers being reckless, breaking into a haunted house for fun. So, here's the thing about that, though. As you remember, breaking into the house was originally Jacob's idea."

I nod.

"And now that it turns out Jacob is probably the rightful owner, or at least JJ is, we were basically breaking into his own house. Long story short, we're probably getting away with it. LAPD isn't going to charge us unless Morrison and her mom are pushing for it, which, like, this is the last thing on their minds right now. And even if they did, the fact that Jacob and JJ will ultimately own the house will probably end up sinking any charges they bring. Adams straight up told my dad's lawyer that the DA doesn't want any part of this mess."

"I hadn't even considered the fact that Jacob was breaking into his own rightful house."

"I know. And check it out. They found our tapes in Dallas's room and a bunch of stuff on her PC. It was clear that she was planning your murder, Jacob's attack, everything."

"She's the one who dug up our tapes," I whisper. "Oh, Zoe, I'm so sorry for assuming it was you."

She shrugs. "I mean, I was the only other person who knew where they were."

"She must have been following us when we buried them. Oh wow. It just gets creepier and creepier. How did we not see her?"

"I'm telling you, nature is bad. If we hadn't been in the forest, there wouldn't have been so many trees to hide her."

I'm about to tease her about her hatred of the outdoors when a nurse comes in to check on me. We lobby her into getting me a wheelchair so we can visit Jacob in the ICU, and when my grandma returns, she helps me transfer from bed to chair. In the elevator, as it whooshes up, Zoe turns to me. "Get up," she says.

"What?" I ask as my grandma makes a noise in protest.

"Trust me. Real quick. Two seconds."

I pull myself up, and she takes my place, then yanks me down so I'm sitting on her lap. The elevator doors ding open, and she says, "Yahhhh!!" and wheels us out at top speed. I can't help but laugh. She can't see over me, though, and immediately steers us into a wall.

"Oh my lord," my grandma says, but she's chuckling. "Let me push you guys."

We arrive in the ICU giggling (Zoe) and coughing (me), my grandma laughing behind us, complicit in our nonsense. The nurses buzz us in with disapproving looks and make us sign the visitor log before we head to Jacob's room. We burst into what looks like a somber scene between Jacob, his dad, and Eddie and his parents.

"Sorry," I say, descending into a new wave of coughing.

"Oh, we're interrupting, I'm so sorry," my grandma tells the adults. Zoe extricates herself from underneath me.

Jacob, sitting up and looking less pale than when I last saw him, beckons us forward. "It's fine. Come on in." I notice bandages poking out of the neck of his hospital gown, a couple of tubes and sensors connecting his wrist to a machine next to his bed.

"Jacob, honey, be careful," Eddie's mom says. She's in a black dress and heels, glossy blond hair tumbling down over her shoulders. She's sitting in a chair beside the bed, toned legs crossed, while Eddie's dad stands nearby, hands in his pockets, dressed in designer jeans and a blazer. Eddie looks translucent with anxiety, hovering by Jacob's shoulder.

Jacob's dad pushes off from his post by the sink, kisses my grandma's cheek, and looks down at me. "How you holdin' up, Casey?"

I start coughing again, and my grandma hustles to get me water. "I'm okay," I croak.

Jacob waves us forward. "Zoe, roll her over here."

She pushes me toward Jacob's bed and sits on the sheet by his thigh. Eddie looks down at his feet, and Jacob glances from one of them to the other. Clearly, something is up, but with all the parentals in the room, I'm not going to ask.

I meet Jacob's eyes. "So, wow. Your family tree."

"Yeeahh," he says.

JJ salutes me with a forefinger. "I'm fancier than I realized."

"What now?" Zoe asks.

"We've been talking to a lawyer," JJ says. "It looks like I'm the heir to the whole Valentini estate, house and all, which is weird as hell." Eddie's dad glances over at him, a little amused.

"Didn't expect that, huh?" he asks.

"Nope," JJ says. "It's a hell of a shock."

Eddie's mom puts a hand on her husband's shoulder. "I'm so sorry, but I do have to get back to the office. We're casting for a few—"

"Wait," Eddie says. He looks almost green, like he's going to throw up. "I need to tell you something." He grips one hand with the other. "I need to..." He trails off.

Jacob looks up at him, eyes full of pity. "It's fine," he murmurs. "Don't."

"No," Eddie says. He closes his eyes and takes a deep breath. "Jacob and I are together. We're not just best friends. Do you understand?" He opens his eyes and folds his arms across his chest. His jaw is square, clenched. In this moment, he looks like a little boy sticking up for a friend, heart-wrenchingly vulnerable in a display of toughness.

His parents look shocked. They meet each other's eyes, then look around the room at the rest of us. The air is stifled, hot with the feeling of everyone holding their breath. Even JJ is frozen.

Eddie's mom breaks the silence. "I mean, that's...I'm sorry, but why..." She gestures to the room. "Why all this? Why the need to make such a big announcement?"

Eddie's brows furrow. "I just...I don't know. I wanted to tell you."

His dad says, "If you're worried we'll be upset about a gay relationship, I'm sorry. I don't know what we did to give you that impression. If you're safe and your life is in order, that's all we care about. You should know that."

"How could I know that?" Eddie says, his voice breaking through its usual calm reserve into something much more visceral than I've ever heard from him. "I don't see you. You say you want me to *be somebody*, but, like, we're all just people. Everyone is somebody. I—I didn't think you'd approve because you're always telling me I need to be around the kind of people who can help me get ahead." His voice turns bitter. "And anyway, it's not like we talk about deep stuff. We barely see each other."

We're all holding our breaths.

His parents exchange a look, and then his mom gets up. She comes around the bed and stands in front of him, just a little shorter, in her heels, than he is. "We love you, and we love Jake. I know he's somebody. You don't have to tell us that." She glances at JJ, obviously worried about what he'll think, but he's looking out the window, almost like he's trying to give them their privacy. Refocusing on Eddie, she says, "We have big dreams for you, babe. You're incredible. But so is Jake. I love him like another son. You hear me, kid?" She says this last piece to Jacob, who presses his lips together like he's holding back a smartass comment.

Eddie puts his fingertips to his eyes, clearly feeling overwhelmed. She pulls him toward her and hugs him. Beside me, Zoe is sniffling and wiping her face on the sleeve of her sweatshirt. JJ and Jacob seem to be having a wordless conversation through eye contact.

I glance at my grandma, realizing I'm going to have to come out to her if I'm going to tell her the truth about Dallas and everything that's happened. She senses my gaze and bends down to whisper in my ear.

"Don't worry. I already know." She gives me a playful little smile. My cheeks are burning. She pats my head and returns her attention to the other adults, and I'm grateful not to have to say a single word.

After Eddie and his mom pull away from each other, JJ says, "Hey, adults, how do we feel about going to get a coffee before you head back to work? I could use a pick-me-up, and I'm sure the kids want to talk without us. There's a little Mexican place next door."

"Glad you're feeling better," Eddie's dad tells Jacob, ruffling his dark hair. "You're gonna have a hell of a scar collection. Very punk rock." Jacob grins, delighted, and I'm reminded that these families have known each other for almost ten years. Eddie's dad kisses Eddie's forehead, pats his cheek, and says, "We're good. We'll talk more later."

My grandma squeezes me and Zoe, and the adults siphon out, leaving the four of us to stare at each other with wide eyes.

"Damn," Jacob says, breaking the silence.

Zoe looks a little more uncertain than usual. She glances between Jacob and Eddie. "Are we cool?" she asks.

Eddie nods. Jacob, however, gives her an appraising look. "I don't know. Are we?"

"What are you guys talking about?" I choke, descending into a coughing fit.

"You didn't know?" Jacob asks. He points at Eddie and Zoe. "These two were hooking up."

"What?" I gasp, shocked to the core that Zoe didn't tell me this. "For how long?"

"I had no idea he was also hooking up with you, by the way," Zoe snaps, tossing Eddie a sharp look. "Maybe let's talk about *that*."

"The whole thing is completely my bad," Eddie says, face distraught.

"Of course it is," Zoe says. "Who else—"

"Wait, *what?*" I say again, dissolving into a gut-deep coughing fit.

When I come out of it, Zoe is saying to Jacob, "You can't blame me. Look at him."

"True, girl." He holds up a fist, and she bumps it.

"Can we please not?" Eddie begs, beet red.

"This is just the beginning," Zoe informs him, and Jacob nods in smug confirmation.

"Wait," I say, and everyone turns annoyed eyes on me. "Never mind. I think I'm all caught up." Later, I will make Zoe go into extreme detail.

"If you want to talk about bad decisions, Casey was dating an actual murderer," Eddie says, gesturing to me.

"Don't try to deflect," Zoe says.

"She was really cute," I manage between coughs, and everyone falls apart laughing.

Jacob is the first to recover, a hand pressed to his chest and a grimace on his pale face. His injuries must still hurt a lot. Eddie slides onto the bed beside him, and Jacob tucks himself under his arm. Zoe takes Eddie's seat, and the four of us sit in companionable silence for a minute.

"Are you going to live in the murder house?" I ask Jacob.

He shakes his head. "It's all burned up now. My dad's going to have it torn down and sell the property. He'll give Morrison whatever money is part of the inheritance, and then he and I will keep what he makes off the sale of the land."

"Wow." I consider that. "Your dad is a really nice person. And Rosalinda Valentini was your *grandma*. That is unbelievable.

But, like, not shocking if you think about it. You definitely have that star quality they talk about."

"Obviously yes." He strikes a little pose, then smiles gloomily. "I think my dad just wishes he could have known her. For real, you know? Not how she was in movies."

"Tell him that Dallas had a bunch of letters between her and his adoptive mom. He'll want to read them. They're probably in her room somewhere."

Eddie asks me, "Are you sad about her? Did you get attached?"

I try to answer, but the words get stuck in my throat. I had felt a connection with Dallas I'd never felt before. I don't know if I'll ever find it again, and I don't know how much of it was an act. I can't put this tangle into words, so I just nod. Zoe makes a compassionate noise and reaches for my hand. I'm so glad they're all right, that we're alive and healing.

Though sometimes the dead feel as real as the living. It's such a shame, such a waste, that Dallas died. It's so tragically sad that she fell prey to the same greed and darkness that her relatives did before her. There was something bright and special about her. She could have done so much more. She could have been a real actress, for one. She was gifted, unusual, one of a kind.

But then, we're all one of a kind. That's the point, really, in the end. None of us is replaceable. When one of us dies, it leaves a hole that can never be filled.

Ever.

THIRTY-NINE

Saturday, April 22

I ARRIVE WITH ZOE IN THE RANGE ROVER HER parents bought her in light of our recent trauma. She's in a designer black dress and heels that seem ill-advised for grass. I'm wearing a black dress, too, but something thrifted, with a scarf to cover up the deep purple bruises that circle my throat.

It's been two weeks to the day since we broke into the Valentini mansion. I've been thinking a lot about how disorienting it is that things can change so much so fast.

"Well," Zoe says in a pseudo-bright voice, inching through the understated entrance of the Hollywood Forever Cemetery, in a line of cars that's clogging up Santa Monica Boulevard. "How are you feeling about attending the funeral of your fake ex who tried to kill you?"

"Feeling amazing," I reply, wiping my sweaty palms on my scarf. At least I can talk without coughing now.

She sighs, hands tight on the wheel. "This is surreal."

"Indeed."

We follow the procession into the narrow lane that winds through the iconic cemetery and pass by expanses of grass interspersed with custom monuments of guitarists, actors, animals, and angels. Gravestones dot the ground, and family plots bordered in wrought-iron fences tell intergenerational stories about the wealthy, the famous, the worth remembering.

It's a reminder that my mother has no gravestone. She was cremated, and we scattered her ashes off a boat in Santa Barbara. Grandma says my mom had always told her she was freaked out by the idea of becoming a skeleton and grossed out by the idea of being embalmed. I completely get that, but right now, I wish she had a gravestone. She deserves to be somewhere fancy, somewhere special. People should know her name.

But, no. She wouldn't have wanted that, and what does it mean, anyway? Immortality is a farce. At some point, everyone you know will be dead no matter how famous you are.

Eventually, we find a parking space on the shoulder beside a casual flock of roaming peacocks. Ahead is a stretch of still water, a wide, peaceful pond. Zoe and I get out, and I fill my lungs with fresh, warm air. No wheezing.

We follow the map past marble monuments to various rich and famous people, each of the more notable ones surrounded by tourists snapping selfies. Eventually, we join a small group in front of a family plot guarded by a marble cupid.

VALENTINI, reads the plaque at the cupid's feet. To its left, a gravestone reads, ANDREW VALENTINI. HUSBAND, BELOVED SON. A gaping rectangular hole lies open beside it, a white coffin stationed on a stand, covered in flowers. Rows of white chairs are filling up. Photographers are stationed nearby, probably the press. Zoe and I find a spot toward the back and watch as mourners arrive. I wonder how they knew Dallas. Could these people just be sleazy onlookers, fans of the murder house?

When I'd heard that JJ wanted Dallas buried beside Andrew Valentini, and that he was willing to pay for it, I thought he must be joking. Why would he help the girl who tried to kill his son? But now, I'm glad he did it. She belongs here.

I look down at my lap and feel tears well up, hot and unwelcome. Zoe puts a hand over mine. "You can be sad," she murmurs. "Eddie was never really mine, but that doesn't mean I don't miss what could have been."

I meet her eyes. It's the first time she's volunteered information about this. Every time I've brought it up, she says she'll tell me another time. That's how I know that whatever happened really hurt her. When she's truly sad, she prefers to lick her wounds in private.

She tweaks one side of her mouth into a smile. "It was just a few times. To be fair, I don't think he and Jacob were, you know, committed at that point. I . . . I kind of knew he didn't care the way I did. It didn't mean the same thing to him. But, you know. It's Eddie. He's amazing. I couldn't help getting a little bit attached."

I wrap my arm around her shoulders, and we sit in quiet solidarity, homesick for people we never had in the first place.

"I'm really, really sorry I accused you of being the one to stab Jacob," I say. We've already been over this, but I'm pretty sure I'll be apologizing until I'm ninety years old. I feel completely horrible, like the worst best friend on earth.

She pats my knee. "It's all good, Case."

"I never thought you had it in you to hurt anyone. It was just that you were the only one who wasn't on camera when he was attacked, and Dallas told me nobody else could have entered. I shouldn't have believed her."

"You were blinded by lust. We've all been there."

I remember why Zoe and I gravitated toward each other in the first place. The way we're able to talk, so honest and real, is like nothing I've experienced with another friend. She's truly the sister I never had. I take a breath, letting the warm air fill my lungs, feeling like a massive weight has been lifted off my chest.

Jacob and JJ arrive, Eddie alongside them, and sit in the front. JJ beckons to us, asking if we'd like to sit with them, but I shake my head. I don't think Dallas's mom or sister will want to see me, knowing I was part of her death.

When Camila and Morrison arrive, it's worse than I'd imagined. They look like ghosts of their former selves. Camila has aged ten years since we first saw her. And Morrison looks like a small, lost girl, full of a horrible grief I recognize too well. I want to reach out to her, to make a connection, but I know I'm the wrong person to do it.

And then JJ is greeting them, hugging them in his big arms, and an older couple I hadn't noticed stands and starts talking to them. The woman keeps touching JJ, and I realize—this must be Mary. I watch her with fascination, trying to picture her and Rosalinda as kids.

A robed man—the minister—stands and begins the ceremony. The sky is blue, and the view behind him is all palm trees and peacocks. Dallas never got her chance at celebrity; she never got to grace the covers of magazines as Dallas Valentini, heir to the Valentini mansion, but maybe this will bring her peace, knowing that at least in death she was famous.

Someone reached out to me yesterday, a writer working on a book about the Valentinis. She wanted to interview me. I told her I wasn't interested. But it made me happy for Dallas in a twisted way. She's getting what she wanted. I only wish she'd wanted something different. I'm choosing to believe that some of what I saw was real, that she didn't fake everything. I'm choosing to remember her as more than greed, ambition, and destruction.

✧

It's dark, and I shouldn't be here, but I couldn't bring myself to go home after the funeral. There's something I need to do.

I get off the bus on Fairfax and turn south. My footsteps are heavy, and my chest is tight, though not because of smoke inhalation or strangulation. It's tight because of what I'm about to do.

There's a bar on Fairfax with an alley and a little parking lot behind it. The bar has a martini glass statuette on its storefront. This is where my mom used to work. Its location is tattooed onto my brain.

Fairfax is busy as always, full of lights and cars and

pedestrians, but I walk slow and somber, clutching the dozen white roses I'd picked up at Trader Joe's on my way over here. My fingers are trembling, and I keep reminding myself not to squeeze the stems too hard. I don't want to break them.

And then, it's there in front of me. The martini glass, the red-lit sign, the open door, just as they looked in the police photos. I pass the bar and a few more shops, then turn right on the side street. I take another right, and I've arrived.

My footsteps falter, and I find myself stalled out, staring with terror down the dark alley. I clutch the flowers and make my way forward. It occurs to me that, walking slowly like this, I must look like I'm practicing being a bridesmaid. The thought brings no comic relief, not now.

The parking lot is obvious; it's the only one back here. I stop across the alley, breathing erratically. Her car was parked on the right, in the second spot. That night, there were three other cars in the lot. Their owners were in the bar, all accounted for at the time of the attack.

I step toward the second parking spot. No one is parked there now. This is where she died. This exact spot.

I've never come here before. But after my experiences in the Valentini house...

Here's the thing. I was fighting against the zip tie that held my wrists. And maybe it was defective. But I keep remembering the way it popped off, snapping open. Then again later, when the railing had crumbled under Dallas...and the wind had blown through at the exact right moment...

It was probably nothing, just an old, fragile house eaten through with termites. It was just a faulty zip tie. It was just an open window letting in a breeze.

But no windows had been open, had they? And it wasn't a windy night. So here I am, worrying about my mother's soul, desperately needing to prove to myself that she isn't stuck in this terrible place.

"Mom?" I say, my voice incomprehensibly small in the night. Of course, no one answers. No breeze rises up to whip my hair around. The only sounds are traffic noise and a faraway siren.

I find the spot where I think she died and lay the roses on the asphalt. "Mom?" I say again, and my throat closes up with sadness. I can barely get the words out. "I just wanted to make sure you weren't here," I say, my voice reduced to a squeaky whisper. "I needed to know you were okay." I wipe my wet cheeks with my palms. "I thought you might be worried about me. Maybe you felt like you needed to hang around and protect me."

I wipe my nose on my scarf. I take a deep, shaky breath.

"It's okay, though. Look, I'm almost all grown up. I'm going to college. I made it. Grandma is taking good care of me. And I'm taking care of her. I'm going to stay with her, and we'll keep helping each other. All right? You can rest. You can move on. In case you haven't. But if you have, that's great. I'm just . . . talking to myself in an alley." My voice fades.

"I love you," I say, squinting my eyes shut against the pain it brings to say this out loud. "I'm never going to forget you. Even if I don't remember all the little details, I'll never forget what it was like to have you. Some people don't get to have a mom who loves them like you loved me." I remember Dallas, and I wonder if she would have been different if she'd had a mother like mine, one who hugged you all the way. "I love you," I whisper, one last time.

A breeze flutters the grocery store roses' cellophane wrapper. I watch the bouquet closely, but it doesn't happen again.

I stand there for a long time, soaking it in. I don't think I'll ever come back here. It's the end of an era, the closing of a book. It's time to be done with my Notion pages, my secret research, my decade of dark and bottomless grief.

I'll never be done remembering her. I'll take Grandma to that motel in Carpinteria. We'll eat pancakes at McDonald's. I'll go back to Griffith Park and sit on the green grass, summoning mental images of the picture I'll always keep on my wall. But I won't continue to dwell on those last few unthinkable minutes. Because my mom is not what happened to her; she is not her death. She is her life.

April 14, 1972

Dear Mary,

Thank you for sending me photos of the family.
Jonathan is getting so big! I loved seeing him in
his little cowboy outfit. I often wonder how he's
doing, what he likes to eat, if he's happy—things I
didn't expect to worry about late at night when I'm
supposed to be getting beauty sleep before filming
the next day.

Your jokes about marrying Hank and becoming
Mrs. Worthington Hardware are funny, but I'd be
lying if I said returning to Culver wasn't tempting.
Thinking about our days romping through the woods,
building campfires, fishing in the summer, running
around barefoot... It makes me downright sad.
Here in LA, everything is so bright and shiny on the
surface, the sun out every day, the sky a brilliant
blue, but underneath is all this... I don't know...
a heaviness or something. It's like a pretty picture
painted on top of a scary one, and every so often,
you get the feeling you could actually see what's

underneath if you just turned your head a little faster.

You're going to get all biblical and start talking about angels and demons. That's not what I'm saying. I mean in this town, you bury everything that doesn't belong in that pretty picture. And at the same time, everyone is so blasé about their parties, their trysts, their wild escapades. You're supposed to be a free spirit, floating from experience to experience, but none of it can touch you. You have to stay beautiful and thin and young and perfect. Maybe we're all fake laughing, just a bunch of fools locked in a room, each of us determined to outperform the other.

When I close my eyes at night, I see our lake and the stars shining so bright with no city lights to fog them out. I hear the woods, the rustling of trees. I see the deer stepping out of the forest and nibbling away at the tender grass. I see bunnies, their little white tails twitching as they try to hold perfectly still. I see you and me in our cutoff shorts, carefree children who never worried how we looked in a bathing suit.

When I'm old, when I've become invisible, I think I'll move back home. I'll buy a little lake house, one with a dock of its own. By then, Andrew will have moved on to a second, younger wife, and no one wants to cast an old lady as anything but a mother or a witch anyway.

And then maybe we can tell Jonathan the truth. Maybe he'll forgive me. Maybe he'll join me every once in a while, and we'll fish together on a little boat in the middle of the lake. Maybe we'll stay out there past sunset to see the stars, and I can tell him stories about when I was young and pretty and everyone in Hollywood was taking my picture, just for a moment.

Anyway, I have to run. Andrew's brother, Rudy, is in town for a few days, and I need to figure out dinner. I love you and Jonathan more than I can say. Kiss that little boy for me.

Love you always and forever,
Rosie

FORTY

Saturday, July 15

THE NIGHT AIR IS COOL AND HUMID AS WE gather, silent, at the base of the eight-foot wall. Nothing as straightforward as a wall has ever kept us out.

"Security isn't scheduled here for an hour," Zoe whispers.

Eddie pulls the rope ladder out of his backpack and tosses it over. It catches, dangles, and he grins at us. "Let's do it."

Jacob slow-motion sashays to the ladder, grips it, then flings his head back in a dramatic pose. "Jacob Valentini takes the stage," he singsongs in a low voice.

"Oh my god," Zoe groans.

Eddie shoves him gently. "Move it."

"Such an alpha male," Jacob croons, then darts up like a spider and lands softly on the other side.

Eddie makes a show of praying for patience, then follows Jacob. Zoe and I exchange a little smile. They're incredibly cute, and if Jacob is being his obnoxious self, it means he's feeling all the way better.

I'm last over the wall, and I pause at the top to gather up the ladder. Hopping down, I see we've landed in a dark, wooded corner behind a bank of bushes. I follow the other three out onto a concrete walkway and take the lead. As always, I'm the one with the map memorized, though Zoe has the flawless sense of direction.

"Feels wrong to be doing this without cameras," Zoe whispers behind me.

"I like having my hands free," Jacob says, and Eddie makes a hissing sound that tells me Jacob probably grabbed his ass.

"I personally love not dealing with the ski mask/glasses situation," I say, leading them along the walkway until it lets us out onto a wider path at the back of the rows of seats.

The Hollywood Bowl stretches out beneath us, endless rows down to the pit and the darkened stage. In the huge, charcoal-and-gray-marbled sky, a pair of spotlights crosses, then splits, then finds each other again—the last vestiges of an all-night party somewhere nearby.

"That was too easy," Zoe murmurs, and I realize we're standing shoulder to shoulder in a line, eyes focused on the stage far below.

"Next time, we'll break into the Pentagon, okay, sweetie?" Jacob croons.

"There is no next time. She's leaving," Eddie reminds him.

"Come on," I say, unwilling to process that right now. Single file, we head down the stairs, from one landing to the next, until we're at ground level with the VIP boxes. These are the best seats in the house, right below the stage, which is bigger up close than I'd expected and shielded with a loose curtain of netting designed to keep birds out.

Zoe leads us between the waist-high partitions, along the paths the service workers take as they deliver food, and then we're in the pit, pushing the net aside and climbing up onto the black-painted wooden stage.

Zoe and Jacob immediately start dancing, nothing choreographed, just an intense and immediate reaction to being onstage, arms and hair flying, butts gyrating. Eddie and I double over in soundless laughter and sit down to watch them, raising silent fists in the air to cheer them on. When they've exhausted themselves, they collapse onto the boards between us, and we dangle our feet, looking out into the empty seats where the audience was earlier and will be again tomorrow.

I can't help but drop some trivia. "Frank Sinatra performed here. Nat King Cole. The Beatles, Miles Davis, the Who, the Doors, B.B. King, the Dead   "

Jacob says, "Wait, did you just list those in chronological order?"

"Maybe."

They guffaw quietly.

Zoe says, "We never got our finale. No last episode."

"That's true," Eddie replies.

"Maybe I made the wrong choice, going to college so far away," Zoe says, almost inaudible.

I put an arm around her shoulders. "You didn't. You belong at MIT. They need you."

Jacob flings his hands up. "This is stupid. Who says we can't ever film another episode again? Zoe, don't tell me your loaded parents aren't going to fly you home to visit once a month."

We lock eyes. All four of us.

"I mean...," Zoe begins.

Eddie says, "Think about all the gear I'll have access to in film school."

I point out, "You know, we could explore beyond LA. There's a whole world out there." They turn surprised eyes on me. "What?" I ask.

"You've never talked about traveling before," Eddie explains.

"I guess I never really considered it as an option."

"Look at you." Zoe squeezes my hand. "All grown up."

"I actually..." I clear my throat. "I do have some news. I convinced my grandma to move into a new apartment."

"*What?*" Zoe whispers, shrill. She knows how attached to that place my grandma is.

"If I'm going to stay home for college and help pay the bills, I need an actual bedroom. You know? If Hollywood is too expensive, we can move to the valley or the east side. With me contributing, we can afford a little more. There are options."

"That's great," Jacob says emphatically. "Seriously. How are you ever going to get laid if you don't have an actual door on your room?"

Zoe snickers, and I can't help but agree in a completely nonjoking way. I have a new job working four days a week in a bookstore, and classes at LACC start in a month. It's time for my grandma and me to build something new.

We lapse into silence, eyes on the rows of seats that stretch up, up, up. We're occupying a space that has been walked on by icons, celebrities, and one-off hopefuls whose careers never rose past their one night at the Hollywood Bowl. All together in a stew, audience members and servers, rich and poor, famous and infamous, the Hollywood menagerie.

"Sometimes I think about Rosalinda," Jacob says in a low, serious voice.

"I still think about Dallas," I reply. "Sorry, Jacob. I don't mean—"

"I know." He smiles sadly. "I get it. She was something. Those *eyes.*"

Eddie laces his fingers through Jacob's. "They were beautiful."

They were. Both Rosalinda and Dallas, with their shining blue eyes, shuttered windows to their unknowable interiorities. Like the house, Dallas contained hidden depths. Was her fate sealed at birth, a legacy in her blood?

Since the moment we set foot on that property, I've wondered—is it possible to commit a crime so heinous that it leaves a spiritual mark on a place? If you tear the house down, does it wipe the slate clean? Or does that darkness live on in the ground, a scar reaching down to the core of the earth?

A breeze whispers past, ruffling my bangs. It takes me back to the night of the fire, to the mysterious wind whipping through Dallas's hair. The house is gone now, demolished by the contractors JJ hired to prepare the land for sale. The lot sits flat and empty, secrets intact.

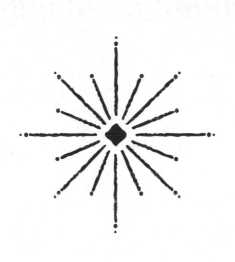

ACKNOWLEDGMENTS

What a pleasure and privilege it was to write this book. Every Angeleno knows the Los Feliz Murder House, and of course that was the inspiration for the Valentini murder mansion. Growing up in LA, the site of many infamous crime scenes, including the Hotel Cecil, I've always wanted to explore the idea of cursed locations. Thank you, Jessica Anderson, Christy Ottaviano, and the team at Little, Brown Books for Young Readers for giving me the opportunity to explore these dark waters, and thank you for your commitment to queer stories. Again and again, I count myself lucky beyond reckoning to publish books with you.

As always, this journey would not be possible without my agent, Lauren Spieller, with whom I've navigated endless twists and turns. Lauren, thank you for your advocacy and support through another book.

Behind every author is a cadre of friends and readers. Thank you, Layne Fargo, Halley Sutton, Mike Chen, Diana Urban, Aiden Thomas, Dea Poirier, and so many others who have proved invaluable along the way. They have read my words, helped me through difficult moments, and provided crucial feedback in the drafting of this work and others.

And of course, I must thank my family. They've tolerated

this author through yet another publishing cycle, and I love them dearly. This book is dedicated to my mother and daughter because, in writing Casey and her grandma, I had to imagine a world in which our three-generation trio was separated. I'll hold them both a little tighter after writing this one.

Wendy Heard

WENDY HEARD

is the author of the acclaimed YA novels *Dead End Girls* and *She's Too Pretty to Burn*, which *Kirkus Reviews* praised as "a wild and satisfying romp" in a starred review, as well as three adult thrillers: *You Can Trust Me, The Kill Club,* and *Hunting Annabelle.* She has spent most of her life in Los Angeles, California, which is on fire more than she would honestly prefer, and can often be found haunting local hiking trails and bookstores. She loves all things vintage and has a collection of thrillers from the eighties. Wendy invites you to visit her at wendyheard.com, where you can read her short fiction through her free newsletter, or find her on Twitter, Instagram, and TikTok @wendydheard.